NIGHTMARE BALLAD

By
Benjamin Kane Ethridge

JournalStone
San Francisco

JOURNALSTONE
YOUR LINK TO ARTISTIC TALENT

JournalStone books may be ordered through booksellers or by contacting:

JournalStone
www.journalstone.com
www.journal-store.com

ISBN: 978-1-936564-83-5   (sc)
ISBN: 978-1-936564-76-7   (ebook)

Library of Congress Control Number: 2013932044

Printed in the United States of America
JournalStone rev. date: May 17, 2013

Cover Design: Denise Daniel
Cover Art: Alan M. Clark

Edited By: Dr. Michael R. Collings

ENDORSEMENTS

"A darkly imaginative tale from a rising genre star. Ethridge plays a wicked tune in Nightmare Ballad." - **Scott Nicholson**, author of *The Home*

"In a field where the twin juggernauts of vampires and zombies have rolled roughshod over the literary ground, leaving barren earth in their wake, Benjamin Kane Ethridge's *Nightmare Ballad* blooms like a resilient flower amidst the desolation. My optimism over horror's artistic viability is due primarily to works like this. *Nightmare Ballad* is edgy, original and unclassifiable, and Ethridge is a fresh voice whose bracingly modern take on surrealism may very well point the way to the genre's future." - **Bentley Little**

DEDICATION

For my parents April and Gary Ethridge, who never once
dissuaded me from my nightmares.

Check out these titles from JournalStone:

That Which Should Not Be
Brett J. Talley

Limbus
Anne C. Petty - Editor

Vale of Stars
Sean O'Brien

Terovolas
Ed Erdelac

Twice Shy
Patrick Freivald

The Donors
Jeffrey Wilson

The Devil of Echo Lake
Douglas Wynne

Pazuzu's Girl
Rachel Coles

Available through your local and online bookseller or at
www.journalstone.com

ACKNOWLEDGEMENTS

I wish to express my gratitude to family, friends, colleagues and especially fans for their continued support. The process of telling certain stories can be, I imagine, like mapping the nervous system of a recently discovered life form. Nightmare Ballad most certainly fell into that category for me. The fractured mind that often accompanies such endeavors can only be tempered with the help of others. So thank you. Thank you all. For the pleasant dreams.

Verse 1: The Frogmen

Chapter 1

Luke awoke with it in his head.

He struggled to remember the notes, the rhythm, some kind of progression or beat. Had it started in a dream last night, or had it started a minute ago? And was this a song he'd heard before? Or a song he wished to compose? He worked the dissonance around in his mind a little more, hunting for an associative memory, but nothing came to him. After swim class, if the girls weren't busy, maybe he'd dust off the classical guitar and the song would work itself out through major and minor chords.

Or had they been diminished chords...?

This slippery music was driving him nuts! And he hadn't even started to consider the cruel-happy tone of the singer's voice, or that the lyrics echoed from some inhuman language.

He wanted to say that the words sounded like the telling of a story, both old and new.

One of his swim students, Petunia, paddled up to him with the reluctance only a fourteen-year-old girl can express. He knew she resented the fact that her parents made her take these swim lessons, being the oldest kid in the class by far. Most likely to pay them back, she was something of a flirt, and had absolutely no qualms about it. To get his attention, she lightly put her hand on his stomach, just above his swim trunks. He floated away from her touch.

"Mr. Rhodes, we gonna use those raft things again?"

"Maybe, Petunia. If we don't run out of time. We still have to work on the dead-man's float. Get back with the others, okay?

She rumpled her freckled face and shrugged before kicking nosily away in the water.

The sound of the splashing reminded Luke of the dream song—if he hadn't had to concentrate on his class, he might have already remembered the song completely. In an effort to redirect his frenzied thoughts, he scanned the Rec Center pool. Beige plastic umbrella tables, over twenty half occupied; an anorexic lifeguard up on his towering chair, camouflaging his nose with pink sunscreen; a gentle chlorine breeze through the dying spruce trees invading the fence line. The brittle limbs cast threadbare shadows over a third of the crystal-blue water. It was heating up quickly, and the shade would rapidly recede. By noon the California sun would forge the Olympic-sized pool into a bar of blinding radioactive blue. Luke was thankful his parent-assisted swim class would be over long before it came to that point.

"Form a line," he instructed over the random splashes. "Parents can come to the side here with me or sit on the stairs."

Adults broke away from their children, who reacted accordingly with shared yips, yippees and splash-bombs. Petunia's mother, Alice Stedding, predictably glided within schmoozing distance of Luke. It wasn't difficult to see where Petunia got her flirting from.

As the woman came at him, freckled breasts first, Luke craned his neck to the spot where her husband, Ralph Stedding, lazed on a beach chair, the nearby umbrella's shade falling just short of him. Because of his buck teeth everybody called him Mouse, but Luke had always felt uncomfortable with the nickname.

"Hey, Ralph!" hollered Luke. "Sure you don't want to come in? Must be hot out there."

Ralph shook his baseball-capped head and gave him a feeble thumbs-up. The lenses of his sunglasses captured the cloudless azure sky.

"He's lazy," Alice complained, the pool's shimmering luminance coursing across her face.

Luke made a dismissive sound. "Ah, he's wiped out from overtime at the plant though, right?"

Alice half-smiled. "Let's just say he needs to put in some overtime as a father for a change. Petunia's almost forgotten he lives with us."

Luke nodded out of politeness. The only noteworthy memory Luke had of his own father, Harold, was that movie he took him to see during the Summer of Classics down at the dollar theater: *CAPTAINS COURAGEOUS*. Spencer Tracey starred.

Luke had always remembered the title as singular, "*Captain Courageous*," until he saw the box in a video store as an adult. Great film, from what he remembered, but the finer story points were foggy now. It was the ending–the Captain fatally injured, hopelessly caught in some ropes and topsail canvas and going down with the ship, so to speak—that had stayed with Luke more than the actual plot. That image was permanent but hazy... dreamlike.

Luke snapped out of his ruminations. Shards of the strange song sank into his mind again, and he returned to his students. "Kids, go to the side here. We're going to practice holding our breath. Hold the sides and go up and down like last time—go at your own pace. Raul, buddy, you're only eight years old, but you're one strong dude—don't hold Martin down like that or you'll have to get out and sit. Miss Katie, don't make yourself dizzy again. Take plenty of breaths of air. Nobody's going for any records here."

"Why don't you teach adult only classes?" asked Alice. "I need to become a stronger swimmer. Didn't you almost make it to the Olympics?"

"Junior."

"But still. You should be charging for these classes with your experience."

Luke could feel her close to him. He turned to watch the other parents, who were chatting or relaxing on the pool's steps. Her husband Ralph was clearly snoring, the sound sputtering upward from his beach chair.

Sure, leave me alone with the she-wolf.

"Everything costs something these days. It's nice to know some things are still free."

Alice caressed her wet, brown pony tail. "True. You're very generous, though."

"Totally selfish," he replied. "I love teaching. It beats the heck out of working in an office."

Luke started to approach the class again, but Alice caught the side of his trunks. He wheeled around. She put her hands up, acting more surprised than he. "Sorry, I meant to grab your arm."

"Okay…"

More zigzag reflections of light scrambled her facial expression, but the heavy breathiness of her voice supplied all that needed to be known. "I'm sorry, but when would I ever get you alone?" She let out a small giggle and Luke's face swelled with heat.

He laughed it off like she'd made a joke, quickly moving away. He wanted to say a lot of things and at the same time he wanted to ignore her advance completely. The old Luke would have gladly taken her up on her not-so-subtle offer. Now he had Maribel and Dara. He'd never dream about betraying them.

Dream.

The word stuck with him.

The song.

In his head.

He remembered it and the whole world dimmed. Every color flickered, like he was seeing everything with a new pair of eyes…

What's happening?

The music fused together in his mind, an appalling, frightful ballad. All at once, he heard the entire song, every note and every word, and as familiar as it all sounded, it was like hearing it for the first time.

The real world drowned at the corners of his vision. Not far from the Rec Center, a silken black curtain slipped down from the sky.

"Where did that come from?" he asked himself. He stared at the rippling fabric for a moment, wondering what was behind it.

Luke let out a gasp in surprise. Something slimy had thrust past his leg, causing him to stumble back. He jerked his body around and searched the area below.

Saw only rippling water shadows.

His flesh still tingled from where it had brushed him. That thing hadn't been a person. *Some type of sea creature that got into the pool somehow?* He accepted this as possible, maybe even probable, and didn't question it as outrageous, not in the least. He was thinking strangely, like he was in a dream. *So accepting of the absurd.*

He gazed across the pool but still couldn't find anything—the thing had vanished.

The water had changed color. It was murky. Rust colored. Dangerous.

"Everybody," he said hoarsely. "Get out of the pool. Now!"

The children began hopping out of the pool, their wet, dripping forms blurring into the murky backdrop of the Rec Center. The adults were out-and-out oblivious to his command. They let loose full-throated laughs, some hooting, some splashing backward in the water like big kids. Luke's stomach fell.

"Hey, stop, parents OUT too," he said over their roar. "What's the matter with you people?"

He panicked as something dull struck his leg again and buckled his knee. With several jelly-slow movements, he got himself turned around but again found nothing in the iced-tea colored water.

A voice rang out.

Alice's. Her face was drawn, eyes wide with alarm as she searched the pool. "Petunia! Where are you? Mouse! Get in here! Go get her. Oh God! Petunia! She's in the deep end! The deep end!"

Before Luke could cast his eyes to where Alice pointed, a resounding splash disturbed the water.

Ralph Stedding's beach chair was empty.

Luke looked up at the life guard. But a different man sat in the majestic white chair, a spear resting over his black-feathered lap. He looked like a witchdoctor or some type of tribesman, but his skin was darker than human pigment could ever be, and charred bones penetrated the flesh of his legs, arms and face. Fiery, yet impassive eyes stared down and made Luke's heart race. He turned away in dread.

A purple raft floated in the deep end of the pool.

"Petunia?" Luke shouted. His heart hammered and the blood went hot in his face. Luke dove through the water as fast as he could.

The pool smelled indescribably awful, and only got worse. How he could actually smell while underwater, he had no clue, but the burning, rotting funk made itself known in the core of his sinuses.

Luke opened his eyes. Below him, the pool's floor moved and a human shaped swam off. It was a man in a scuba outfit, exactly the same rust color of the water. Fleetingly he recalled another movie he and his dad had seen about World War II...what had those divers been called?

Frogmen.

Luke yelled out a torrent of bubbles. He suddenly knew the frogman had evil intentions for Petunia. He just *knew*.

Luke swam faster but made no progress. Invisible fingers caressed his belly, and he flopped over, foul water going up his nostrils. It tasted better than it smelled but not by much: bitter chocolate and iron. He broke the surface and spat. Despite the taste, he ducked his head underneath again. He could see a little better now...the iced-tea atmosphere had thinned to a light-brown haze. Dozens of frogmen swam around the bottom as if they'd been doing this since the dawn of time. Luke's mind responded: *Those air tanks last them forever—they can be down here forever.*

He came back up for air and heard Petunia just behind the raft. "Hey, Mr. Rhodes? This yours?"

She let out a scream and threw something up in the air. The object came down with a splash, a small red thing in the water. Luke closed in on the raft and swam to the other side.

Everything was quiet now. He grabbed the side of the pool and looked to the other end. Nobody was there. They'd all taken off. How had they done that so quickly? Petunia was just here!

A red rubber ducky floated just beyond the raft. Instinctively, Luke reached for the toy. It bobbed away. He extended farther, and his struggling sent the duck down the length of the pool. Luke inspected the raft again, then pushed it away. He had to get her out of here before those things...

Above the surface of the water he saw.

On the bottom of the pool lay Petunia, curled in a tight ball.

He dove down after her.

Underwater, a striking sound echoed.

Plink.

Plink.

Plink.

Deranged music pursued him as he plunged deeper. Luke's eyes widened. There were no frogmen. He was alone. He had to prove he could do this. Of course he could. Captain Courageous showed how much he cared. That's what a real man does. Out of high school Luke had been a lifeguard for four summers. Only had one person come close to drowning, though.

Please don't be dead, Petunia.

The girl looked gray. It could have been the water, which seemed to darken the closer he got to her, but her skin had taken on the color of eel or shark flesh. *That's how dead people look, isn't that right?*

Luke hungered for air. Only ten feet down, his lungs squeezed and burned. When he reached the bottom of the pool, his vision went black, he was dying, he couldn't make it, he had Petunia's ankle, so cold it stung his palm—he tried to swim back up to the surface with her in tow. Something halted him. His vision cleared and he saw…the pool seethed with the shadowy figures in wetsuits and flippers, all forcing people to the bottom to drown them. There, twitching in the middle, were Ralph and Alice Stedding. Other parents had joined them in this mass execution.

Luke halted. One of the frogmen held Petunia. Luke ground his heel into the creature's face, and its goggles snapped in half. The eyes should have been animal, but they were darkly human, so human that the sight made Luke's muscles go limp. He almost let the girl slip through his fingers, but he renewed his grip and pulled her upward.

When they broke through the water, the end of the pool had reconfigured. It reminded Luke of his parents' pool at their house in Glendale, but in Olympic proportions. On the other side, the recreation center still stood but had several more stories, with red trim rather than blue.

He hadn't heard her get out of the pool, but Petunia ran for the exit, now located where the restroom and showers should have been. Before making it outside, she stopped and vomited a stream of iced-tea water. She made a face at him, part sickliness, part accusation. "Why didn't you tell me that was your duck?"

"What are you talking about? Petunia, wait—"

A great rumbling from beneath the pool carried a tapestry of froth over the side and soaked the concrete above.

Petunia moaned and charged off, puking again.

Luke grabbed onto the railing and pulled himself out of the water.

A frogman ten times the size of the others emerged in a frenzied splash and chased after him, the clanking of its enormous scuba tank like a god's hammer striking an anvil. *Plink, plink, plink.* Violent eyes beheld him beyond the giant square diver's mask.

Luke scrambled among the umbrella tables and burst through the side door. Petunia was long gone. Vanished. Like so many other things, Luke didn't bother to question how that could be; he just ran down the street, the concrete under his bare feet rough and burning. He headed for the black curtain in the sky, his only point of reference in the glittering dark madness around him.

A growl came from directly behind, he didn't want to turn and see what the massive frogman could be changing into. It was destroying the road with its flippers. He heard concrete and dirt crunching. Road shrapnel struck his neck. Looking back would be too much, so he just ran as hard as he could, the truth more apparent with every step.

This frogman thing wanted him dead.

Chapter 2

Luke didn't recognize the lime-green house.

But as the tip of a frogman's claw sliced through his back, he turned toward the end of Maple Street and rushed in its direction. Fifteen minutes of running without a destination in mind and he'd wound up in an unknown neighborhood. He'd never been to this side of Maple before, and all the unfamiliar houses began stacking up on each other. A lime-green house caught his eye, but really, he didn't know any of these track homes; his way back from work never took him through this neighborhood.

Sounds of the snarling creature faded as he took this new course, so he didn't doubt himself. Just ahead, the heavy black curtain he spotted earlier hung like theater drapes from the heavens. There wasn't time to stop and he barreled straight through it.

The fabric parted for Luke, then vanished.

And on the other side, the music fell to the back of his mind, colors enlivened, and the sun shone brighter. He stopped in the road for a second before crying out in pain from his burnt feet. He ran onto some stranger's lawn.

"Holy—aye!" The toasted, tight feeling in his feet made him cringe.

After he composed himself, he looked up the road. The concrete was disturbed, uprooted, like a major earthquake had occurred. "The hell?" he whispered.

He looked down to the next block. A middle aged woman in a bikini top and jean shorts ran a hose over the roof of a mini-van. Two ducking and weaving boys played with water-guns on the nearby lawn. Several houses down from them, a goggled gardener edged around a flower mound.

Why weren't they running over to see what happened to the street?

For that matter, why wasn't everybody outside their houses right now, investigating the upheaval?

Luke nodded as an easy resolution popped into his head. *They must be used to this kind of thing.* Doubts dissolved. Or rather, were pulled away, by something external, forcing him to accept the reality before him. Regardless, fragmented memories still nagged at him. He couldn't explain what had happened. He must have been out for a jog and didn't wear his shoes, but what kind of a dumb ass thing was that to do?

He considered maybe he'd gotten dehydrated and become delirious. Maybe he took his shoes off somewhere? *Oh great, Dara's going to chew my ass out for this. I probably have second degree burns on my feet.*

He smelled like chlorine.

Of course! This was swim-class day. So he'd been swimming earlier. He could hardly recall anything from today's class. Jogging on such a hot day had been a massively idiotic thing to do.

A bead of sweat ran down his back. He intercepted it and felt a stinging pain at the spot where his finger touched the wetness.

Blood.

He rubbed his fingers together and inspected the maroon stain on his fingertips.

"Can I help you?"

A teenage boy stood on the front porch. He looked as though he'd been heading out. The faded green van in the driveway must have been his.

"Hi."

The teenager blinked impatiently. "Hi."

"I'm uh…kind of in some trouble. I lost my shoes. Wouldn't be able to give me a lift, would you? I live in town, not far."

The teen raised an auburn eyebrow and looked halfway between intimidated and irked. "You can use my cell, but then I have to go. How's that sound?"

"Sure. I appreciate it."

He tossed a cell phone in a blue case at Luke. Surprised, he dropped it onto the grass.

"Sorry," muttered the teen.

"No problem. It's *me* who is sorry." Luke had only one phone number memorized and surprisingly, it didn't belong to either of his wives. He recalled the number because of how often he'd avoided it on caller ID. Today, however, finding himself in swim trunks on some stranger's lawn, the soles of his feet feeling like barbequed steaks, the only person who wouldn't scold him happened to be Alberto Cruz, or as he insisted on being called—

"Johnny?"

Static crackled and somebody mumbled on the line.

"Johnny? You there? Hey man, I'm in some trouble here. I really need you to come pick me up."

"Who the fuck is this fucking shit?" The voice blared through the tiny speaker.

With a nod of reassurance, Luke smiled at the teen, who folded his mole-spotted arms.

"It's Luke."

"*Luke?*"

"Luke Rhodes, you jerk."

"Calm down, just bustin' your beebees."

"I'm kind of in a…I need help, man." Luke checked the number on the curb across the street. "I'm at 255 South Maple Street. Can you come pick me up?"

The teenager stood on the curb and surveyed the destroyed north end of the street. It looked like a gigantic rabbit had burrowed through with ten-foot claws. The young man's face had a placid indifference that made him appear robotic until annoyance creased his features. From the look of things, this major disruption in the road hadn't awed him in the least, just superficially pissed him off, like a bad traffic jam might piss off a late-to-work commuter.

"Johnny, you there?"

"Yeah, yeah. I'm kind of busy on my bike mods," Johnny replied. "When do you need me over there?"

"Can you come now? I'm really screwed here, man."

A jaded laugh rattled in the speaker. "How? Did *both* your old ladies kick you out?"

"No jokes right now. Please?"

Johnny breathed noisily through the phone and groaned. "I'll need to gas up first."

"255 South Maple."

"I remember the address shithead," Johnny snapped.

"I'll be here." Luke ended the call.

The teen walked over, hand extended. Luke dropped the phone onto his palm. Without a word, the young man went to his van, wiping his phone against his shorts.

"You mind if I wait here?" Luke asked. "Please? I don't have any shoes."

An ugly frown creased the boy's face. "Yes I mind. So would my parents. Go across the street. That place is foreclosed. Nobody cares if you're over there."

Luke glanced at the street, still glazed with the white-hot shine of the afternoon sun. "Right."

The teen smoothed back his hair, checked his palm, and opened the van's driver-side door. Luke, trying his damnedest to delay his fire-walk across the asphalt, piped up, "Weird about the street, huh? How did it get that way?"

With a shrug, the teen shook out his wad of keys, then said, "I don't know why it's like that. All I know is I've got to go down Sycamore now to get to the freeway and that street has like a million friggin' stoplights."

"Has it been torn up like this way for a while?" Luke asked the question, but the frenzy of dust particles still suspended in the sunlit air told him otherwise.

"Nope. Just happened. Maybe an earthquake did it."

"You're taking this kind of well, if you don't mind me saying so."

"It's one of those things that can happen. Hey, are you leaving my yard or what?"

"I'm gone."

The teen got in the van, and a second later the old engine coughed to life. It revved a few times to signal Luke to get walking.

Luke waved a thank you to the asshole and sprinted across the asphalt. He didn't feel the short trip, thankfully, but the lawn on the other side wasn't particularly refreshing: mostly dead and yellow, full of bald spots. The heat from the exposed dirt and brittle grass aggravated the painful blisters on his soles, so he retreated to a square of cool shade near the dirty front porch and sat.

He put his hands on his head. *What will my two wives think of this? That I'm drunk? Screwing around? Shit…*

His hair had the telltale starchy texture from chlorine. He'd been at the pool recently then…but why was it so difficult to remember? It was like trying to recall the events from a dream, but it couldn't have been a dream, because this was clearly reality. The aching in his feet and back were too persistent not to be real.

Luke recast his mind to this morning and a chill ran through him: Dara, fretting over her job interview, had silently made them breakfast; Maribel, busy with her lesson plan but otherwise in her usual good spirits, had flown around the house, room to room, corner to corner, picking up the messes they'd made. Regardless of the shitstorm Luke had faced the past week at work, this day started as good as it possibly could have.

After breakfast, giving each of them a full kiss, Maribel left to get her classroom in order for a new batch of students this week. Taking a chance, Luke had shared a moment with Dara. *See, I think you're worrying too much. She's fine. Just worry about your interview—I mean, don't worry. Just prepare, okay?*

Dara seemed to marginally agree, if not take it to heart. Too bad it wasn't what Luke had really wanted to tell her, which would have been more like, "Why are you getting a job all of a sudden? Years have gone by. *Years*, Dara. And you choose *now* of all times. Why couldn't this interview have taken place before every middle-management jerk-off elected me as their favorite fall-guy? My career is on the line and even if GeoGreen hires you, you won't last long—that'll be my fault, too. Everybody is learning about us and Maribel, and it's only going to get worse. You're going to be smack-dab in the middle of it! Christ! I thought you were happy keeping house and taking care of us."

He hadn't said that.

Any of that.

Hell, no.

The Luke of old would have buried himself in emotional fallout. It'd been a while since he had made Dara cry, although it used to be a norm for him. No, the reinvented Luke had done what his second wife, Maribel, taught him to do; he tried to imagine the most reassuring thing for Dara to hear before he said anything. The result was magic. It almost always worked. Dara had hugged him, smiled her best smile, tweaked his chin, and told him to go shave.

Now, sitting in a strange neighborhood, on the porch of a foreclosure, Luke felt his face. He had shaved this morning. He remembered doing so because he was on his last razor, and it had reached that irritatingly blunt, but still usable, stage. What had he been thinking about in front of the mirror? A song...*a song from a dream*. He couldn't recall the tune anymore but it'd really bugged him this morning, all the way to the pool.

Yes.

He'd gone to class.

Alice Stedding had put the moves on him right in front of her husband. Their daughter, Petunia, was at the bottom of the pool, but she hadn't drowned. The events were vaguer than vague.

Men in scuba suits?

Frogmen.

Luke grimaced at the recollection and watched a wasp do circuits around a lopsided bush before flying off. Had he suffered from head trauma? He checked his scalp and found nothing. There were, however, tiny scrapes on his neck and one razor-thin scratch down his spine, but none of those even qualified for a Band-aide.

He swooped his fingers around his face and clasped his chin. Had he been drinking? When he was a teenager he'd woken up drunk on a kitchen floor, even once on a front lawn, but this was altogether different. The memories he struggled to recall were real, but they *couldn't* be.

A rush of anxiety flooded his guts. *Is this what a breakdown is?*

That last thought stayed with Luke until he heard the rumble of a Harley Davidson up the street. Johnny Cruz struck the curb as he pulled over and the motorcycle tipped a bit. His old friend had lost a little weight this summer, but still looked well into the three-hundred-pound range. Pulled tight in a ponytail, his long, black, Native-American-looking hair stressed his widow's peak to the limit. From behind the fish-aquarium lenses of his glasses, his magnified eyelashes clashed together.

"Luke?" Johnny leaned off the bike a little, squinting. Half of a Swisher Sweet cigarillo poked out of the side of his mouth, an inch from setting his bandito mustache ablaze. "I can't tell if that's you? Oh shit, it is." A grin crossed his wide, stubbly face.

"Yeah, yeah."

"What the fuck did you do? Look at you. What a sorry piece of shit."

"Nice to see you too, Johnny." Luke waded out of the shadows. "I don't have any shoes...it's...I'd like to say a long story but I don't even know what the story is."

"Say no more! Hop up." Johnny snapped his fingers. A coil of sweet smoke framed his face for a moment as he watched Luke climb on. "Grab the helmet, fucker."

Luke took the black soup-bowl helmet off a hook on the side and placed it on his head. "Ouch," he said, curling his toes at the diamond plate runner board.

Johnny glanced down. "You can put your feet on top of my boots. People will talk anyway. You already got one of those haircuts from some gay-boy salon poster."

"I'll take it over looking like a two bit Hell's Angel version of Hurley from *Lost*."

"Aye *cabron*...."

"Guess you didn't notice the street?"

"Duh, I noticed it. Big deal."

"Something must have happened right?"

"You think?"

"An earthquake?"

Johnny shrugged his giant shoulders. "I didn't feel nothing. Then again, I've been drinking all morning. Ah, weekends!" He poised to take off.

"I thought you worked at the plant on Sundays?"

"Fuck those people. Let that mouse-faced doofus take care of that stupid fucking shit farm."

"Yikes, sorry I asked."

Mouse Stedding. Luke recalled him diving into a pool filled with reddish-brown water. Going to save his daughter Petunia. The man had all his clothes on. His rodent face was tight, stricken with fear.

"Does Ralph even work Saturdays?" Luke asked.

"Ralph don't ever work. Ralph just bitches about floating holidays and pay increases and how he's not getting any overtime like the rest of those useless village idiots. To answer your question, I don't really give a fuck."

The Harley roared from underneath and Johnny took them on a sloppy trajectory to the nearest stop sign.

"You really are drunk off your ass today, aren't you?"

"Silver Petron, all the way, son." Johnny punched it, and Luke grabbed his friend's broad back.

"What about your real son? How's he doing?" Luke asked over the motorcycle's trilling roar.

"Beltran's fine. Who wouldn't be? Living it up with that fuckbucket stepdad of his at that big-time university."

"Did you call him on his birthday like Maribel asked?"

Johnny glanced back, an agitated knot of skin bunched between his eyes. "I didn't ask anything about why you're alone in swim trunks in some weird neighborhood. Do we really have to go through this discussion again?"

"No," he said simply. Luke realized then he'd probably just tried to dredge up Johnny's problems to mask his own. "Sorry."

"Forget it. Only one person in this world is unlucky enough to have me in his life and that, my friend, is you. Speaking of which, are you coming over and tying one on tonight, or what?"

"Say that again?"

Johnny shouted in a pseudo drill-sergeant staccato. "Are. You. Gonna. Get. Fucked. Up. With. Me. Tonight. Mother. Fucker?"

He pulled up to a stoplight at the corner of Sycamore and Pine. A police cruiser stopped beside him. Two cops, both looking straight out of the academy, sat there, eyeing them with unprovoked disdain.

"Don't say anything," Luke told him. "Please."

Johnny leaned back. "Not even the pork sandwich joke? Those fuckers' balls haven't even dropped yet."

"Just don't."

"Oh fine." Johnny blew them a kiss as the light changed.

During the rest of the ride through town Luke held on for dear life. Johnny blew through stale yellow lights and two reds. He stopped painfully close to a jacked-up pick-up truck and leaned against its door while he lit another cigarillo. The man in the cabin rolled down his window and glared, as though that would accomplish more than heated words, but Johnny ignored him completely.

When they arrived to the house, Luke started formulating a way to tell Dara what had happened. The motorcycle came to a stop, and as it did, Johnny gently extended his leg and kicked over the neighbor's recycle bin.

"What the hell, man?"

"It was in the way. Why doesn't that jackass put it closer to his property?"

"You're...out of control."

With a wheezing cough, Johnny bent forward, into his handle bars, like he wanted to take a nap right there. "So you're not coming over?"

Luke placed the helmet back on its hook and stepped onto the lawn. "I would be afraid of what would happen, tell you the truth. Thanks for the ride, I'll text you later."

"You calling me reckless, then? Hey, fucker, answer the question."

Crossing his yard, Luke replied, "Yeah, Johnny, I'm calling you reckless."

"Well ain't that a load of shit. You think I'm reckless? Reckless! Me?" Johnny stood on the running boards of his Harley, watching Luke go. He raised his fist like a Mongol conqueror.

"You're the dumb asshole with more than one spouse."

Chapter 3

Dara's appetite was officially curbed.

At this time of day she was usually thinking of what to make for dinner. Nothing sounded good right now. How could she be hungry with the churning sourness in her stomach? Too many things pressed on her. Those strange vibes Maribel gave off, the interview tomorrow at GeoGreen, and now this weird behavior from Luke: it was enough to make her start smoking again. And why not? Her teeth were already hideous anyway. Maybe she'd keep this low appetite and lose the fifteen pounds she'd put on from sitting in front of the computer all day?

That's it, she thought, worry about the *important* stuff.

But she couldn't stop concentrating on the heaviness of her breasts. She didn't care what Luke and Maribel said. Every pound she gained had gone straight to her chest. It was obvious, standing naked before the mirror. Not yet returned to what they once were, she certainly shouldn't be freaking out, but how long before she was back in a triple-D bra? It wasn't just the size, either. Unshapely and huge, areolas too big and too pale, too short nipples like bug bites…she knew Luke and Maribel must have thought so too, deep down inside.

Another surgery and stretch marks, here I come. And yet, if she allowed her weight to go unchecked, her back muscles would spasm her into early cripplehood. Despite her breast reduction a few years ago, her portions had gradually reinstated their old claim on her body.

What a waste! She'd wanted the procedure since high school but never saw it happening. She was shit at saving money and had become resolved to going through life being fodder for flat women to crinkle their noses at and for men to ogle like milk-hungry babes—until her bra came off and revealed the unprepossessing reality of overlarge breasts. It wasn't fair, but life could go down that way.

And it had, until her soul mates had saved her.

One of those people was asleep back home with his feet wrapped in aloe vera soaked bandages, but the other was here, slowly nodding her head to a Green Day song. As Maribel drove them to pick up Luke's car at the Rec Center, where, for whatever reason, he'd left it, Dara gave her wife a sidelong glance, appraising her, wondering. Maribel had a perfect button nose. If Dara hadn't always been so boob-conscious, she was sure she would have been nose-conscious. Nobody had ever implied so, but Dara felt her schnozz could badly use a Beverly Hills trimming.

Maribel's head slowly dipped with the conclusion of *Jesus of Suburbia*. It was cute how she got hypnotized by her favorite bands. You'd have to set off a firecracker in her ear to pull her out of it. Maribel could tune everything in the world out, and with Dara's stupid self-consuming thoughts about her body, which she knew were vain and borderline obsessive, she so, *so* wished she could do the same.

If not with her body, then with that strange song that had been playing in her head for the past few days...

At any rate, all these issues swarmed around Dara, sharks and vultures, vultures and sharks. Luke wasn't thrilled with her interviewing at his engineering firm, but she actually had an "in" there, which was a job-hunting advantage she'd never had in the past. He wouldn't really come out and say anything directly negative about it though—before Maribel came along, they might have fought, and in the end Dara would have let him have his way.

Not so anymore. The dynamics had changed with their new wife; she'd made both of them feel like dumbasses for ever rallying against each other's happiness. That was a rule. You never interfered with happiness. You were the facilitator of making it happen—and that's why Maribel took out half of her savings and Luke sold his wave-runner to make Dara's surgery happen.

Hopefully, it would always be like this. Lately there had been some cracks in their newfound holy trinity. Last night Luke had grumbled a few disparaging things about the interview, and Maribel hadn't interceded. She might have had her classroom planning on her mind because it often possessed her when she began a new school year, but still, it wasn't like her to let slide any caustic or judgmental quips, especially when directed at each other. Luke even seemed to notice the absence of her enforcement and corrected himself, hoping for Maribel to chime in.

She hadn't.

Dara remembered exactly what Maribel had been doing. Sitting in the recliner, legs bent beneath her, fingers absently fiddling with the white horse earrings one of her students gave her. She'd been watching a water polo match on TV in a trance, the worn-out paperback of the autobiography of Mark Twain resting on her lap, a leopard-print book mark sticking out of its center. Luke asked if she wanted a salad with her chicken, to test whether she was even listening. She turned her light brown eyes to him. "You know I don't."

Of course not. Maribel only ate one thing at meals. She wouldn't eat a hamburger and fries. She'd either get a hamburger, or a large order of fries. One or the other, not both. At their first Thanksgiving together she just ate stuffing. The next year she had turkey. The next, green-bean casserole. But she never feasted. Dara and Luke had both tried to figure this out, but it was just one of Maribel's quirks. She never ate plain dinner salads because that'd be the only thing she'd have, and it would leave her hungry.

A wave of commercials came on the radio. Maribel turned it off.

"Are you proud of me, doing this interview?" asked Dara.

Maribel's eyes flitted to her. "That's a silly question, Dee. You know I am. Luke is too. It's all the static he's getting in his job from the rumors. He'll work through it. We'll all be okay."

"But what about today? Do you think he's having a breakdown over it?"

"You're not going to be there when he gets home," said Maribel, pulling into the Rec Center parking lot. "He's prematurely missing the housewife he thinks he has."

"Yeah, I'm not much of one of those."

"That's not what I meant."

Dara leaned over to kiss Maribel on the side of her mouth, but the flickering lights of police cars and fire engines made her freeze. "What's all that?"

"Oh my god," Maribel whispered.

Several gurneys awaited transport in one of the four coroner's vans parked amongst the other vehicles. Everything came in flashes, Dara's breathing quickening with every image. Bodies under white sheets. Men in sweat-soaked collared shirts scribbling on legal pads. A policeman pointing to some unknown thing near the pool. Freeze frames of an aftermath. Of what, Dara couldn't tell yet, but it opened a pit in her center.

Luke had been here. What if he'd been part of something horrible and couldn't tell them about it yet? Her mind flitted to all those shootings in public you read about or saw on the news. Massacres from militant wackos with 180 IQs and Facebook walls brimming in hate.

"Look over there—look at the road," said Maribel. She put a hand up to her lips, and her eyes looked as frozen as Dara's heart felt. A tremendous cataclysm had shattered the street, making the concrete roll like a wave of stone.

"What did that? A bomb?"

"I don't know, but we have to get back to Luke. We have to ask what happened here. You okay to drive?"

Unwisely, Dara shook her head to dispel the dizziness that had overcome her. "Yes, sure." She took the spare keys from the center console and popped open the door.

"Careful driving, honey," said Maribel.

"You too."

As Dara walked over to Luke's blue Chevy Volt, the only ambient sound was the secluded 60 freeway. Her ears unintentionally perked for the floating vibrations of loved ones crying, something tragic and grim that would make her heart fall; she remembered the echoing of such pain. It'd once come from her own throat, rang in her own ears, the day Uncle Sal came to the house and described her parents' accident. *On their way to church, couldn't be helped, big rig carrying eight thousand gallons of corn syrup couldn't brake in time on the downgrade and just went through the intersection. Took them under, crushed the station wagon, back to front.* Had Dara gone with them, she'd have died first. She'd made them late by pitching a fit about wasting her Sunday morning. In the end they'd just left the house, both in bitter moods, promising to discuss her attitude when they returned.

That discussion would never happen.

A case could be made that Dara's lack of respect and stubbornness got her mother and father killed that day. For many years that was all she could behold in a mirror: a heartless soul, a bad daughter, an ugly leftover from two wonderful people. Uncle Sal and then Luke had tried their best to calm her self-loathing, but nobody except Maribel had ever scratched the surface.

Dara studied her shape reflected in the Volt's window and door. It was never enough. She would never be the person she wanted to be. Accepting that fact was probably the only answer, but how did someone pull that off?

The song from her dream shimmered to the front of her mind again. It wasn't the whole song…just maybe one layer of a thousand. *Strange.*

"Excuse me ma'am."

Dara jumped. Lifting a hand to calm her, a young cop with a raspberry birthmark on his left cheek took another step closer to her, his heavy utility belt squeaking as he did. "Sorry, I just wanted to caution you to the east side of the parking lot. The street department has not arrived yet for detour signs. You weren't at the pool today, were you?"

"No, my husband was."

The man's entire face turned the color of the birthmark.

"He's fine," Dara quickly said. "I guess he left before everything…happened."

"Good. All is well that ends well."

Dara blinked, uncertain that she'd heard him right. "Certainly. What went wrong in the street out there?"

"Likely a sewer explosion. We're still looking at it. But, you know, that's what you get when this type of thing occurs."

"What type of thing?"

The radio on the cop's shoulder chirped, and an authoritative female voice began to rattle out information. He held the radio, walking back toward the Rec building. After a moment he replied, still walking, "No I think the pool's always been shaped that way. Yeah, yeah. Well we have…" His voice trailed off.

Dara took a deep breath and opened the Volt. She dropped into the muggy cabin and rolled down the windows. After getting the car started and taking off the brake, she checked the external temperature gauge. It read 108 degrees. *Yes, this is a Southern California August; no doubts there.* Maybe there had been a madman at this place, and he'd gone crazy from the heat.

Maybe Luke had been the one to go crazy…

She headed west out of the parking lot.

Luke couldn't hurt anybody. He had made mistakes but had also paid his dues. She reminded herself that had he been faithful in the beginning, they no doubt would have broken up for other reasons. She wouldn't have been hurt, betrayed, whatever—she wouldn't have moved temporarily back in with Uncle Sal down at the beach and wouldn't have gone for that walk where she met Maribel.

At the time Dara understood that something existed between her and this exciting new woman, that it was more than a passing friendship. She was terrified of losing it, just about as much as she was terrified to discover what it might actually become. Taking a great risk, she told Maribel she still loved her husband and couldn't do to him what he'd done to her. That's what she thought she *had* to say. That she couldn't break the vow she'd made, and that she wasn't ready to leave him. Instead of the whole relationship unraveling though, Maribel wanted to meet Luke. Dara hadn't thought it a good idea at first. In fact, she thought it might isolate her from both these people she had feelings for.

She couldn't have been more wrong. It was almost immediate. Beautiful. Complete. The last puzzle piece snapping in place. And above all, the wonderful thing was knowing everybody felt the same way. The three of them were united. They would adore one another forever. They would support each other until their bodies gave out or the world ended, whichever came first.

Dara flipped her hair off her shoulders. Maribel fondly called her blonde waves a unicorn mane. On sweltering days like this, Dara just called it a pain in the ass. And speaking of pains in the ass—

"Yuck," she commented, already feeling sticky sweat dampening in her bra. Hoping to let a little air in, she adjusted herself. *Should have just stuck sponges under the girls.* She resentfully nudged the A/C dial higher.

She avoided gridlock on Pine Street and took Maple to the freeway. Maribel drove like an ADHD bat out of hell, and Dara didn't expect to keep up with her most days. Yet, she actually caught up with her. Today Dara's wife piloted the mini Cooper just under the speed limit, making no attempt to beat out any lights. Respecting the horror that car accidents had to offer, Dara couldn't feel anything but grateful. *But why now? Nerves because of Luke?*

Don't question it. Be thankful.

It just doesn't seem like her though.

She drives crazy-fast in every mood I've ever seen her in.

"What's up with you, Mari?" Dara whispered to herself. She turned on the local radio station and checked for news reports about the Rec Center. After an extremely worn-out Red Hot Chili Peppers song, the news came on. Dara increased the volume.

"*...Riverside Recreational Center where eight people drowned.*"

Dara gasped and caught her mouth.

"*...over a dozen in brown scuba gear were also found dead in the pool. No air was found in their tanks. The Riverside police department has confirmed that the frogmen had their arms locked around each victim, possibly drowning themselves and the people in their grip. Two of the frogmen were empty-handed, yet still drowned with the others.*"

A text came on her phone. Dara never read texts in the car, but this time she picked up the phone without hesitation. It was from Maribel.

Listen to the news.

They arrived at a red light and Dara answered. *I am. Dont txt & driv.*

Fifteen minutes later they were home. Not saying a word, they rushed to the front door, unlocked it and went inside.

Luke had tossed the mail over the kitchen countertop. Along with a recent copy of the *Federal Register*, which kept him updated on new environmental regulations, a copy of Dara's new *Game Informer* magazine had arrived. She'd seen the issue at Target earlier that week and thought the cover artwork for Dragon God III stunning. Now the Orc hovering over corpses of its fallen victims, battle axe raised above its head, just stared at her, fire in its condemnatory eyes. As Maribel unstrapped her purse, Dara slid the magazine away.

Another letter fell out of the pile. It was from the bank, and judging by the size of the envelope and the type of block writing at the top, it seemed to be the same notice as before. The bank wasn't willing to short sale the house and wouldn't budge on their offers. Shocking as it was, the lender had suggested, indirectly though not subtly, to let the home go into foreclosure. They might have been able to get topside on their mortgage if Maribel and Luke hadn't blown their savings earlier on Dara's surgery. She'd ruined their chances of moving up north.

Luke sat in the living room, watching the news on TV, both of his feet submerged in a large square container of crushed ice. On the coffee table a few Heineken bottles stood in formation, along with an opened tube of aloe vera and a wad of damp rags. He looked at them, his face pale and eyes red. In the background, a video showed a sheeted body being pushed into a coroner's van. The next shot was of a red rubber ducky floating on water so brown it might have been put through a sepia image filter. Maribel capped the aloe vera, took the rags to the sink, and hurried back.

Twisting away from the TV, Luke said, "I was there to teach my class. I remember those frogmen now. Couldn't happen, right? And then again...that's how it all went down."

Maribel sat down beside him, Dara at his other side. They were quiet for a few minutes. Dara grabbed the remote control and muted the TV when an obnoxious toothpaste commercial cut through their fugue state.

Luke looked intently into the den, at nothing in particular, his lips slightly parted. "Ralph Stedding and his wife, Alice, died in the pool."

"He's the one Johnny calls Mouse?" Maribel asked.

"Yeah."

Her honey complexion yellowed. "Was Petunia there, too?"

"She got away with me, I think." Luke put a hand on his forehead and looked up at the ceiling. "I think so—it's like remembering an acid trip. I don't know if that's what happened."

"Did they say anything about her on the news?" asked Dara.

"No," he said. "They only talked about Alice and Ralph."

The house phone rang, breaking the calm. Maribel grabbed it and answered.

Dara squeezed Luke's knee. "Don't worry. You're okay."

He nodded and remained quiet.

Maribel sat back down by Luke and spoke with a detective named Reese. Evidently, her aide from work, Allie Banks, had tipped off the cops that Luke had a swim class this morning at the Rec Center. Allie habitually interfered in other people's affairs, citing loose ends as her justification. She was always jumping for a chance to screw Maribel over, but would explain it as *just trying to help in a bad situation*. Dara didn't understand how Maribel could even work with the woman anymore. She'd have strangled her by now.

Maribel crinkled her nose in disbelief at something the detective said, then turned on speakerphone.

"My husband is listening in now, too," she said, carefully leaving Dara out of the equation, which she appreciated. "So if you have questions for him, he'll answer anything. He might be involuntarily suppressing some of what happened right now, but he will of course come down to your office and cooperate."

A polite, almost jovial voice replied, "No that's quite all right ma'am. That's completely unnecessary. As I said before, we have all we need here."

"I know, but how can that be? It just happened today—are you serious?"

The man laughed, but wasn't mocking in his tone. "It wasn't complicated. Petunia Stedding released a statement about the frogmen. We have no reason to doubt her version of the story because it fits with everything we've put together."

"But how did you...it just happened today," Luke repeated Maribel's statement.

The man's voice got louder. "We're certainly glad you're all right Mr. Rhodes and let us know if you need any medical attention. There are post-traumatic stress groups that meet at the community center every Wednesday. Do you want me to send an email with the information?"

"We don't understand," Maribel insisted. "Something very bizarre happened at the pool today. Why are you being so...tolerant of this?"

"Oh, yes, well, it isn't so bizarre," answered Reese. "You see, there were frogmen in the pool, and in circumstances like this, that's what they do. Right? Not much we can change about that. Yeah?"

It did make sense to Dara, actually, and as she searched Luke and Maribel's faces, she discovered that it also made sense to them. *That's what frogmen do.* Even the reporters on the TV had moved on to basketball scores. This event wasn't a big deal at all. What else could you expect from frogmen?

"Is there anything else I can help you with?" The detective's voice sounded bland.

Dara felt bad about Petunia. Losing both parents at once... She unfortunately knew how that was. "What will happen to Petunia now?"

"Like the other children, she's with family, from what I understand. Otherwise, I'm not part of that proceeding."

Luke nodded. Some life flooded back into his face.

"Thank you, Detective Reese," said Maribel.

"Call me if you have any further questions."

"We will. Thanks again."

Ten minutes of silence passed. It was uncomfortable silence. Dara thought of the song in her head. She wanted desperately to put it together, so she could recall the tune.

"Did we all just space out at the same time?" Maribel blurted out suddenly.

They all shared a laugh.

Another cell phone rang.

Luke's.

He'd left it on the mantle over the fire place. Dara began to get up, but Maribel touched her arm and nimbly pushed off the couch. She hurried to the phone and answered it. "Hi, Blake, yes, he's here. Oh yes, he's okay. He can talk. Here."

Luke nodded thanks and accepted the phone. "Hey, man. How are things?"

He leaned forward and pushed some ice off the top of his toes. "Yeah, I'll be there tomorrow. No, it's no problem…what? Well what is the status? Come on Blake, you can't put that out there and then expect me not to ask."

Slowly, Luke leaned his face into the fist that held the cell phone. "So the Los Angeles project is gone then, too?"

Dara and Maribel exchanged anxious looks. Luke's main project was water remediation with Los Angeles County. Some of the funds had been "mismanaged" at the top of the corporation, but it seemed like Luke had received all the blame for it. He had reassured them it would all work itself out, but the plowed-over expression on his face now told another tale.

"Well thanks for calling. Yeah, thanks, it was pretty unreal. Never seen frogmen before." He chuckled uneasily. "All right, buddy. Good bye."

He pushed the end button and tossed the phone on the coffee table so hard it skated off the glass and went over the other side.

"Bad?" asked Dara.

Luke sniffed and looked down at his buried feet for a moment. "I'd say that of the two of us, you are the more likely to be working for GeoGreen next month. I might have trouble finding engineering work anywhere locally after this."

"No way." Maribel shook her head. "We won't let them tarnish you like that. It isn't fair. You work so hard for them."

"They don't care about that," Luke said. "The people at the top know a sacrificial lamb when they see one, and they want to keep their jobs. It's an easy call as far as they're concerned."

"It won't be an easy call," Maribel promised. Dara forced a smile.

Luke patted their legs. "Let's be calm for now. I'm going to take a bath and relax a bit."

"Your feet up for that?"

He pulled them out of the ice. The skin was bright red from the cold. "I forgot about that," he admitted. "Probably not a great idea. Do we have any poison?"

"You two drank all the Tequila on the Fourth of July," Maribel said pointedly.

"Want me to go buy something?" Dara asked.

"No, no. You have to study for your interview. I'll give Johnny a call. I have to *not* think about this stuff for a while, and it's easy to forget just about anything when he's around."

"Just don't bring him over here." Dara folded her arms. The last person she wanted to see right now was Johnny Cruz.

"I know, I know." Luke got up, slightly wincing.

Maribel clapped her hands, as she always did when a plan was made. "You have your boy time, then. Dara and I are making spinach bake."

"Bleh." Luke opened the bathroom door in the hall.

"Sound good?" Maribel asked Dara.

She smiled faintly and nodded. She did love the spinach casserole under normal circumstances, but her stomach still churned from the events of today, not to mention the butterflies for tomorrow. Maribel pinched her skin below her ribcage. "You know you want some."

"Don't," Dara cautioned. For some reason she couldn't get Maribel or Luke to buy into the fact that she hated to be tickled.

"So sensitive!" Maribel tittered and headed for the kitchen.

"Hey, you okay with all the stuff I told you about Stobecker?" Luke stood in the darkness of the bathroom, his hands bracing him in the doorframe.

"Hope so," said Dara. "He hates you, so I might be tainted."

"He doesn't hate me. He's just very Christ-y. But there are two very nice atheists on the panel. They probably aren't going to go to bat for me with this Los Angeles deal, but that's neither here nor there."

Dara didn't want to address this new development. Luke *couldn't* lose his job. They didn't have the right to take it from him. "Are these other folks as conservative as Stobecker?"

Luke paused. "I don't know their politics, Dee."

"You know what I mean."

"Just try not to mention Maribel."

"You said the rumor's already going around."

"Yes, so don't add gasoline to the fire. Just concentrate on your business. They should concentrate on theirs."

"I don't have to go, if it bugs you."

"If you want a job there, then I want you to have a job there."

She sighed. "Go take a leak."

"Your wish is my command." Luke shut the door. She could hear the toilet lid flip up.

Dara hummed part of the song from her dream last night. She had the interlude right, but couldn't quite get the next part worked out.

The bathroom door swung open. Luke stood there, pants unzipped, backlit by the bathroom's florescence. "What was that? What were you humming?"

Dara almost blurted out where she'd thought the song came from, but she didn't want him to think her foolish. "Nothing…just something on my mind. I don't know where it's from."

"Huh," he said.

Maribel shut the refrigerator firmly. "Sounds like something from one of my dreams."

Dara turned to Luke, wondering if he'd say the same. But he said nothing.

He shut the bathroom door, looking disturbed.

Chapter 4

Johnny just couldn't feel sorry for Mouse.

It was a tough break, what happened to him and his wife at the pool, but the man had been a lazy-sack-of-shit vampire who sucked the city of every drop he could. Dead or not, you couldn't mince issues here. Workers like Mouse made it harder for everybody to get their jobs done. He showed up late, took long lunches, napped behind abandoned tanks, yapped all day long with the secretaries down at City Hall, on and on; he was a dingleberry of the first caliber.

But he was the city's favorite dingleberry, it seemed. Mouse and Johnny had the same grade of mechanic certification, but the city handed him the Lead Mechanic title last year, which carried a significant raise, not to mention an ego blowjob for someone who didn't deserve one. Never to go silently into that fucked-up night, Johnny bitched high and low about Mouse's piss-poor performance maintaining the plant, his abuse of sick time and floating holidays, and—to show he wasn't just a jealous jerk— Johnny pointed to data to support this. Nobody wanted to listen, though. Minds were made up. Eyes and ears and assholes were shut tightly.

Johnny then made a few not-so-veiled threats about quitting and leaving everybody in the lurch (they needed him so bad it was pathetic— with him gone just two days, all of Redwood Boulevard would be under three feet of sewage), but even with the threat of overflowing sewers, nobody considered his candidacy. Somehow, the superintendent of Water and Wastewater was more impressed with all the overtime Mouse put in. This supposed overtime really amounted to Mouse abusing union rules. The man checked a sewage lift station on his way home from work every day, a ten-minute job, and since this was considered off-the-clock, he logged the time as a call-out and granted himself the union-sanctioned three hours overtime. To Johnny Cruz, this amounted to stealing, but to those schmucks standing before him in the operations room, it amounted to a dedicated employee.

So why was Johnny so surprised? It shouldn't have come as a shock that with Mouse now gone, these dunces would not only pass the Lead Mechanic job to someone else, but to a guy with less experience and a lower certification.

"Grover Franklin? I trained that fucking guy. He doesn't even have five years under his belt!"

From the break room, Grover shuffled in, a tanner, slightly more muscular version of Jim Carrey in an orange city shirt and black Dickies. He was a hard worker and a good kid, but Johnny hadn't decided yet if it wasn't all just kissing asses.

Grover took off his sweaty LA Angel's cap; his hair was an oily dark mess. "Hey, I don't want to interrupt here, but maybe Johnny is right," he said with a shrug.

"Well done, candy-ass, but they aren't going to change their minds and you know it. You've made yourself look good without losing anything."

"Come on, Johnny," he mumbled, face flushing.

"Meanwhile, I've been faithful to this city my entire adult life, and now it's turning its back on me. Mouse was a fucking idiot, and now you're replacing him with a rube!"

The superintendent, Fabian Rove, a short, bald, dodgy-looking guy in a button-up baby-blue shirt and maroon tie, just about took a step back. He was courageous, though, in his Superman colors, and locked eyes with Johnny. "Let's calm down here, Alberto. I know you lost a friend today. I appreciate that."

"My name's Johnny."

"Okay, Johnny."

Johnny whipped around to the silent man in the corner of the dim trailer. "You're not really endorsing this, are you Jack?"

The plant manager, Jack Portiere, head and shoulder above all three other men, idly brushed his calloused thumb against the canary cage hanging in the office, making an irritating noise that reminded Johnny of a song he'd once heard. The plant's mascot, Shit Bird, a brown-and-black finch, cycled around, making a racket but also adding to the song. Johnny tried to recall it for a moment and then refocused his thoughts.

"Grover isn't ready," Johnny said. "He's just hardly a grade two."

"I aced it, though. I'll be able to go for the three in no time," Grover pointed out.

"He pulls a lot of overtime," Jack said, in the weary monotone of a man about to retire. "Puts in the extra hours. We need that dedication."

Johnny smacked his own face, hard. "Oh my damn god. Have you even asked what the overtime is about? Does common sense mean nothing to you people?"

"I don't want to take sides," Jack replied, shrugging his thin shoulders. He didn't even look at Johnny and instead studied Shit Bird again.

"There won't be any new hires. You'll have to use what you have," said Rove. He folded his arms, sweat ovals running from his underarms down his sky-blue shirt, maroon tie soaked in his own brine.

"Okay. It'll get done," said Jack. "We'll make it work. Johnny can show Grover the new lift stations on Cedar and how to maintain surcharges on Redwood."

Johnny's mouth dropped. He was furious at himself for being so shocked. Jack Portiere had less of a spine than Mouse Stedding had a work ethic. He was actually the other extreme—the guy required his head buried in an engine or pump at all times, and human conflict, moments like these, he avoided at all costs. Johnny never could understand how such a jellyfish had become manager of an entire sewer-treatment plant for a large city.

"You're both fucked in the head if you think I'm training Grover for a job that should be *mine*."

"Hey!" Rove pointed a thick little finger at him. "You're getting a lot of chances to vent here. Remember what I said before. There's no need to be uncivil. We can get through this without being rude."

"I'm not being rude. You're just not important enough for civility."

Rove stepped right in front of him. The guy had to look up at Johnny, who nearly busted up laughing at the intense pale face and beady hazel eyes. "I think you should leave now," said Rove.

It was a trial of temptation not to slam his forehead into Rove's stupid face. "Tell you what, get your ass away from me before I choke you off."

"How about I terminate you instead?"

"You gonna let him do that to me, Jack? After I showed up on every flippin' rainy day this city's ever had?"

Jack gave him a glance as though to say *hey, come on, don't drag me into this.*

"I don't need his approval, just his statement for the record," Rove fired back. "I'm not afraid of you, if you hadn't noticed."

Johnny balled his fists and exhaled through his teeth. The lenses of his eyeglasses had fogged a little. He wasn't stopping to wipe them. It was on now.

"You still have a chance to stop this fit of yours and go home." Rove took a step back, not so macho after all. "I will take into account what happened today to Ralph. Just go home and reflect a little. You a family man, Alberto?"

It was all over. *What the hell right did he have in asking that?* In just a moment's time fate had changed everything. Johnny lunged forward, caught Rove by his sickeningly wet shirt and threw him into Jack's desk. Rove went backwards, ass-over-elbows, and struck the stem of the canary cage. The cage went sideways and wacked Jack Portiere hard in the face. He was jumping out of the way as it happened, and the blow sent him staggering into another desk overflowing in paperwork. The cage door popped open. A black-brown bullet zipped out and headed toward the engine room, tweeting merrily.

Johnny stormed down that same hall, not even looking back at the calamity he'd caused, trying not to feel anything more about the shouts and challenges coming his way, because with all his strength he could easily cripple any of these men. He came to the exit for the pump room and kicked the door open. As he went outside, the finch flew past like an apparition loosed on the world.

Freedom, Shit Bird. It's called freedom. We're both flying out tonight.

Johnny got on his Hog and pulled a cigarillo from a pocket in his cargo shorts. The tip was a bit scrunched, but it would do. He lit it. Puffing away, he started his bike and blew down the side road along the plant's sludge beds. As he got to the end and stopped at the street to wait for some cars, everything surged inside him.

"Son of a fucking fuck!" he yelled. His cigarillo fell out of his mouth. "Fuck," he added in a whisper.

If they canned him over this…they'd be sorry. That's all he knew at this point.

The drive back home normally took about fifteen minutes, but with all that was running through his mind, it didn't feel like more than five. He listened to Cannibal Corpse the entire way; the death metal band hadn't even seemed to get warmed up when he pulled into his driveway. Johnny decided he'd put them on in the garage and do some fab work tonight.

His garage door hadn't even opened all the way when a car pulled up behind him. The sun was setting, but he recognized the Chevy Volt and his friend behind the wheel. Luke slid out of the car with a black plastic bag from the liquor store. Bottles clanked inside.

"Holy shit," Johnny muttered. "You're a sight for sore eyes. I must be turning gay."

"Thanks?"

"It's just that I didn't think I'd see you again for a while."

"Happy?"

"What'd you bring me?"

"Corona."

"Good man. The shop fridge has room."

Luke nodded and headed up the grease-streaked driveway. "You just get home?"

"They called a meeting about Mouse. He had one of those positions that had to be filled right away with an interim."

"How'd that go?"

Johnny sighed. "I don't know, man. I think I'm gonna quit that job."

Luke tilted his head. "And do what?"

"Who the fuck knows? Maybe I'll be an engineer. I can spend Sundays barbequing my feet in front of strange houses."

"Be nice."

"Yeah, okay, weirdo. I don't know what the hell I can do. There's not enough money to start my own metalwork shop. But I don't mind taking a government check for nothing, rather than actual work."

Luke bent down before the little fridge, opened it, put the six pack inside, less two bottles. He used the opener on the wall, careful to collect the caps and set them on the drying machine. Johnny took the beer he was offered and drank half of it in one tug. "Thanks for coming over man...I mean it."

Luke brought up his bottle. "My pleasure. Neither of my wives wants you in our home, so it's always my pleasure."

Johnny smiled. He couldn't help it. In that moment, he was so damned grateful. He might not have a wife and son anymore, but this he still had. Friendship. Tonight would have been about drinking alone, beating off to porn, maybe a little welding if he got ambitious, but honestly probably not. Instead, his best friend was here. He was lucky to have Luke. And Johnny would do anything for him. Hell, he'd do anything for Dara and Maribel, too, just because he believed Luke really loved them as much as he said.

"Come on, let's watch the tube. There's this one show I want you to see."

"It better not be lesbian stuff again, man. Really."

"Hey, fact versus fiction. You have to admit it's impressive. I just wanted to know if Dara and Maribel could get that same rhythm—"

"Enough."

Johnny opened the door to the house. "It's a fuckin' sitcom, by the way, you douche."

"Sounds good."

"A lesbian sitcom."

"What?"

"Just kidding."

"Johnny, you are a depraved man."

"Deprived, not depraved."

Johnny decided everything would work out. Luke was going through his own shit at work and it didn't seem to bother him much. You just had to have some kind of resolve was all. It was settled. Johnny wouldn't apologize for these fuckers trying to railroad him, but if they let him come back to work, he'd shut up and do his job. Of course, he wouldn't teach Grover how to do anything. The kid didn't deserve the bump in pay. The title. None of it.

And if everybody's tit was in a ringer about what had happened tonight, if Johnny did lose his job of ten years over a momentary lapse of judgment, he would sue the city for psychological harm or some shit. That might take time and money, though... Hell with that. Johnny knew a guy that bought stolen copper fittings. Perhaps he'd take a tour of the city and steal every bit of copper from every city backflow device. He'd use the money to open his custom motorcycle shop. See how those dick-smears liked that.

Yeah. Good. That wasn't a bad idea at all. They'd see. They thought he was like Mouse? Some no-good, union-hugging slob? A grimy little flea or tick? Or what were those other things called? Louses? *Mouse the louse.* Sounded about right.

Well fine. Let the city think of Johnny Cruz whatever they wanted. He'd laugh all the way to the bank. They'd see. Soon.

They'd feel the full potential of this louse.

Chorus:

He thought about what the dreams meant.

In the playground structure, They have built many shapes, shown many colors. Harnessing fire-engine red, sunshine yellow, baby blue, sweet-pea green, this three level fixture of metal composites and plastic would likely call attention to itself in an unaffected world. Here, the eyes beg to look away.

The smaller slide that once spiraled to the ground, collecting static and giggles along the way, now spirals up into the sky through the black clouds that drip with long, icy incisors. Looking close, They would see something indistinguishable riding the slide down (or up?), and this something, this indistinct enigma, is the red kind, the one They squint to focus on and exclaim silently within their loud, loud hearts, *it's bloody, whatever it is, it's bloody.* They look away. Sure They do.

Except for one. The man on the bench across from the playground. He's listening. He's waiting. He's watching. His attention is on the leering clown-face tunnel beneath the play set. The man cannot recall a time when the tunnel merely led to open air beneath the second floor. It hasn't been long, and yet, this tunnel before him has always stretched to the farthest darkness his eyes can discern. In his ringing ears, beyond the eternal song that rests upon the sky, earth and brain, come the taps of a xylophone, and children are screaming and laughing and living, or screaming and cackling and killing. In his mind, he longs for answers and hatches questions like an overstressed hen. In his eyes, he beholds the mixing of shadows and flashes of light and slashes of blood at the far end of the tunnel. He bites back a sob. Of course, he does. He's one of Them.

"Can you hear me in there?" he asks. "Don't let it find me. Please…I want to live. Did you hear me? Say something. Just make a sound. Anything. Tell me you'll keep it away. I can't see it again. My mind…won't take it. *Please.*"

Verse 2: The Interview

Chapter 5

Days like these, Luke played goalie.

It wasn't enough that the Los Angeles contract and his job were in question. Hell, due to the tight-knit network of environmental agencies, the shit-splash went fairly far, so Luke's ability to find anything new might be in question. That particular raincloud followed him to work every day now, but it didn't stop at that—there was also this little matter of a man married to two women.

People's opinion about his relationship with Dara and Maribel varied on many levels of disapproval, and he deflected endless attempts, subtle and not-so-subtle, to score points against his wives. It had been several months now since their secret became public domain, but the barrage continued with renewed vigor every day. He could feel the eyes of people he didn't know, but they were easy to ignore. Some people here at GeoGreen had been familiar faces for almost a decade. Friends. Some almost like family.

Mildred Betters from accounting had once treated him like a son, and although she didn't abandon their half-hour long talks about her granddaughter's water polo team, she stopped asking him about Dara completely and never mentioned Maribel. Luke wanted to believe she did it to spare him any awkward moments, but then again, Mildred had several Christian fishes on the bumper of her car, which told him her silence might be for more sanctimonious reasons. It bothered him to judge her like that, but when in Rome...

At least she didn't confuse Dara with Maribel.

At least he didn't feel like a walking hard-on around her.

At least, at the very least, he'd never overheard the word "mistress" or "Mormon?" whispered from her cubicle.

The list of known offenders went on. For some reason, Jane Wiles in plan check and the CEO's secretary Maria Rosa, who had always flirted with him, had now become aggressive with their advances; Blake Jackson, a fellow engineer, while still polite and professional, no longer asked Luke to *Cowboy Burger* for lunch; and Denise O'Shea, who ran the storm water contracts, rumpled her nose whenever he came walking down the hall. She may have always been a bitter woman—he couldn't recall if she'd ever been cordial, even before the rumors started swirling—yet it didn't matter, because Luke still had to deflect it. Captain Courageous had to absorb every attack, even those he conjured himself, and he had to remind his black-and-blue heart, *they just don't know.*

Some days he did this without any extra effort. Others were more difficult.

Today was shaping up to be one of the difficult ones.

He took three aspirin and drank them down with black coffee. The beers last night with Johnny wouldn't have had an effect on him back in the day, but at thirty-two he got banging headaches if he went over three drinks. It was difficult to focus on his emails. The song had crept into his mind again. Tapping. Wind. Crying. Laughing. A xylophone. Static. Life and death sounds. He had the idea that while he slept the song was just as elusive. It was like the soundtrack to his unconscious mind, and the song wanted to be free again; his mind had to mold it and bring out the tenor and bass and vocal progression. The tone, too. The song would need to have some dimension before he could completely recall it.

He wondered about the red rubber duck. He wondered about Petunia Stedding. Was she really okay, like that cop had said? He hoped so.

Luke highlighted a couple important emails. He found one from Maria, the CEO's secretary. The subject line: *Don't you wish you had a mouthful of those?*

He sighed. Once he deleted an email from her with a provocative subject but Maria had actually included some business items in the body of the email. He'd never seen it and failed to call the west coast project manager, who patently had an ego that required people call him back the same day.

Luke opened the email to a photo of a woman with enormous breasts. She wore a translucent bikini that left nothing to the imagination. Below the photo it said: "BIGGIES, BUT YOU & THE WIFE HAVE SARA, SO YOUR PROBABLY USED TO THIS. STUD! LOL! :)"

Sara?

He twisted the flesh between his eyes, hoping to kill the lingering ache there.

Sending something like this was pretty ballsy after the recent security upgrades and internet monitoring the company had invested in.

After he deleted the email, Luke sent Maria a request to keep all correspondence business related. He might have corrected her about Dara's name and the fact that she was his legal wife, but knew it would do little good. Luke had sent similar emails to her before to no avail. He'd even thought about going to HR to file harassment charges, but Maria had been with the company since its inception and was like a daughter to Kris Thacker, the president. Filing for harassment was a pile of shit Luke didn't want to step into, for sure.

"Have you finished with those P sheets?"

Luke glanced up from his monitor.

Derek Stobecker.

This was the gray little man who would make or break Dara at her interview. He, like Mildred, had proclamations of his faith stickered on his mini-van, but unlike Mildred, he brought up the Lord any chance he got and usually at Luke's expense. In fact, by the pinched look on his face, he seemed to be thumbing through the bible in his mind, for ease of use.

"Didn't you ask Blake for those?"

"No." Derek sighed. "I asked you."

"I'm kidding. It shouldn't be a problem. I have the isometrics done for the third site already and the fact sheet on the dissolved air flotation system is in your inbox—"

"How long will the P-sheets take? LA County is being...insistent."

"By the end of the day."

Derek dropped into the chair across from the desk. He looked weary, but then Derek always looked weary. "I want to talk a little with you. It's personal, so I hope you don't mind. It seems I'm doing an interview with your girlfriend—"

"Wife. Yeah, yeah, she's excited."

He blinked for several moments. "This is the one you're married to?"

"Derek...I don't really want to talk about that again, if it's all the same to you."

His face went long. "I still have a responsibility to see that things don't get too complicated around here if we are going to hire your, um, *wife*. It's this Los Angeles deal—"

"Are you refusing Dara an interview?"

With a snort, Derek shook his head and looked away. "Try not to be personal about this. Think about how you've turned this department upside down on two fronts, only in a matter of months."

"Completely my fault. Yeah, I get it."

"You know I don't believe that."

"Belief won't help me with the LA contract," said Luke grimly, "But if it does...Dara and I will be in completely different departments, so it's within company guidelines. I work at home three days a week. Shouldn't make for many complications I don't think."

Derek licked his lips and, with a sour expression, stood up. "Yes..."

"So I'm going to get to work on those plumbing specs right now."

"Just so I know. Who was it I saw with you at the grocery store last Sunday?"

Luke stretched out his mind, waiting to fend off the incoming puck. "That was Maribel."

"And I hate to press, but this *is* a unique situation. Who holds her health and life insurance, can I ask?" The man dissected him with his bright blue eyes.

"She has her own. Maribel's a teacher, and Dara is currently on my insurance. We aren't legally...married...to Maribel, so she's separate financially."

You happy now? Asshole?

Something made Derek turn abruptly, as though prodded with electricity. "Can I offer some advice?"

Luke swallowed. "Absolutely."

"This is a bit risky way to go about things. You should come down sometime, you and Maribel, to discuss Dara. We know how perilous the world can be sometimes."

"Pardon?"

"My church has family counseling. You and your wife—oh did I say Maribel again? She's the other one."

Luke felt his fingernails digging into his palms. "We aren't religious and don't need any therapy. Thanks though. I mean it. I appreciate your concern. We're good. No problems at all."

"Oh, it's not therapy—sorry, I didn't mean to be pushy."

"We've been together for over three years now. We're very happy."

"So you don't go to church then? *Ever*?"

"Dara used to be Catholic, but no—"

"You're atheists?" The surprise in the man turned him a shade of green that almost made Luke bust out laughing.

"We have nothing against it. Maribel actually finds studying books on religion to be a fascinating pastime."

Derek frowned. "I'm very sorry for bringing all of this up, Luke. I had the impression you were Christian, since you're such good friends with Mildred. I hope I haven't made you feel uncomfortable."

"No, no. It's okay. My parents were Christian."

"I'll pray for you guys." He got up from the chair, resolute.

"May I offer a suggestion, Derek?" asked Luke.

He raised his eyebrows, but nodded curiously.

"Those children at the Rec Center who lost their parents sure could use your prayers more than us. I was there. It was very scary. They and their families would probably appreciate your thoughts."

Derek snorted. "Hardly...we all know that's what frogmen do. No prayers are necessary."

Luke stared at him for a moment, until what he said sank in. "Oh yeah," he replied. "Sure."

"Well then, back at it." Derek gave an awkward thumbs-up that scarcely cleared his pointer finger. "I'm sure Dara will have a fine interview tomorrow. Tell her not to worry. We're all nice people here."

"Yes, we are."

After a tight-lipped smile, Derek left the room.

Putting that conversation behind him, the song began seeping into cracks in the foundation of his mind again, Luke tried to get some work done for a change. He'd been daydreaming for the past couple of months about quitting this job and opening his own small environmental engineering firm. It'd be better if they moved out of Southern California, somewhere with less hellish weather, perhaps to a mountain town or something. Maribel wouldn't like the idea of living like a hermit, so it would have to be somewhere within reach of a big city, and she would need to keep teaching children. Dara would go with the flow.

Wait, though. What if she got the job here?

Unlikely now.

Luke put his mind back to reviewing the plumbing diagrams for the latest bio-digester he'd designed for the water reclamation plant, or as Johnny called it, "the shit farm."

Thinking about Johnny, he took another aspirin (now at the max dose) and swallowed his last sip of cold coffee. He decided that a fresh cup was in order and headed for the break room. Halfway there, he felt someone pacing him.

Maria had too much rouge on her cheeks, and one of her silver hair clips appeared to have lost its grip on her long, wavy, night-black ponytail. She wasn't a hard woman to look at most days, but when she was busy or flustered, all of her attractiveness diminished to the stress wrinkles around her eyes.

"You didn't have to be so serious with me in that email," she told him, breathlessly trying to keep up. "I thought we were friends. Can't you take a joke? You know I'm the only one here who defends you? Do you even know that?"

Luke faced her. "Wait up a minute—"

"Do you know how you made me feel?" Maria asked.

"Wait, wait. Take it easy. It's all good. I'm not mad. Just trying to be professional is all. Let's get you a cup of coffee."

"No, I've got to get back to my desk. You aren't going to say anything about that picture, right? It was a joke. A damn joke." Her voice shrank, the words sitting in her mouth. She looked away from him. "Thought guys liked that kind of thing."

"Let's just forget about it. Better head back, okay?"

"I just can't believe...you would be offended."

"I'm not."

"It's not fair." A smile started to form on Maria's full lips, but she apparently willed it away. "You led me on."

"No, he didn't," said a voice behind them.

Cup of herbal tea delicately held in his large hand, Blake Jackson stood there, his frame almost filling the doorway. His heroic face had African features but there was an exotic, almost Asian appearance to the set of his eyes.

"I'm sorry, Blake, but this is actually a private matter," said Maria.

"Like heck it is. Maria, just go back to your desk and play Angry Birds. You aren't doing any good here."

She glanced at Luke and started away, her heels snapping on the tile floor. When she was gone, Blake cocked his head and rolled his eyes. "Such is your life."

"Such is my life," answered Luke. "Thank you."

Blake shrugged and made a face: *don't mention it*. Luke wondered for a moment what it would be like to have Blake as his best friend, rather than Johnny. Life would be easier, no doubt. Johnny probably would have egged Maria on.

"Well, I'm gonna get some Joe."

"Go for it, man," said Blake, stepping aside.

Luke went in and grabbed a cup from the stack. "Hey, isn't your barbecue bash this month. Gotta get me some of those jalapeno cheddar hot links."

Blake's shoulders sagged. "It was last weekend...sorry."

Luke reached for the powdered creamer. Words stuck in his throat. "So...uh...scaling the event down huh?"

"Shawna and I thought you'd be busy with your swim class."

"It's only an hour long, man."

Blake looked around outside, then stepped back into the break room. "I don't approve of how folks treat you here. That's on the record."

"I'm glad you feel that way."

"But come on, Luke. You'd show up to my house with *both* of them."

"We've brought Maribel for three years now!"

"It was better when everybody just thought she was a family friend. Why did you even start telling people?"

"You think *we* would?" Luke raised an eyebrow.

"Johnny?"

Luke shook the creamer into the cup. "He said a few things at a bar to his friends from the treatment plant, and we're still doing contract work over there, so his blabbing trickled over here."

Blake took a deep breath and a sip of his tea, while Luke poured and stirred his coffee. "How was the turn-out this year?" he asked. "Did you make the beer chicken again?"

Blake glared at him.

"I'm just asking."

"Look man.... My wife doesn't get it. Okay? Having Dara and Maribel there—she'd take it out on me."

"Why?"

"She would. Trust me. *Is that the kind of thing all men want?* I can hear her now."

"We could talk to Shauna, make her understand—"

Blake shook his head fiercely. "No, no, no. Maribel and Dara are nice women, and you're a good guy, but there's little hope of getting that across to Shauna or my kids."

"Who's telling the kids?" Luke almost spilled coffee on his wrist.

"These things find a way."

"Bullshit, man. Honestly. That's bullshit."

Blake took another sip of tea, steam still emanating from inside the cup. Luke stared down at the oily surface of his coffee, and his stomach knotted.

"Johnny, man..." Blake finally said. "I don't know why you're still friends with that guy."

"Because he wouldn't last long knowing I was gone, too." With a sigh, Luke raised his coffee to cheers. "I'll see you around. The P-sheets review shouldn't last too long."

Blake nodded for a moment, seeming in a trance. He came out of it, shaking his head. "Oh the hell with it...come here a second. Near the fridge."

Luke gave him a sidelong look as he came over. The hum of the compressor kicking on made him nervous for some reason. It reminded him of that song.

"Look..." Blake began. "I've been thinking about what's happening to you here, with the Los Angeles contract, I mean."

"Yeah?"

Blake checked the hall for a moment. Satisfied, he pulled back into the room. "There's a San Francisco division opening up next month. I got the low-down on it with Terry Archer in logistics."

"They've been talking about that location for a while."

"It's really happening. Building is there and everything now. Staff isn't where it needs to be yet, though."

"I see."

"But here's what I'm thinking. Couples get transferred all the time. It's actually preferred to keep them separate. If Dara gets that job, I could move you into a satellite position for the San Francisco office. You would be working from home all five days a week."

"Wow," Luke said, head suddenly spinning. "But we'd be in different departments. There isn't really a need to separate us."

"You're still in the same building and with all the stuff floating around right now it would be more than justified. Look at John and Jessica Myers. They were in separate areas, and they got relocated over that bathroom rumor."

"Don't remind me."

Blake's narrowed eyes held Luke's for a moment. "If we make the transfer before the Los Angeles contract is up, it would muddy the waters a bit. These directors are idiots. They don't have much on you right now anyway, just a bunch of hypothetical stuff that the board won't question or dare to research. So whoever falls into your current position next will be safe, and yet responsibility over the life of the contract wouldn't be all on you. You'll be in a different area, and the directors can play like they'd already remedied the problem."

"You should have been a politician."

"Soon," said Blake with a grin. He put a hand on Luke's shoulder. "If Dara's interview is impressive, she can eventually transfer to public relations at the new office, and you'll already be there. Maribel can start looking for schools, all that. You guys could go up north like you've always told me you wanted."

Luke hadn't considered that option. "You think we could?"

Blake pulled his hand away and took another sip of tea. "Why the hell not?"

"I love you!" Luke embraced him.

"Easy, just don't marry me, too."

Luke pulled away. "Touché. This is a great idea. Thank you so much."

"You're welcome so much, but remember, it's all about how well they receive Dara tomorrow. If she doesn't get the job, it won't be easy to justify the transfer. I can still try, but that might look like I'm hiding you from scrutiny."

Luke nodded. "I understand. Pressure's on."

"She'll do great." Blake smiled. "Now go on, get your shit done."

Luke headed back for the solitude of his office. Three conversations in a row about his wives, but the last one had ended on a great note. This blindsiding avalanche could have buried him, but the force of its impact had instead taken him to a more hopeful place.

When he returned to his desk, the phone was ringing. Luke swore that if this call had anything to do with his home life he'd probably rip every last hair from his head.

"Mr. Rhodes…"

It was Petunia Stedding.

"My god, how are—I mean, it's, um—you okay?"

He could hear her softly breathing into the phone, but she didn't say anything more.

"I don't know what to say about that day, honey. You're parents…were both good people. Are you okay? Do you need anything?"

"I touched the rubber ducky in the pool," she whispered. "I wasn't supposed to, but I did. I don't think *it* wanted me to."

"The frogmen?"

Petunia laughed. "No. Not them. That was your ducky, Mr. Rhodes. I wasn't supposed to touch it. I'm sick now."

"Sick about what happened to mom and dad?"

"I shouldn't have touched the ducky, because now it knows. It's treating me like an alien. I don't belong. This connection is not mine. It should be yours. I'm hearing the song through you. It's unnatural, and it knows."

"What? Who?"

"The Balladeer. The one who sings the Nightmare Ballad."

"Honey, I don't understand."

"The Thing that rides on the Balladeer's shoulders wants to kill me now because I know. It doesn't like people to question. What happened that day in the pool wasn't real life, but *it happened* in real life."

"Can I talk to your grandmother?"

"I got a Japanese steak knife and opened my bunny rabbit from crotch to throat. I haven't decided yet how to use what I've learned. I either gut myself next, or you."

"Me? Petunia…"

"You brought those things to the pool. They drowned my parents. I don't know if you're the Balladeer, but opening you like I did Mr. Fluffs would feel good. Maybe it'd pull the song out of my head. Your song. Get away, Grandma! Goddamn it don't touch me!"

A tired voice came on the line. "Hello? Who is this?"

"Luke Rhodes," he said.

"Hello, Mr. Rhodes. I'm sorry—I've been trying to keep her away from the phone. She's dealing with this really hard."

"No, I understand. It's so horrible. I…I really don't even have the words."

"Don't let whatever she said disturb you, Mr. Rhodes," the old woman said.

"Did she really kill her rabbit?"

"Just a stuffed animal."

"I see… Please let me know if I can help."

"It'll take us all a long time, but probably more for Petunia. I'm trying to be patient with her. I keep explaining it, but she just doesn't seem to understand. The poor thing cannot accept this is what frogmen do."

"That's true," Luke agreed, slowly.

Chapter 6

Some days Dara felt defeated, that the blind would stay blind.

She didn't have any childhood friends, and after her parents went in the crash and Uncle Sal from cirrhosis, no other family existed beyond her two mates. Dara was, nonetheless, hyperaware of the outside world. After word about their second marriage got out, the people from Luke's work reacted differently when she bumped into them, whether it be at a desolate gas station, a crowded mall, or a boring line outside a movie theater. It was like they'd all got together and decided to get on the same page, take the same stance. They had this guarded expression, the kind older people reserve for teenagers with a piercing or tattoo or pink hair. *Look at the freak*, in other words.

Dara knew the real question, the only question on their simple minds. The answer wasn't what they sought however. The idea of a sexual paradise for an ever-grinning man might have existed for those fake idiots on reality shows, but not for the Rhodeses. Sex, in fact, was a complicated experience that needed many factors to be bright, shining and perfect before anything could be initiated. Although sex was wonderful when it did finally happen, activities like those tonight were more common.

While she sat gluing goodie bags for Maribel's Back-to-School night, Dara watched pro-wrestling, one of her vices that her wife and husband endured out of love (they both enjoyed "real" sports, and there was no convincing them how much athleticism it required *not* to hurt someone hurled over a turnbuckle).

She blurted out laughing as two beef-heads challenged each other in an interview, their eyes wide and white like hard-boiled eggs, lips pursed in quiet rage. They were new wrestlers and she hadn't learned their names yet. One of them wore a too-small blue-flamed Speedo, which looked like the pattern on the electric guitar Luke had wanted to buy a while back.

"Luke, should we get you a pair of those butt-huggers?"

Maribel looked up from her halibut sandwich and smiled at the wrestler stomping around on TV. Luke placed a cut-out of a pencil on a dab of glue he'd placed on the paper bag. After he finished, he glanced up and grunted.

Sour puss. What was eating him? He'd been weird since coming home early from work. Dara wondered if he'd gotten some bad vibes about her interview. Unconsciously she stuck her fingers in her mouth, but the nails were nubs by now.

Crunching sounds at the dinner table startled her. Maribel had moved on from her halibut steak on Hawaiian roll to a bag of salt-and-vinegar chips...but she never ate more than one thing at a meal. Her ritual about eating a meal the size of her fist was sacred. *What's up with that?* She couldn't be pregnant; they'd used birth control since the beginning.

Troubled, Dara paid attention to putting glitter on her batch of goodie bags.

"Thanks for the help, guys, I'm almost done," said Maribel, stuffing a few more chips into her mouth.

"You made dinner, take your time," Luke said.

"Yeah," Dara agreed. "Hey, Luke, did you hear anything about the interview today? Anything I should know to prepare?"

"Nope," he replied after a moment. "Nothing important."

Maribel crumpled her bag and gave him a look that included a silent directive. Luke sighed and shook his head. "Just do your best Dara. That's all I can say."

"I plan to. Thanks for making me feel confident. I appreciate it."

"Can we not do this? Don't turn this into me making you feel small. This is about more than just your feelings. People are out to get me. Out to get *us*. I'm trying to protect what we have and at the same time not freak you out."

She leaned over the arm of the couch and squarely met his gaze. "I'm not a fucking baby."

"You don't have to curse me out."

"Are you kidding me? I wasn't cursing you out. Dummy."

"Stop calling me names."

"What? Ever heard of sticks and stones? Shit!"

"Damn it Dara, why can't you understand—"

"*My loves*," Maribel announced loudly over them. "Please sit on the couch with me for a second. I have something for you both."

Luke got up slowly from the floor, his anger at bay but not completely gone.

Maribel had two sealed envelopes on her lap. "Dee" was printed on one, "Luke" on the other. Giving them time to take a few breaths, Maribel smoothed her long hair behind her ears to reveal a pair of ruby earrings she rarely wore. Dara looked at the envelope with her name on it and felt a spasm of dread.

"What's this?" Luke's voice sounded apprehensive.

Good, so it's not just me.

"We've gone through a lot, us three," Maribel began, "and you've made me a better person than I ever dreamed I could become. I don't like to see you fight. You're both scared. And we don't even need to know why or what about—Luke is scared of this, and Dee is scared of that." She glanced at him and then at Dara. "There's nothing to be scared of. No matter what happens, you will both be okay. Just as long as you keep trying to make each other happy. I know that might be too simple and that it might not address everything you think it has to, but just consider it for a while. For now. Deal?"

Dara was confused. What could this little speech mean? If Maribel was leaving them, wouldn't she just write one Dear John-Jane letter? Or did she think this a better approach?

"Deal?" Maribel asked again, breaking the stunned silence.

They both nodded. Dara wished she knew how Maribel could speak to them in such a way and *not* make them feel like two of her students. But there was nothing but respect in her voice. She wasn't condescending or holier than thou. Her maternal grandmother, who raised her, did a hell of a job. Dara wished she could have met her.

"Kiss," Maribel instructed.

Dara glanced at Luke. His face wasn't filled with anger anymore...he actually looked afraid. She leaned over Maribel's lap and met his lips. After a moment, she felt Maribel kissing her along her neck, across her jaw, her mouth, over to Luke, to his mouth, jaw, neck. They all pulled away. A pleasant daze fell over Dara. Luke looked content. *He must get so tired of my feeling sorry for myself all the time. All my self-image BS. He must hate me. Without Maribel where would this fight have gone?*

Maribel pensively studied the envelopes. "I want you to open these alone, on our anniversary. Please don't open them before. It's important. We've come a long way, now. I want you both to be happy. Remember that."

"You" both?

Not "us?"

She said no more and headed to the collection of decorations scattered over the carpet. The air conditioner kicked on, the vents rumbling. It was the only sound in the room. Dara and Luke sat there, holding their letters, unsure. Without a word, they pocketed them.

Dara hated waiting for special dates. She would probably peek at hers before then.

It took another hour to complete the task and load the bags into the back of Maribel's Mini Cooper. Afterward, they set up a mock interview that stretched into the remainder of the evening. Luke had prepared the questions beforehand, and Maribel had practiced reading and rereading them so she would sound more fluid and knowledgeable. Each provided Dara the opportunity to find stumbling points in her answers, with a third interviewer offering a completely different scenario—Johnny Cruz had been brought in as a wild card to destabilize the perfection of their fake interview.

"What the shit is a FROG ordinance?" Johnny sipped his beer and leaned his magnified eyes closer to his paper.

"Fats, Roots, Oil and Grease," Luke replied. "It's for sewer systems, Johnny. Haven't you heard of one? You work at a sewer plant."

Johnny thumbed his glasses farther back on his nose. "Do I look knowledgeable to you?"

"Just...read the question."

"I thought I was being the aggressive interviewer."

"You're doing fine with that, but you have to read the questions, not ask them," Luke pointed out.

Maribel took a deep breath. "I knew we shouldn't have asked him over."

"I bring balance to this house," Johnny said.

Maribel rolled her eyes.

"FROG will most likely be communicated to the public through brochures with Best Management Practice for restaurant grease removal and root abatement." Dara searched Luke's face to see if she'd gotten this one right.

A light smile touched his lips. "Dead on. You're going to do great, honey."

Johnny stood. His knees crackled under his three-hundred pounds. "Youch. Good, well, I'm out of here. I got real business to attend to at the bar."

"Thanks for helping, Johnny," said Dara in her most diplomatic voice.

"You got it," he replied and disappeared into the kitchen. "I'm gonna take another beer for the road."

Dara followed him. She didn't think he'd take anything except the beer but still.

As Johnny tugged at the tightly sealed refrigerator door, she opened the cupboard beneath the sink. "Let me get you those old towels for your shop."

"What?"

"Remember I said I had extra towels with holes in them, and you said you could use them in your work shop."

"I did? I must have been drunk, but sure I'll take them." He finally opened the fridge, leaned down to take another can of beer. His glasses dropped onto the floor.

She regarded the thick-lensed monstrosities. "I'd be getting laser eye modification if I were you. Those glasses...don't really suit you, Johnny."

Picking the glasses up and slipping them back on, he laughed, shaking his head. "Dee—you and I are the same animal, you know that?"

Now she laughed. "You're high."

"Not yet I'm not," he said and pursed his lips. "Yep. I can see it clearly, but there's only one big difference."

"One?"

"Yeah. You still give a fuckin' shit what other people think." He drained the entire beer in four big swallows and set the can on the counter with a burp. Sweeping the towels up under his arm, he said, "Good luck tomorrow."

A moment later the garage door banged. She couldn't see how they were the same at all. God, she hoped not. Dara smirked at the thought of accepting insight from Johnny Cruz in the first place.

"Want to watch the late shows tonight?" Luke asked when she returned to the living room.

"No, we should get ready for bed," said Maribel. "Dara needs her rest for tomorrow."

"Guess you're right."

The women got into their nightgowns, and Luke stripped to his boxer shorts. Maribel slept in the center of their California King, between Luke and Dara, but depending on who got up in the night to go to the bathroom, the arrangement would shift. Luke was the first to fall asleep, then Maribel. The only real snorer was Dara, so it was always a good thing when she nodded off last. Sometimes she'd go to the computer and play a few campaigns online after they drifted off—they'd be in a deeper sleep when she returned, and the snoring wouldn't be an issue.

Tonight she wouldn't be sleeping anytime soon. While she was excited and terrified about the interview, that strange song wormed around her brain, looking for a way out. A fretful question fused with its insistent, broken rhythm: *what if I'm late tomorrow?*

She told herself to stop worrying and thought instead about what she'd set out to wear. Her black blouse showed a little cleavage, and she was starting to reconsider. Nothing else fit right, though. Her clothes were too baggy and old, all pre-surgery Dara. She just hadn't had a reason in the last couple of years to buy anything new, because she didn't care to go out to fancy restaurants or night clubs. That was more Luke and Maribel. The damn blouse was what Dara wore when they dragged her to those kinds of places.

For a few moments she mulled over other outfits but systematically disqualified them.

Just wear the damn blouse. Don't over-think this.

She just had the jitters. She was ready. She had prepared and prepared. In the morning, she would get up, get as pretty as she could possibly get, eat a micro-bowl of cereal, and then head out early, because one of the interviewers liked punctuality. Another liked visuals, so she'd printed some distribution graphs and public outreach spreadsheets, which highlighted her knowledge of office-based programs. Maribel had helped her with those and had created a fairly info-fluffy résumé. It was all there. It was more than enough to qualify her for an entry-level public relations position. She had memorized all the correct answers, and, barring any stammers or nervousness, the only thing that could mess this up would be the people on the other side of the table.

Dara really hoped she got this job. She wanted to show Luke she could do this. Over the past year she'd felt more worthless than she could ever remember. Luke and Maribel were good at what they did, but Dara had never found a career path. The height of her experience in the work place was as an assistant manager in the fragrances at Macy's. She'd been considered to manage her own department briefly, before the company eliminated several positions, and she refused to take a pay cut. Commissioned retail wasn't for her, anyway. She wasn't pretty or smart enough to drag in a bunch of sales.

Time worried her more than anything. She wasn't getting any younger, and her marriage with Luke and Maribel wouldn't keep working if they grew in success and she continued to wither in failure.

Her mind wandered for an hour. Her eyelids dipped once or twice. She was starting to let sleep take her, but the stir of butterflies in her stomach got her pulse racing again. She needed a sedative, or a good stiff drink. There wasn't any booze in the house, though. Maribel and Luke were so out of it, Dara imagined slipping out to Shasta's for a quick rum and coke. *Oh, but Johnny is there right now.* So much for that fantasy.

You thought about going to the bar, though—maybe he was right, maybe you are alike.

As much as Dara tried to change the tangent of her thoughts, they remained on Johnny Cruz, sitting in that dive bar, alone. It was the last thing on her mind before the song came. The memory returned, not in pieces, but all at once, heavy and imposing, the bottom of every crevice in her consciousness surging up in harmony. She thought the violence of its presence would wake her up, but her eyes shut and she drifted off.

And all the while she slept, it reached out its shadow-dripping claws to the waking world. Normal dreams would not come to her in the presence of something so dominant. It metastasized with a promise to wake her when it was potent enough. On and on, it spread. A solved puzzle inside a lock-box. A death mask draped over the world. Crazed sanity in the drooling mouth of reason.

The strident song echoed through the colonnades of her mind.

Chapter 7

In this life and in any other, Johnny had just one simple wish.

Succeed. Just finish one damn thing he could look back on and say *yeah, I did that and I did it the best way it could be done.* Sometimes he wondered why he bothered to still care, seeing that he had burned every major bridge in his life.

The biggest bridge still seemed ablaze, slow roasted for his displeasure. His son from his second marriage, Beltran, was living in Arizona with his stepfather, Charles Reinhardt. He was calling this guy "dad," a man who'd been a stranger just a few years ago. But it wasn't as though Johnny hadn't had another crack at fatherhood. Fate gave him another chance. After a stroke and series of unexpected heart attacks brought on by chronically mismanaged diabetes, Beltran's mother, Lisa, slipped into a coma and passed away. A month later, Charles put Beltran on a plane to California to live with Johnny.

A weird feeling tugged at Johnny and a shiver ran through his bones. He shook it off and took a sip of beer. There was nothing to be ashamed of. He and his son both gave it their best shot.

Only lasted six weeks.

When it got really tough for them, the Rhodeses had suggested that they watch over Beltran while Johnny got his shit together; they'd be sort of like godparents with more authority. Beltran loved all three of them, so it'd seemed perfect at the time.

But when exactly would Johnny get his shit together? That was the problem they didn't want to see, but one that Johnny picked up on right away. Alberto "Johnny" Cruz would never rise above his own bullshit. He'd still be in Beltran's life, and being nearby, with unlimited access, was dangerous.

Like the afternoon he promised to take Beltran to the drive-in, but had a few too many Coronas after lunch and ended up napping until ten. When he woke and went out into the living room, his son, only five at the time, sat on the couch watching an infomercial about bread-making machines.

Can I go back to my real dad now?

It'd felt like Johnny had been smacked with glove full of rocks. *Charles isn't your real dad. You're no Reinhardt. Look in the mirror,* mijo. *You're a Cruz through and through.*

What about Maribel's house then? I don't like it in this house.

No, you just don't like me, Johnny told him.

Beltran bowed his head and said nothing.

Mama's gone. I'm all you got now. We're family.

Can we just go see my dad? Please?

Look you little bastard. We're going to the movies! Now get out of those pajamas and put on some real clothes.

They went to the drive-in theater in Rubidoux. The last movie showing was some shoot-em-up cop flick. Beltran fell asleep right after the opening car chase. Johnny watched the movie but didn't really pay attention to it. He just kept flogging himself inside. *What kind of a fucking asshole calls his son a bastard? The little boy just lost his mother and you can't handle it like a man. He doesn't deserve this. You're going to keep hurting him like this.*

Lisa shouldn't have been the one to go.

Johnny remembered Beltran looking through the back window of Charles Reinhart's car, the love of his father melting in his eyes. That was the moment—Johnny should have taken note—the moment he still *had* Beltran. But he let him go...

No, fuck that, I made the right choice.

Johnny wiped the mist out of his eyes. He'd only left the Rhodes house about half an hour ago, but he was already pretty drunk and getting emotional on top of it. *Better calm the hell down. Focus on the matter at hand.*

And it was good timing for that. Lou Parcette had just walked into the Shasta Bar and Grille. It wasn't safe meeting at Lou's seedy little pawn shop in downtown Riverside, so Johnny had called him here. Getting involved with a guy like Lou wasn't a great idea, but something had to give after what happened at the plant. He'd be damned if he was going to work for Grover Franklin even one minute, though. Better to take his chances now with Lou, if this was going to happen.

Lou hadn't changed. He still had the posture and featheriness of a scarecrow left out in a field for a hundred years. Although the man went through sports cars like underwear, he normally wore a wife beater and a pair of khaki slacks. Tonight was no exception. He sat down and shook Johnny's hand. His was wet and cold, and Johnny almost said something snarky but shut up for once.

Glancing at the bar and raising his eyebrows, Lou beckoned the waitress. She came over, and he ordered an Irish car bomb. Johnny noticed that the man's complexion had worsened over the years. The acne on his cheeks and jaw not only looked hideous but also painful.

"I got a lot to do tonight," said Lou, leaning his head against his thumb. "So what's up, four-eyes?"

"The price of copper."

"You said you had a family and didn't want in."

"Well that's changed, okay?"

Lou's eyes thinned, seeming to humor him. "Okay, okay. Let's keep this quick big guy."

Johnny took a quick sip of his Tecate, and said, "So, I figure we take like five devices and meters, one double check, and one construction meter, and that's like what, five thousand per site?"

Lou's close set eyes narrowed. "Are you joking? You didn't think I'd let you...oh I can see you're not joking." Lou glanced at the ceiling and shut his pale eyelids. "You simple motherfucker."

"Calm down there, Lou."

"You think I'd allow some three-hundred-pound jerk to go copper farming in this city? With my name tied to him? It's disrespectful for you to even think I'm that stupid."

"I did it before."

"Times are different now."

"Well, let's start over."

"No, let's keep going," said Lou. The waitress set down his cloudy white drink, and he pushed it aside. "This isn't a silly little game for extra pennies. You have to be fast on your feet to strip devices now. The cities are losing money, and they're more likely to pounce now when their copper fittings end up gone. You're bound to get on camera at some point. Police don't usually move on it because there's nothing for them to go on, but you're unmistakable—"

"Sure, there are no other fat guys in the world."

"Even if you had a head-start, most coronaries in a rent-a-cop outfit could catch your blubbery ass—"

"Okay then, your point is friggin' taken. I'm confused, though. Why even meet me about this?"

Lou cocked his head and stuck his bony chest out. "If I've got your attention and respect now, let me lay this down, and don't interrupt me again."

Johnny lifted his hands, palms up.

"I know a place...it's, well, it's a storage yard for someone else's take—this city, Corona, San Bernardino, Upland, Cucamonga. These guys are everywhere, and they take their time with exchanges, so there's probably over a million in value crated in their yard. Every other Thursday they pack a trailer to drive out at night. They don't show up until the afternoon. My buddy has a truck—"

"Hold the fuck up! I'm not as simple as *that*."

Lou shook his head and frowned. "If you interrupt me again..."

"Well, explain it to me, shithead."

"You're lucky I need some help. First of all, let me come out right now and say you're not getting any copper on that trailer."

"Why am I not surprised?"

"But if you get me and Jimmy into the yard, help us hook up the truck...shit, while we're in there you can take as many crates as you want."

"I only got my bike. Sold my truck a year ago."

"Rent something then and load that shit up."

"Sounds wonderful." Johnny took a breath. "When?"

Lou took a long, thoughtful sip of his car bomb and then wiped some cream off his thin lower lip. "I'm out to Vegas in a few days, so let's do this first thing tomorrow morning. Best shot is around six sharp. Bring your U-Haul or whatever and show up with your best tool box, too." Lou took out his smart phone and began typing on the touch screen.

"What are you doing?"

"Texting you the address. You'll get inside and take down the control box for the cameras that face the driveway. Go around to the field, north of the facility. We figured out they only have dummy cameras back there. Jimmy already cut the fence open— even you can wiggle through it."

"Thanks."

"They haven't noticed the opening in the fence either—that was kind of a little test we set up. These guys are too busy making money to notice much, but all the same, you should probably bring a piece with you."

Johnny shrugged. "No problem."

Hell-fucking-no, I'm not bringing a gun.

Suddenly Johnny's leg vibrated. Lou's text message had come in.

"Got it?" Lou asked.

Johnny took his cell out, checked the screen, and repeated the address.

"That's it."

Lou killed his drink, stood, and knocked on the table. Shadows tumbled across his face, like brawling tigers ripping each other apart. Johnny rubbed his eyes and winced. The strange feeling from before returned.

A loud whisper rattled through Johnny's ear: *Dara.*

"Excuse me?" he said.

Lou lifted an eyebrow. "I said delete that text when you can."

"Oh...yeah." Johnny put his phone away.

"What happened to your wife and son?" The man must have felt the need to end on a different note, a sentiment Johnny didn't quite share.

"They're free now," he replied lowly.

Lou snorted and knocked on the table again, before heading for the exit. "Six o'clock. Don't stay out drinking."

I guess I have to buy the bastard's drink too? Goddamn it.

Six o'clock in the morning would be rough at this rate. Johnny flagged down the skinny-minny waitress for a menu. Needed some food to soak up all the poison. She was bent over another table, talking to a woman with curly red hair and a squat man who seemed in perpetual pain. Nodding, nodding, smiling at their inane blather, she spotted Johnny, and he imagined she might have been happy for a release from the conversation.

"Can I have a menu?"

She pulled one out from behind the napkin dispenser right in front of Johnny. "There you are."

"Oh...what a dumbass."

"Pardon?"

"Not you, *me*."

Her thin claret lips peeled away to reveal some awkward-looking teeth. "So, are you going to have another twenty-four ounce of Time?"

Johnny blinked.

"Tecate?" she repeated. "You want another?"

"Oh, yeah, yeah."

"Do you know what you're ordering to eat yet?"

"Can I have a minute?"

"Just let me know. There's no rush."

Johnny already had the chicken nachos in mind. Extra jalapenos, extra sour cream. He reviewed the menu a few times to be sure that was what he really wanted. Now and then he'd look up at the vague figures lined up on the bar stools. It looked like everybody was drinking. Some drinks boiled white in the neon glow of the beer brands suspended in the vacuous space above, others appeared muddy and red, curdled almost. The sight of the beverages made him queasy, and Johnny pledged to not order another drink after this next one—he wasn't even buzzed, but he'd been throwing them back at a considerable velocity lately and getting shit for sleep and all-day hangovers as a result.

Out of the corner of his eye he noticed that the remaining inch of Tecate in his mug had the same bright, white glare as some of the drinks at the bar. He pinched his eyes together. It was hot in this joint. *All the money they made on crap beer, you'd think they'd spring for better climate control.*

Johnny swept up his mug, now warm, and finished his drink. It crackled and sparked against his lips, more like electrified soda pop than lager. A strange sensation pulled at him, but he decided it wasn't from the drink—this sensation had been growing, strongly, since just about midway through his conversation with Lou. A familiar song banged in the unfathomable depths of his mind, the melody also playing from farther away. Like a storm, lightning rich clouds slowly expanded and sought a conductor. Johnny recognized that, somehow, the storm wasn't originating from him. Not yet anyway.

Dara Rhodes. This nightmare's for her. Her mind sleeps now, but when she fully awakes, IT will too.

In the back of the bar, in a brown leather booth, sat five tribesmen, spears and all. Nobody questioned their presence. The waitress even asked the large-muscled warrior at the end of the booth if he wanted to order something. He didn't answer, and she left. He and the other four stared at Johnny Cruz with dreadful interest. Their maroon eyes were the same color as the drinks at the bar, and the bone piercings through their noses, necks, and biceps appeared ethereal purple from an ultra-violet Jagermeister sign.

"How…" Johnny began to say, then thought his question. *How do you know Dara?*

The Bone Men glanced away now.

A sound on the table made Johnny jump. The waitress delivered his next beer. She crinkled her nose. "Sorry. Deep in thought?"

Johnny took off his glasses and cleaned them on his shirt. He chuckled and shook his head. "Must be drunker than I thought. I'm at that point where I'm wondering if this is a dream or real."

"It's both," the waitress replied. A disgusting, lustful expression entered her pale face for a moment and then vanished like a fleeting hallucination.

Johnny licked his lips. "It's coming from that song, isn't it? The one I can't remember?"

The waitress smiled. For a moment he could see her skull behind the flesh. Blood filled the spaces and hemorrhaged from a curdled brain.

"I need to get out of here." Johnny tried to stand, but his muscles refused to work.

"You're stuck here. Dara thought of you just before she remembered the song. Only Death can free you now. And why not? It's still happy hour. Would you like to order one in a 24 oz. glass?"

Johnny struggled to stand. It wasn't always easy to pull his heavy ass up, but this was like moving with a two-story house tied to his back.

"A glass of Death? It's the dark-red drink."

"No, thanks," he barked, vein about to burst in his forehead. He gave up with a breathless gasp.

"Maybe then you'll keep drinking Time. Maybe Dara will sleep for ten years. For thirty? It won't matter. Just order a glass of the red stuff, Johnny. Do something right. Save these people. Your boy might hear about it someday and think you're a hero."

Sweat dotted Johnny's forehead and prickled along his back. "I just want the chicken nachos and then the bill."

The waitress's face softened, and she made to leave. "Coming right up."

Johnny checked his glasses again. The beer in his mug flashed white and he looked away, accidentally, back to the bar. Those drinking the dark red drink regarded him with rotten faces, their skin sloughing off in clumps. Those with the bright-hot white drinks had the sunken appearance of advanced age, but were no less disturbing to behold.

One guy, with a faded trucker's cap, considered Johnny with insane attention. "I let it all get away from me. *Time*. We fucked up, you and I. We thought there was enough to go around. There isn't. Now, there will be nothing to look back at. Nothing to love. There will be nothing to look forward to."

"Look forward to us," the corpses cackled. Everybody joined in singing parts of the appalling song, some of the dead resting their arms around the necks of the rapidly aging. They changed back into normal people for a moment, then transformed into another ghastly crowd the next.

Johnny managed to move his hand down to his pocket. If he could reach his cell phone…he could call Dara and wake her up.

Would that be worse?

"Nothing is worse than this," he mumbled.

"Wanna bet!" roared a skeleton. Coagulated blood and vomit shot from his unhinged jaw across the bar top.

Johnny's left arm moved independently of him. He grasped the full glass of white, glowing sludge, tipped his head back and drank.

The sun came flying up outside. Shadows skittered across the room from the violent resurgence of sunlight through half-closed vertical blinds.

He took another swig and felt tired…so damned tired…like he'd been up for thirty hours or something.

Yellow light and gray shadow had quick intercourse in the room and deepened with dark offspring.

It was night once more.

Johnny noticed it had taken him almost an entire day to take his phone out of his pocket. He'd opened the menu to his contacts and had scrolled down the short list of people he kept track of. His thumb quivered before the screen.

Someone screamed, and he heard a body thump on the floor.

"Fuck," he said through gnashing teeth.

Johnny took another chug of his beer. He watched it dump toward his mouth. Nothing looked wrong. Yellow. Friendly. Beautiful.

They order Time and Death. The drinks are the same, just different strengths, of course.

What's going on here? thought Johnny.

Not much at the moment, replied the Bone Man, *but wait until Dara Rhodes awakes…the Mare will ride again, twice as fierce as it did with Luke Rhodes.*

Johnny's thumb suffered a painful spasm as he tried to stretch it toward Luke's number.

"Why is this happening to me? If this nightmare belongs to Dara?"

Dara's thinking about this place as she sleeps, explained the Bone Man. *And so this is wonderful territory for foreplay.*

Are you here to help me?

All side conversation in the bar suddenly stopped. The Bone Man spoke. "Yes of course. You will bear witness and when Dara brings the nightmare here with her, we will spit you both over a well-kept garden of flames. We'll cook that same expression into your face and hers. Panicked meat tastes better."

"Good one! It'll taste better!" said a corpse at the bar, slapping his knee, bone exposed through the rotten material of his blue jeans. He hummed with fading amusement, leaned forward and pulled a cheese-bound tortilla chip off his plate of nachos.

Then the room flickered and strobed.

Everything appeared normal again. No rotting people. No sagging, frail, aging people. Just a bar with a bunch of very tired drunks. What you'd come to expect, for the moment anyway. Johnny was still bound to his seat though, his thumb still poised and struggling to touch Luke's number illuminated on his cell phone. The once-skeleton man scarfed down a wad of gooey nachos and made a gagging sound.

Johnny looked at his menu again and opted for a different dish.

Chapter 8

Through the slider, the meddlesome sun shined.

Again? She could have sworn she'd felt the heat of its rays on her face earlier. Muscles stiff, stomach in a sailor's knot, Dara picked up Luke's cell phone off the nightstand and checked the time. He'd missed a call from Johnny this morning. That's what had awakened her.

Wait, Johnny called this morning?

She wondered if he'd been thrown in jail again.

She'd answer the call. Whether it was a plea from jail or just a pocket call, Johnny Cruz had finally done something helpful. She had an extra fifteen minutes before her alarm went off, and on this big day she could use it. From the sounds of things, she wasn't alone. The California King was empty, the rest of the comforter pulled tight across its length.

In the den, slow minor chords rang from Luke's guitar, while Maribel nosily rummaged through the kitchen cabinets.

Dara swung her legs off the bed. Through the slider she spotted a row of luminous violet insects, each the size of her fist. Outside they joyfully trekked across the balcony. The bugs struck her as memorable, though she didn't much care to investigate. *Let them stay out there. I've got an interview and can't be troubled with some super-large Brazilian insects.*

She took another moment to wake up, stretching, rubbing the crust from her eyes, running her tongue over the sleep-film on her teeth. As she reached over to retrieve her own phone from the charger, she froze.

What had that date been on Luke's phone? Unplugging her cell, she felt a horrible fear wash over her. She reached out and touched the screen.

"Holy shit!" She threw the comforter off her bare legs. It was impossible. There had to be a mistake. She couldn't have possibly slept through all of yesterday! Somebody would have woken her up long before this.

"Luke! Mari!" she yelled in a panic.

Guitar chords.

Rummaging through the cabinets.

"This can't be true. Can't be." Dara awkwardly thumbed through her contact list, going past GeoGreen several times before getting to select it. She would cross her fingers and leave a message. Maybe she could explain it as a misunderstanding. Maybe she could lie. A death in the family? Something. Anything to get this chance back. She was calling at the crack of dawn, so she would have to wait for hours before they even got the message. *You don't have any fingernails left as it is. Better be careful you don't eat the fingers to the knuckle.*

To her surprise and absolute horror, a secretary picked up. The woman sounded exhausted and bitter.

"Finally," Maria rasped. "Are you coming yet, Sara? They're still waiting in the conference room."

"Waiting? *Still?* Since—"

"Yesterday."

"Oh my God, yes! I'm so sorry. Tell them I'm sorry. I...I'm on my way. Please tell them I'm sorry."

"Get here quick, Sara. They are...very upset."

"Absolutely. Absolutely. Bye." Dara powered off the phone and shrieked.

She stormed into the walk-in closet, found her slacks and put them on, along with her favorite bra. Where was her black blouse though? Great! The only thing that fit her half-way decently and she'd lost it! She smacked away some clothes on hangers. *Not there. Not here. Not fucking there!* She went through another series of older clothes, some of which belonged to Maribel and shouldn't have been mixed in with hers. Maybe Luke accidentally put them in the laundry pile in the corner? Dara tossed clothes over her shoulder, the pile seeming endless before her.

Guitar chords.

The song, the song she remembered the other day, just before falling asleep.

Cluttering pots and pans.

A beat to set the rhythm.

Tears flooded her eyes. "No," she babbled. "No…"

Dara leaned back and realized that she already had the blouse on. Her hair was also pulled back neatly, held by a black clip.

Oh, okay!

She must have forgotten! At some point, she'd gotten ready and putting the blouse on just completely slipped her mind.

It made sense.

Dara ran through the house, colors running murky and stagnant, slow underwater erosion, ominous like thousands of unknown fingertips slipping down her back.

Luke sat in the den playing his acoustic. His hands were wet and bloody, the pick-guard streaked red.

"You're bleeding from your fingers," Dara yelled at him. "You can't play that way. You're not a martyr. Go clean up. I'll check on you when I get back." She hated herself for leaving him that way, but there was no choice. This had to be done. She had to show him she could do this.

She stumbled through an obstacle course of pots and pans in the kitchen. Maribel had half her body inside the lower tier of the pantry.

"I'm late. Bye, Mari," Dara said, grasping the doorknob.

"Don't go that way," Maribel said, scooting out. "This way is faster."

"Really?"

Maribel's honey skin took on weathered tone. Her eyes were bloodshot, dark circles orbited them, as if she'd been up for days. "I'm not kidding. Go, Dara, hurry up, before you miss the interview. In the pantry. It's a short cut. It's always been there."

"Really?" she said again and got down onto her knees. She pushed away a box of saltines and entered the pantry. She had only crawled a few feet before she noticed a purple glow ahead. The sound of laughing and conversation increased as she got closer to the end of the tunnel. One of the voices sounded like her dad's. He was arguing with another person. Dara's mother. Another voice interrupted them both. Her uncle Sal's. They sounded like they hated each other.

They didn't though.

They loved each other.

She loved them.

Never got to prove it.

Never got to prove anything.

Dara crawled faster. They must still be alive. She wanted to hold them, tell them so many things about her life. But Mom and Dad never died, really. Existence was the lie here. She had no problem accepting that the huge hatchet wound to her life, the accident with the big rig had never really occurred. It was easy to let go of something so unwanted.

She climbed out of another cupboard, parting bottles of Triple Sec and Midori liqueur out of her way, and found herself behind the bar, at Shasta's of all places, only a block from GeoGreen. Maribel had been right—this way was quicker!

"Awesome!" she shouted, wondering why in all the years they had lived at that house she had never used the passageway before. She would be using it again. "Hell yes!" she said triumphantly.

Her smile faded. The bar was littered with moldering corpses. Ten of them spread out over the bar, glasses of blinding white light and glasses of red mud in the others. Out among the tables, slumped shapes indicated that the massacre, whatever it had been, had claimed everybody.

Except for Johnny Cruz, who staggered from his table like he'd been torn free from a piece of Velcro. Like Maribel had, he looked as if he'd been awake for a week.

"You brought it here—all these people died because of you." He bumped into a table, which shrieked loudly behind him. "Get away from me, Dara!"

She moved around the bar, stepping over the powdery, wrinkled face of a bartender, her eyes unmistakably two martini olives. Dara's heart trilled. She pushed a table and a chair out of her way. "I'm just trying to get to my interview, Johnny," she said. "I don't need these games."

"Games?" he whispered in disbelief. "Leave me alone!"

Shadowy figures started converging on her from the walls. They had barbed bones jammed through their skin. Black feathers sprouted from their stringy, ash-laden hair. Spearheads moved above them like a collection of fangs grinding on the darkness.

Johnny broke through the front, door and sunlight filled the bar. The group of Bone Men stood there, dazed, blinking through the light.

Dara put her head down rushed outside—

—to a completely different layout of Sycamore Street.

Rather than GeoGreen's main office being on the corner of Redwood, it was right across the street, the sprinkler-wet concrete steps leading from the curb to the front lobby. Elder trees lined the ivy-covered hill at the bottom. The obscenely large purple bugs she had seen earlier crawled through the tree branches and laced around the trunks, a jubilant natural energy.

The rattle-roar of motorcycle engine startled Dara. Zigzagging, Johnny took off on down the street, trying to gain control of a vehicle that looked halfway between a Harley and something from a post-apocalyptic wasteland, all rusted gears and sprockets clasping, flexing, and releasing dirty smoke from carbon-smudged stacks in the back.

Dara turned her back on the road, just to make certain the Bone Men hadn't come after her. For a moment, she'd almost completely forgotten them. They were there though still, in the doorway of the bar. One of them licked his fangs. Another moved his hand down into his feathered loin cloth and massaged the thickness there. A third, his face smashed apathetically against the door frame, mouthed words she couldn't hear.

She ran across the street and took the stairs as quickly as she could in heels. Disquiet hammered her heart, demanding to take over every inch of her.

The portfolio she'd put together—it was back at home.

Or was it in the car?

She hadn't driven but still searched the parking lot. Ten cars down, sat Luke's Volt, gleaming metallic blue in the early morning sun. Flash frames of time passed: she was in front of the door, the door was open, and she was rummaging around through a sea of papers with graphs. Many of the papers had been marked up in crayon, and none of the sheets were actually the final version she'd settled on.

These were the old graphs! How was this possible? She'd deleted those! Where the hell was the new one? The good one? She needed to show these people, to show Luke...

Glancing out the window, she saw pages drifting in the air. Did they fly away? No, she'd made four copies and put two in the back seat, just in case. So many of these papers, all over the place. *Wouldn't it be funny if it started raining graphs or resumes?*

Abandoning all hope, disgusted beyond belief, Dara slammed the car door. Papers began to cascade from the heavens. Thousands upon thousands. Millions. Everywhere. The parking lot quickly resembled the aftermath of a New Year's Eve bash in New York.

They're going to think I did this. Better move!

She hurried on and pushed into the lobby. She had been in the building many times with Luke. The air conditioning and the familiarity of the trickling waterfall over pebbles on the back wall, the black marble topped reception desk, the fake plants suspended in baskets overhead, all of it, made her blood pressure drop considerably.

She'd arrived. She was here. Safe and sound.

After taking a deep breath, she stated her business to the receptionist.

The woman, a drab-looking person in a dress too tight for her frame, reached over and pushed a button on her phone. Her voiced cracked, "She's finally here."

Dara swallowed her fear and watched the woman's reaction as a voice spoke on the other end. Under her young eyes, the woman had grown some heavy baggage from either sleep deprivation or drugs. After a moment, she punched the button again. "They'll see you now."

"I'm sorry...where?"

"Second floor, last door down the hall."

"Thank you."

Dara headed for the elevators but halted at the receptionist's sharp voice. "They're broken. Use the stairs."

She thanked the woman again and walked over to the half-helix stairway. Spider webs stretched from the banister to the wall. More of the purple bugs skittered on the sticky surfaces. Closer to them now, they seemed more of a hybrid spider-wasp, only their radioactive purple exoskeleton brought them into a whole new category of the bizarre. She tore through webs, slowly making her way upstairs. Angry shouts came from behind the walls. *Loser.* It was a word she heard more than once. *That woman. Luke's girlfriend. Luke's concubine. His fuck puppet. No. 1 Wife. Or was she No. 2?*

She had to ignore the voices, had to fight them. Dara straightened her spine and ripped through a particularly oozing web. Strands fell on her shoulders, and she brushed them off and checked her hair. They would not use any of this against her. She'd arrived. She'd done this. She'd come here as quickly as possible.

"Thanks for making it rain paper," said the receptionist down below, her voice echoing in the vast room. "That's going to make it tough to drive out of here."

Ignore her too. Ignore it all. Keep going.

The second floor approached. Luke's office was down the adjoining hall; she'd been up here many times before, but the last room in the hall, the conference room—never. Seeping through the drop-ceiling tiles and falling heavily onto the floor, a black curtain covered the door. The black was deep, void-like, space without stars in the distance.

Out of the corner of her eye, Dara saw a purple bug skitter over the wall. She snatched it, compulsively, just to touch one of the pretty things.

Then *everything* became clear. Just coming in contact with this familiar bug had brought her awareness she hadn't possessed a moment earlier.

Like magic!

This wasn't real.

She was dreaming.

She was still at home, in bed, asleep.

No. *Can't you feel the air in your lungs? The heart beating under your ribs? This is no dream. This is real.*

"Yeah sure," she said. "This is totally a dream."

In her hand, the bug settled down like a dog making itself comfortable. She slowly turned her hand, to let it drop, wary of her fascination. The insect nipped at her finger anyway. She yelped, and it fell on the floor to scramble off.

She examined the bead of blood on her finger.

Concentrated.

Healed!

Dara loved when she got control of her dreams. Self-awareness happened so very rarely. The stranger part of this experience seemed to be *how* deeply asleep she was, because usually alertness made her wake-up. But not this time. If she wanted to, she could stay here for a while and dream up anything she desired. The muted colors of the walls and the carpet made her feel uncomfortable, however; and she wasn't so sure she wanted to stay in this dream. Not after that scene back there at Shasta's. *What a funny thing to dream about, though. Johnny had been there, too, hadn't he? Yeah. He'd been riding some funny looking steampunk-cycle or something.* Where her mind had dug that up, she'd never know!

Curious to see what her mind would conjure up for her interviewing experience, she headed for the black curtain. Before she submerged herself into the velvety nothing of the curtains folds, she glanced back to the hall. No sign of the purple bug. Weird that the insect had brought her awareness, almost like an antidote for her obliviousness. Why an insect? Why was it so familiar?

Dara crossed through the curtain, her skin immediately chilled and prickled with goose bumps. On the other side, the overpowering force of the air conditioner hit her bare skin full force.

Someone. A woman. Gasped.

The dream had ended.

Dara realized, however, standing in the board room only in her bra, that reality had been in sync with the dream. Everything that had happened, had *really* happened, and now she was here, at the head of this long conference table, with four people ogling her in complete disbelief. Despite the whirling air conditioning from above, the room hung with body odor. Had she sleep-walked all the way from the house?

"What in the heck is the meaning of this?" Derek Stobecker slammed his palm down on the table. His red-rimmed, exhausted eyes seemed to bulge to the point of rupturing. "We...we...we've been here over a day...and you show up like this?" He gestured to her breasts, quite visible through her sheer bra. "Like...*that!*"

She covered herself. The CEO, his secretary, and the balding man who ran the community outreach program sat there in perplexed silence.

A scream wanted to escape Dara's mouth, but nothing came. She fell back out the door. The black curtain was gone, but fragments of spider webs still lined the stairs. Outside, through the building's large wall-sized window, she could see the parking lot surging with sheets of paper.

But the dream ended...how are these things still here?

Her ankles bent painfully as she hurried down the stairs. This had to still be a dream! No. No. No. This was reality. Right here now. Those people in the board room had been real, and they'd been waiting there for her since yesterday! You could see it on their faces and *smell* it on their skin. Dara hadn't merely dreamt she overslept, she really had overslept!

It had all started with that song. That horrible, wonderful song. She couldn't recall exactly how it went now. The memory of its tune had disappeared when she stepped through that curtain. There had been words though, right? Someone was singing the song.

Ballad.

It was a ballad.

A story-song about…what?

She stood in the lobby. Outside, papers heaved up into the air like a lesser mushroom cloud. Hypnotized, she watched the flurry, origami leaves tossed every which way.

"Miss, you can't stay here like that."

A car drove through the papers, kicking them out in a festive display from under its tires.

"Mrs. Rhodes…uh, Dara…you have to put on a shirt if you're going to stay in here."

Dara turned to the receptionist. "Did I come in with a blouse on?"

The woman blinked. "Did you take it off upstairs?"

"So you remember?"

"You have to put it back on."

"That's my ride. I'm leaving." Dara raced outside. Luke jumped out of his Volt and cried out in surprise. He embraced her. "What happened?" he asked.

"Let's go. Let's just go."

Through her quiet tears, he ushered her back to the car.

"Didn't I drive this car here?" she asked, confusion calming emotion.

Luke hit the windshield wipers, but they were already thoroughly caught with the graph papers. "No, hon. I think you just walked all the way here."

Another Chevy Volt sat in the parking lot, all its doors and the trunk wide open. Papers covered it like mock snowfall.

Dara shook her head, speechless, and turned away. She noticed Luke's hands on the steering wheel. Dry blood covered them. He had his fingers slightly extended, rather than curled around the wheel.

"What happened?"

"My guitar. I was playing too long."

"How long?"

"I got up yesterday and decided to play a little before work. I couldn't stop. Time just flew by. It happens, I guess, when you're caught in the moment."

"You played for an entire day, Luke. That doesn't *just happen*."

"Where's your top?" The question had no emotion behind it, only mild curiosity.

"I don't know if I was drugged or what, but I've had a very bizarre experience this morning. And I get the idea that if I hadn't found..." She didn't want to tell him about the purple insect. It was just too damned weird. "If I hadn't discovered something for myself, I think I'd still accept everything as normal. God, I think a bunch of people might have died down at Shasta's, too. We need to call there and see if anybody knows anything."

Luke didn't seem fazed by the unusual turn of events. "Just be calm, hon. You probably rushed out to make the interview and didn't even think about your blouse."

"Wait...you can't serious? And I just told you people might have died. Did you hear me?"

He shrugged. "Well, we have a real problem back home."

"What? Is Maribel okay?"

"Yeah, just tired. Same here. We're wiped out. I'd like to take a nap after the plumber gets there."

"Plumber?"

"For the tunnel through our wall."

"What?"

"You know, the one that goes through our pantry, right through the stucco and everything—out to the backyard. Come on, you know the one."

"Uh, what? You act like it's always been there.

"Sure it has."

"It leads to the backyard?"

Luke laughed. "Where do you think it leads, Wonderland?"

He wasn't processing anything she said in a rational way. *What in the hell was going on?*

"Why do we need a plumber?"

"Pipes broke in the tunnel. Don't know how. They don't look corroded or damaged."

"Listen to what you're saying. It doesn't make any sense. Why would we have a tunnel through our kitchen to the backyard? Think about what happened to you the other day at the pool. At the time, for whatever reason, I felt all that business with the frogmen was normal too, but now...I know better. Something is really wrong, Luke."

"How did the interview go?"

"Like fucking shit! I'm in my damn bra! You drove through a blizzard of graph paper! Frogmen drowned a whole swimming pool full of people, and there are zombie skeletons covering the floor of Shasta's! Now why in the hell are you acting like you just accept these things?"

"Don't yell at me. I'm sorry your interview went bad."

"Oh sure, you're sorry."

Luke looked away, pissed. "Whatever."

He pulled into the driveway and got out to pull some papers out of the windshield wipers and the wheel wells.

Dara sat there a minute. Angry. Embarrassed. Out of her mind.

The dream had ended, but what it changed, it destroyed.

She went into the house, saw the disaster in the kitchen, as if a grizzly bear had made a frenzied exit through the pantry. Water had flooded the lower shelves and the entire kitchen floor. Beach towels were set out to seep some of it up. Dara checked the faucet. *Yeah, nothing. He had to turn the water off.*

For a moment she wondered about those people in the bar. What Johnny said about her being responsible...she was definitely responsible for this calamity in the kitchen. Were lives on her hands, too?

Dara felt like passing out, not from lack of sleep, but from all the confusion gripping her. She entered the master bedroom. Maribel slept on the bed, breathing soundly. Careful not to make any noise, Dara shuffled into the bathroom. Her black blouse hung on the door frame, where she now remembered hanging it.

That's what happened. In the dream she imagined wearing the blouse already—*stop this dream stuff, it can't be what happened*–and then when the dream ended, the illusion of the blouse ended. She'd never really put it on, just like there wasn't an actual tunnel from the pantry to Shasta's, but somehow it had been reality while it was happening. So the dream had left its mark.

One of these Lifemares had happened to Luke at the pool. Frogmen? *That's what Frogmen do?* She remembered thinking it. Hell, she remembered believing it.

She had to ask Luke if he'd seen the bugs in his dream. But how could she ask that? He wouldn't be responsive.

A hand dropped on her shoulder, and she started. Luke stood there, eyes beet-red, face drooping. "I'm so freaking tired. Do you mind waiting for the plumber?"

"No, honey, go ahead and lay down."

"Thank you. I love you. Sorry again about the interview."

Her eyes warmed with tears. Why was this happening to them? Why now? She'd been so close to breaking out of her shell, only to come to some psychotic episode?

Oh, but it's not. You have a plumber coming to prove its authenticity.

And those Bone Men. Were they still down at Shasta's? Probably not. Not everything had been accounted for once Luke had ended his dream...that must have meant he went through a black curtain too?

Dara opened her mouth to ask, but as Luke lay down next to Maribel, he gestured feebly to the spot beside him. "Just for a second, okay?"

She nodded and lay at his side. He wrapped his muscular arms around her and took Maribel's hand and brought it up, so Dara could place hers over it. Dara never wanted to leave the safety of this moment. She might be losing her mind, or some cosmic disease had polluted reality, but she still valued this above all. She couldn't lose these two people. They were everything to her.

For now, she could only let this all sink in a little more. Hopefully she wouldn't remember the ballad again. If she did, with any luck, the next reality wouldn't bring any monsters with it, and she could stay here with her Luke and her Maribel, just like this, forever holding each other.

Their bodies together as one, entwined.

Chorus:

He considered how the universe's paradigm had changed.

The playground was awash in primary colors and basic shapes. Without the world trapped under a Devil's eye, the play-set would certainly catch Their hungry attention in this lush grassy field, the cherry-red ladders, the banana-yellow railings, the blueberry-blue flags, the avocado-green bastions. At present, nobody would look on this spot, however. The Eyes. Desire. To flee to brighter places.

He's caused this. They've all caused this. The faded wooden teeter-totter, which once sat unused while hordes of children enjoyed the swings and slides, now has become overwhelmed by purple bugs. Peering harder, They would spot two riders, before adverting their gaze. On one seat, an old black corpse overrun with maggots tied there with razorwire, and on the other seat, a man with a grinning horse face, gently pumping the contraption up and down (again again again; soft soft soft; in the dirt dirt dirt; mangy cloven feet mangy cloven feet mangy cloven feet). Their souls would warn them, *it's a way to have fun, whatever anybody else may say, it's a way to have fun*. Away from it, Their eyes must go. Of course.

All but a single man, who sat on a bench overlooking it all. Eavesdropping—Lingering—Staring. Underneath the play-set, the clown-face tunnel stares back at him. How long has it been a pit to Hell? Wasn't it just an hour ago that it led to a harmless place of playtime? Not an hour…a minute-year ago. The ballad, cumbersome as it was on his senses, did not completely diminish from his ears the idle tickling of the xylophone, or the hollering hyena kids murdering each other with love from the sincerest black beyond. Answers were nowhere; questions were yeswhere; his mind invested in confusion and the yields were amazing. Crawling, scraping things comingled with shadows dripping from their wounds and blood shrouding their deeds, according to his mangled eye-sight. He shrieks, chokes off a whimper. Quite expected. They are always doing that kind of thing.

He asks, "Do you hear my voice down there? Stop it from coming again. I beg you…I don't want to die. Hear that? Answer me! Just something! A sound. Promise me it won't come here. I can't take it one more time. My heart…won't endure that. *Please.*"

Verse 3: The Count

Chapter 9

Startled, Johnny fell off the sofa, startled by a metallic clatter in the garage.

The clock on the DVD player said 9:17 pm. He couldn't remember what it'd said when he came home from the bar, but he couldn't have been asleep for more than an hour, dead tired as he felt.

Something tinny settled on the ground in the garage. A cat might have got inside and knocked down some cans of spray paint, or a rat, or a possum got in the trash—some damn thing. With everything he had, Johnny just wanted to make an excuse not to get up, to put his head back down and sleep off the crazy dream about the bar. The nightmare had lasted for a long time, in the scope of his mind's eye, anyway; and he still felt creeped out by it. He'd probably only been dreaming for twenty minutes, but in the dream he'd nursed too many beers to count. Those from real life had his gut feeling like a bucket of steak knives.

His eyelids bobbed, and he lowered his head, about to knock off again, and then a word got his blood running.

U-Haul.

"Oh, Christ." He pawed at the coffee table for his glasses and then his phone. "Call U-haul," he told the phone. After waiting a moment, it responded, "*Find Carnegie Hall?*"

"Suck my dick," he whispered and brought up his web browser. He found the number for the place off Alder Road. They closed at 10 pm.

Head pounding, arms and legs quivering, Johnny Cruz put on his glasses and got up from the mildewed couch. He made for the garage and hoped that if an alley cat was lurking in there it hadn't pissed on his leather jacket. He flipped on the florescent light. The rods fluttered, illuminating his garage. He halted, his mouth dropped.

His Harley lay in pieces, meticulously, almost surgically dissected. Some parts had finely drilled holes through them, and others had strange welds in the frame that at first glance didn't appear natural. It was as though the motorcycle had been pulled apart to create something completely different, a piece of art perhaps, and then was promptly deconstructed again, left for dead.

Johnny's mind quickly supplied the answer. *You had to get away from the Bone Men at the bar and an ordinary chopper wasn't going to do the trick.*

He nodded and, as though to answer himself, said, "Yeah, I just wish I could have kept the other parts that made it so badass."

The clattering must have been all the parts sliding off a pile. He'd probably organized and stacked some of them (couldn't remember, though). Good thing he was suspended from work. This damn thing was going to take a lot of TLC to put back together the way he liked it.

Fuck, did his head ever hurt. To think he'd completely ignored Lou and drunk himself so silly he dreamt about Death- and Time-cocktails and spear-wielding tribesmen speaking like demons in his mind. They'd been real, right? The Bone Men?

His mind again: *doesn't matter, you just had to get away, right?*

"Right," he breathed and rubbed his nose, thinking for a second. A bus stopped up the street at around 9:30. He'd used it before. Looked like he would be using it again.

Johnny put on the coat his ex-wife Lisa had gotten for him the year before they divorced. It was an old thing, not as stylish as his leather jacket, but he didn't feel right getting rid of it. She'd been the mother of his child. The love of his life, really. His first wife, Mandy, had never come close. Lisa had been the one. It was harsh, but he guessed he was glad how things had turned out. He'd been lucky not to have been around when Lisa's diabetes got the best of her. He wouldn't have been as supportive as Charles Reinhardt, the great and wonderful professor and stepfather of the year.

Johnny stroked the soft green sleeves of his jacket and wondered if something similar hung in Charles Reinhardt's closet.

Johnny wanted to dislike Charles for that time, Lisa's sickness being a more intimate situation than any he had shared with the woman. They'd gone through some shit: Beltran getting put in the hospital at eighteen months old with a viral lung infection, almost losing their house to foreclosure, Johnny wrecking her new car, Lisa losing her sister to cancer. Challenges. They'd gone through them and the bad stuff always brought them closer together. After they broke up, Johnny still felt like he owned those hardships, but he wasn't part of Lisa's greatest crisis. Charles was.

Then she passed away and Johnny didn't feel as jealous anymore. It was one thing to be present to nurse an ailing person to health. Failure to do so was quite another thing. The world most likely judged Charles a better human being than Johnny, and after Charles had gone through that kind of suffering with Lisa, Johnny could scarcely disagree.

He held the cold post to the bus stop sign and closed his eyes, tried to picture Lisa. A song played in his mind. He'd been ignoring it for the past day—week—year? It didn't matter. He couldn't concentrate. All he could do was stand out by this street, washed in darkness, a foot away from oblivion, always just that one step away. Would going to this place tomorrow be a mistake? Maybe that dream had been his intuitive mind telling him to stay at the bar, just forget the copper. The strange dusty taste of Time still slid between Johnny's lips. This might be his only chance to make some real money. One day he'd be too old for these opportunities.

For any opportunities.

The bus arrived at 9:37 and he was shocked to see it jammed full of people. *Don't any of these assholes have jobs to get up for tomorrow?*

After being raped of four dollars for the lousiest (and last) seat on the stuffy, crotch-scented, public-transportation coffin, Johnny felt his mood turn sour. He was crammed into a little vestibule in the back, not actually a real seat like the others, but it counted the same. In truth he was taking up two spots, although the hard vinyl bench hardly afforded him space for one ass cheek. Ahead of him, two bleary-eyed kids played their hand-held video games, their parents seated across from them, both trying to get some sleep.

That'd be nice right about now.

The bus stopped, and an old black lady, painfully slow-moving, climbed through the door. There wasn't a spot for her, and nobody offered one. She grabbed a loop tied to the support beam running the length of the bus.

Johnny thought about giving her his spot, but he was too bitter at the moment. These people didn't give a rat's pink pucker about him. The lady was old, yeah, but nobody else was moving either. Roles reversed, she sure as hell wouldn't move for him, and he could hardly fit in the aisle with all these people.

He buckled a little though and said, "I'm getting off at the next stop."

The lady blinked a few times but said nothing.

When they pulled over, Johnny made his way off the godforsaken bucket of humanity. The still, hot, arid night air outside felt great in comparison. As the bus pulled away, the lights flickered. The old lady still stood in the aisle.

"Stubborn," he reflected, walking across the street to the U-Haul center. *My kind of person right there.*

He went inside the office, which blazed with hot, white light fixtures above, making the glossy gray walls look like shark skin. A rail-thin man bent over the counter, examining a card with a selection of vehicles. "I'm not sure the medium size will do it. Let's go for the large."

The clerk, a blonde woman with a startlingly large mouth, pressed her rubbery lips together and nodded. "We have one more of those. Let me check." Her eyes turned to her computer monitor, and she started clicking the mouse. After a moment, she squinted. "Okay, we have one large sized left."

"Hold on, Monstro." Johnny brushed the man out of the way. "I actually *need* a large size."

"I'll be with you next, sir."

"I came down here on a smelly bus to get the huge renta-truck. You're going to sell it out from under me, when this guy isn't even sure he needs it?"

The clerk hadn't worked up to being flabbergasted yet, but puddles of red expanded from the center of her cheeks. "Sir, I said I'll be with you in a minute. You'll have to come back tomorrow, though, if you want the XXL model. The others are all out."

"Bullshit. When do you open?"

"Eight am"

"Not early enough." Johnny turned to the skinny man, who flinched. "Come on, dude. Do you really need it?"

The man rocked his head side to side. "I...my family's moving tomorrow."

"Got a lot of shit? Now's the time to throw more stuff away. Right?"

"I just want to—"

"So it's settled." Johnny spanked the counter. "Ring me up, mackerel woman. And don't give me looks like that. I ain't no worm on a hook."

The clerk looked around Johnny to the skinny man. "My manager isn't here, but we can call someone. He can't just make us—"

Looking over his shoulder, Johnny shoved his glasses farther back on the bridge of his nose and waited to hear what the weasel said.

"No, no, I'll just get the medium. I don't want to get wrapped up in all this."

"Yes, the big truck for the big guy. That's sensible, no?"

The man moved to the far side of the counter, saying nothing more. The clerk shoved the paperwork over to Johnny. He took up the pen on the little chain and began filling out his information. "What's the date?" he asked.

"23rd," she replied.

"Already? Damn, I'm losing it. Thought it was only the 21st."

That's what staying home from work with not a care in the damn world gets you. That's what drinking and bad dreams gets you.

Lost in life.

No man. It's freedom, shit bird. Freedom.

After he completed everything and the clerk processed his credit card, she gave him the sales slip, told him to fill up the gas tank before he brought it back, and he was ready to go—someone would bring the vehicle up front. *Have a nice day.*

Johnny walked by the other man, who seemed about to burst apart with impatience.

"You'll make do," said Johnny, before pushing through the exit. He wasn't sure if the man heard him, but fuck that guy anyway.

Less than fifteen minutes later, Johnny Cruz sat in the comfortable driver's seat of the moving truck. They'd put the air conditioner up way too damn high, so he fiddled with it a bit. He liked cold air, but not the Antarctica setting.

When he got home, he put his big tool box on the passenger's seat. Then he took another look at the wreck his Harley had become. It pained the hell out of him to see it that way, so he walked away, went inside to his bedroom. He made sure to set his phone for five in the morning. He wanted to be at the yard even earlier than Lou had instructed.

Johnny put his head down and heard himself snoring as he drifted off.

He woke up once during the night to take a piss and felt grateful for the hours of sleep he had yet ahead of him. But those hours went quickly and too soon, the gonging of his alarm registered on his smart phone.

"Shut up," he breathed and switched it off.

He sat up against his headboard. The entire bed hitched and sighed at his weight. It occurred to him the bed had been the last big thing he bought with his wife, months before she left him. Back then, she'd still had a glimmer of attraction for him and joked in the furniture store that with Beltran going off to Kindergarten, there could be some banging of the headboard again. That thought brought a smile to Johnny's face. *I can't believe she's gone. She really is. Buried in the ground. That woman who once loved me.*

Me, of all people.

Not very bright, that one, but then again, she did leave your sorry ass.

His first wife, Mandy, had done the same, but that had been mutual, not to mention welcome. Lisa, not welcome, not at all. That fact pressed into him harder around the second or third week when Beltran had come back to live with him. One day, Johnny couldn't take his wretchedness anymore and got an itch to ride out to the beach.

He and the kid stood there, watching the waves. It felt like hours went by before they even said anything.

"I should have kept your mom happy."

Beltran had looked at him curiously. "Would she still be here, you think?"

Johnny shrugged. "Can't really ever know that."

"It's cock-sucking bullshit." Beltran kicked a clump of wet sand into the approaching foam.

"Don't say that stuff."

"What?"

"You know what. Those bad words."

"But you say them all the time."

"So? I do a lot of things that are wrong."

Beltran's brow furrowed. "But why?"

"I don't always catch myself. I'm not very smart sometimes. Not like you." Johnny smiled down at him.

The boy thought about this for a moment. "I could help you...to catch yourself."

"Really? I'd like that *mijo*. I really would."

Beltran leaned up against his leg, and they watched the gray ocean slowly change to dark blue.

"We're going to be all right, aren't we *mijo*?"

"Yes, Dad. We will."

Johnny didn't remember the rest of the day, but that was a hell of a time. He wished he could have had more memories like that.

He blew out a whistling breath. "You're pretty sentimental when you're sober, Johnny boy."

He got up from bed. He thought about showering, but the idea of loading heavy crates of copper would have him fairly well funkified again; in no time at all, he'd be sweating like a nun in a field of cucumbers. Or so he imagined.

He did put on some organic armpit slick and brushed his teeth; so he wasn't entirely savage.

Even at 5:42 am, the weather was still hot as shit, so the air conditioner in the U-Haul was welcome. He supposed it was a good thing his bike had suffered its Mad Max conversion and fallen apart. He wanted to reconsider his stance about what had happened last night at the bar, how odd the outcome with those Bone Men might well have been, but *these things are bound to happen* was what his mind cheerily informed him, again and again, until he just dropped the subject.

He checked his text messages at a stoplight and read the text from Lou. It was mostly just to make sure; looking up the address wasn't even necessary. Johnny knew the street well. He'd grown up in this part of San Bernardino. In fact, he figured that this place was the site of the old steel mill that went under just around the time the black guy got elected president. Not that Johnny blamed him, or the white-guy president before him, for that matter. For places like these, deep in the heart of San Berdoo, it was just a matter of time before they got caught contaminating ground water. The businesses would scream, "This is how we've done it for fifty years," and the city regulators would say,

"Well, that doesn't make it right," and then the businesses would respond, "Oh, go fuck a tree. In the meantime, we'll be packing for China, where *anything* goes!"

Johnny stomped the brake, lost in images of Chinese people shuffling barefoot through alleyways running in radiant green sludge. That'd be pretty fucked up, but this industrial street, with its sullen concoction of litter and graffiti, its thoroughly cracked and pitted road, its dead shopping carts overrun with weeds and broken beer-bottle glass, wasn't far from such a ridiculous scarceness of spirit. Then again, it never had been. This place was just like he remembered it.

Johnny compared the address on his phone with the painted numbers on the rusted aluminum plate zip-tied to the chain link fence. *Yep, I knew it was the steel mill.* End to end on the large multiple-acre lot, he could see crates neatly stacked twelve feet high. Had to be thousands. If Lou and Jimmy had more time, they could fully load several truck trailers. From the size of the crates, it looked like Johnny'd only fit about eight to ten in this U-haul. How much copper would that be? Depending on how full the crates were and what types of fittings were inside, that could be a few hundred thousand dollars. Johnny's heart hammered. *Not too shabby for gravy money. That could start a little bike shop.* What if it was more than that? *Holy shit. Maybe a bike shop with a brewery attached to it!*

A dirt road led to the back of the facility. Luckily, the stationary security camera pointed at the front gate probably hadn't picked him up, but rather than chance a three-point turn, he backed up and climbed the gravel-dirt ledge where the sidewalk crumbled away.

As he drove the length of the lot, it was impossible not to hearken back to his childhood, when he'd played in the nearby field. So many lazy afternoons spent out here; this desert scrub had been a second home. If his mother, Sandra, rest her soul, hadn't worked so much and his jellyfish of a father had actually stood up to his kid, then maybe Johnny wouldn't have ever ventured into this wasteland of spent condoms and gnarled tires. It was the perfect sanctuary for him, though, even if he got bullied occasionally out here. That was before he grew into his body and flipped the tables on those motherfuckers. No more *Fat Alberto*. He was Johnny, and that meant he didn't take shit from nobody.

He wheeled around the corner. The road got a little wonky in the back. Judging from how far he'd gone, the place had to be around ten acres. He spotted the cut in the chain link and above it on a pole, the dummy camera (pretty obvious, since it didn't look to have a power supply—then again, it probably worked fine to detract teenagers). Johnny parked the U-Haul and got out.

It was damn silent outside.

He checked his watch.

Still plenty of…

Time.

If there was one thing he hated (but there certainly wasn't just one), Johnny Cruz did not enjoy idly hanging out in the sun. It was twenty minutes until the others were due to show. No sounds came from inside the yard, so he felt it relatively safe to take a peek inside. The break in the fence could only be seen if you were looking for it, but the chain link had corroded and gone slack over time, so prying it apart and sliding his wide body through was no problem. Directly on the other side, a panel of blue fiberglass leaned against the fence, as though another barrier of protection. Didn't do a whole lot of good, and Johnny had to wonder why these guys hadn't gotten ripped off before. Perhaps they had. Maybe there was so much cheese here the rats couldn't be bothered with a few other rodents visiting the nest.

Didn't seem likely, though. People enjoyed money too much. Even a slow leak could do damage over time. Although, it wasn't out of the question these guys were the reckless sort.

Johnny stayed close to the fence and peered out over the yard. He could see the shadowy, hulking shape of the old steel mill, a jungle of weeds and wild flowers growing through its many weak points. The crates were stacked at the fence-line, three rows deep. A large rectangular formation also sat in the center of the yard, piled three high. Johnny couldn't imagine they'd be able to get those without a forklift. It'd be smart if they brought one, but that would leave less room in the truck trailer.

The sound of a dog barking, distant, muffled, made Johnny grab the fiberglass piece, ready to flee. He waited for a beat. Nothing else came.

Must have come from another property.

Hopefully.

Many of these yards had dogs. Lou would have mentioned that, though. Unless that asshole didn't know.

The dog barked again, but it definitely wasn't nearby. Johnny felt slightly more at ease. He went over to a crate. Plastic bottom and top, with wooden panels. Sturdy. He pulled opened the clasps. Dust exhaled from inside. A rancid scent lifted.

Fertilizer.

What the shit?

Literally.

Johnny chose a crate two rows back. He opened the clasps on these and stood on his tip-toes to look within. Copper meters, two or three that he could see, and an entire band of copper wire.

Thank fuck.

Johnny guessed it made sense to have some decoys out here if any city official came by to inspect. Still, they'd have to double check these crates before loading them. He didn't want to take home a U-Haul of fertilizer; that was for damn sure.

Six o'clock had rolled around by now, and Lou and Jimmy hadn't shown. He texted Lou.

Here. Want me 2 unplug front camera? Or wait?

A semi-truck came plugging up to the front gate.

That unseen dog started barking again. Johnny looked around, hoping no pit bulls would come rushing out to gnaw his dick off.

He texted again.

Nevermind. Saw u pull in. I'll head up.

Johnny put his phone back in his pants and slid through the fence once more. He grabbed his tool box from the passenger seat and fought off the urge to whistle a merry tune. It took a bit of a struggle to fit through the fence with the toolbox in tow, but in only a few minutes he was back inside and heading for the little shack near the front gate. He thought he heard the dog bark again, but then wondered if it was only his imagination.

This was a hike, going all the way across the yard like this. He'd probably drive his truck up to each crate rather than lug them back and forth. Halfway across the yard, and he was getting winded. He dragged his arm across the sweat peppering his forehead. *This already sucks.*

He heard a padlock clang against metal. A strange face hovered outside, looking through at him with a baffled expression. From the shadows cast by the plastic shade wound through the gate, Johnny tried to make sense of the face. From its fullness, it definitely wasn't

Lou. He'd seen Jimmy once before and maybe he just didn't recognize him. But Jimmy was Korean. This guy looked white.

No, this guy *was* white.

"Oh shit!" Johnny dropped his tool box and ran.

He heard shouting rise behind him. It lanced through the pieces of a dead song in the back of his mind, pushing it forward, *but still inaccessible*. His heart drummed. The veins in his thighs stung with pressure. He might have heard the dog bark again, so possible, too possible.

Dirt exploded in front of him. He knew the sound. Just like a map of the neighborhood, he could probably guess the caliber of the bullet.

"Stop, you fat fuck!"

Johnny did. He put his hands over his head. Heart singing. Singing the song. But his mind still hadn't caught on yet.

"Why you fuckin' shooting?"

"He was running!" said an out-of-breath voice.

"And you couldn't chase *him* down? Asshole. Asshole. Asshole. Goddamnit. You better go out to the street and check."

"There ain't nobody out there. Calm the hell down."

"Thoughtless son of a bitch."

"Calm down, I said. Do we put him in with the ones from the other day?"

"They still in there?"

"Should be. Whatever's left."

The cold mouth of a handgun pressed into the back of Johnny's sweaty neck.

"You come back for your friends, piece of shit?"

Johnny trembled head to toe. He licked his lips and tasted salt and fear. "I...got lost. I thought this was my uncle's tow yard."

"Right. I always visit relatives by sneaking into the back of their place."

"He...always forgets his phone. Thought he was in the building over there."

The gun jabbed deep under his skull. "You're a shitty-ass liar. Two days pass, and you figure the coast is clear?"

"Two days?"

"Since your buddies came down here. They told us another guy would show up. Said he'd be here that day, but he never showed. We thought they might have been making it up to stall us. But now, I'm thinking you somehow figured out your pals Lou and Jimmy got caught, so you decided to try your luck another day. What balls."

"I don't know anyone by those names."

"Well, let me introduce you. Come on."

"No wait—I don't know what you're talking about. Please listen."

"Move your lard." The gun nudged him forward, and Johnny, like a puppet, began walking.

Two days? How could it have been two days ago? He'd just been in the bar last night...he'd only dreamt he'd been there for a long time. That was a dream.

A dream.

(Nightmare).

They led him to the steel mill. The sound of barking echoed from its depths. Johnny glanced at an indifferent Mexican guy examining a random crate, as though to assure that nothing had tainted the goods. Johnny saw the copper inside. It shimmered, burnt red and gold. That could have been his. That could have been his way out. The deeper they took him inside the mill, the vaguer that reality became to him, the less the metal glinted in the sunlight.

He admired the shine until, like everything else, it faded, an old mirage.

Chapter 10

Without doubt, confronting the execs could get him fired.

Luke was already walking on the thinnest ice possible with the Los Angeles project noose hanging around his neck. Blake had called him last night, but he didn't have the emotional strength to hear the bad news. When he finally listened to the message this morning, the voice mail said little other than "Call me back." Could he still be transferred to that satellite position up north? Would that even matter now, seeing that at the interview Dara had some kind of breakdown? What had they done to her?

It had to be Stobecker. He must have made her feel…unwholesome. It had to do with their marriage, that much he knew.

This wasn't something he could let go. Both Maribel and Dara were hurt over the incident. Dara, for obvious reasons. Maribel, for not being able to protect her. She wasn't the sort who allowed others to bully her friends, doubly so when it came to her husband and wife.

This wasn't her battle, though. Luke had to make this right. He had to at least make some kind of gesture to appease both of his wives, and yet, in the interest of keeping any chance of retaining his high paying though pain-in-the-ass, job, he had to step lightly on that thin ice…especially with the fire-and-brimstone wrath of Derek Stobecker.

On his way to work this morning, Luke had decided he didn't care who was at fault for the lack of interview; right now, to rescue any credibility, his words had to be heard. And those words couldn't be the truth. He had to lie, and lie his ass off. Let the damage control commence.

It was difficult to be convincing, however, with such sketchy details. Everything was dim about that day. He and Maribel had been up and around the house for a long time. They kept on talking each other out of waking Dara. *She's resting. She needs her sleep. Resting will get her mind clearer for the interview.* They'd let an entire day and night slip past them. How did that even happen? At some point he'd picked up his guitar (the still-painful pads of his fingertips had scabbed over in a series of deep rifts splitting the skin) and he'd just played and played and played. Music was music was music. The ballad equaled the ballad equaled the ballad. It was perfect. He'd tried to replicate the notes in his head and the song rolling forth from his sleeping wife. Never could get it right. Never could remember it like he did that day at the pool.

The music had faded suddenly, and he'd noticed that Dara was gone. Maribel had told him to drive over to see if she'd gone to GeoGreen, because she couldn't remember what had happened to Dara, and the kitchen was flooding from the broken pipes. It was instant confusion and bedlam.

The event reminded him of that day at the pool. Luke had been thinking about it a lot lately. He should have done more to warn the parents. Maybe that was what Dara had been driving at by bringing it up the other day. Everybody knew what frogmen were capable of doing, so why did the parents go without a fight? Why did they (and he) accept the frogmen so easily? And where had the children gone? They must have seen their parents being drowned, but Luke didn't remember hearing any of them screaming or crying. How could he, with that hopeless song in his head? The kids just blended into the background, and other than what the police officer said on the phone about them going to family, he didn't know the fate of any of those kids, except for Petunia, who didn't seem to be getting along so well.

Luke should have been the voice of reason, just like he should have told Dara never to get involved with GeoGreen. He'd let her do the interview on the chance of saving his own job. Now the whole thing had traumatized her. That was his fault. He was supposed to be there for her.

Perhaps that's what he was doing right now. Going down with the ship, Captain Courageous.

Courageous, yeah sure. That's a laugh.

Luke stepped into the board room. All those who had been present at Dara's interview were accounted for, including Blake and representatives of his largest contracts with the United States Air Force. The atmosphere in the room thickened to rotten molasses as he walked through the door. Luke went dizzy a moment, all those pairs of interested and confused eyes on him.

"Sorry… Can I sit in briefly with all of you after the meeting concludes? I won't take a moment."

Derek stood, an uneasy shift to his broad, bony shoulders. "No, this isn't a good time. Please just return to work."

"It's just that Dara was in a serious accident prior to your encounter, and since then she's recovered. I really want to discuss her interview."

"Excuse me, Luke, but we will deal with this later. Okay?"

"No, no. The Rhodes family won't wait for later," said a voice at Luke's side. Maribel pushed past him into the conference room. "I apologize in advance to others present and not responsible, but those accountable need to fess up right now. Which one of you denied Dara's reapplication?"

Luke's heart stopped. "Mari, no—wait!"

Blake raised his eyebrows at Luke and leaned back in his seat, his face expressionless.

Maribel stood before them, eying each at a time, her hands at her sides, about to draw imaginary pistols. Her honey complexion had darkened, making her face fierce behind her long brown hair. "Tell me to my face why Dara doesn't deserve this chance. Or you can cut the baloney. We know you're doing this because of *me*, so let's have it out right now."

"We're in the middle of a—"

"It can wait," Maribel said through her teeth.

Blake leaned over to his military companion. "Sorry, this will only take a minute."

One of other executives pointed to the phone. "Ask how she got up here?"

"She used her husband's spare badge," said Maribel with a level gaze. "And I won't be thrown out of here until I've said what I need to say."

Derek Stobecker blinked, obviously ready to give consent, but the two-star General at the table snickered. *No way*, he mouthed. *Let her talk.* He sat straight in his chair; before, he'd been slouching, looking rather bored.

Luke didn't want to look at anyone's face. This was the beginning of the end. As much as he yearned to tell everybody at GeoGreen exactly what he thought of them, it seemed irresponsible to self-destruct like this. Not having control of the outcome was even worse. Maribel must have sensed he'd feel this way, because she reached back and clutched his hand.

Dara wouldn't have the vigor to do this, but Maribel would glide through this moment. Luke should have been storming in, not standing meekly at the door with his sorry attempt at passive assertion.

"Well?" Maribel demanded again. "Out with it. I've got work to do. I'm sure you have stuff to get back to as well—like setting up my husband to take the fall for all your mistakes—but I have a substitute teacher who's probably feeding crayons to my students, so I'd like to settle this now."

"Fine...uh Mrs...."

"Rhodes."

Derek chewed on his lip for a second. "Uh, yes. Look, we're more than happy to keep Dara's resume on file. We have other applicants to interview, and we will consider them all equally. We are in a meeting. Can you both please get out of here now?"

"So she gets another interview?"

"She had her interview. We dedicated two days to Dara Rhodes. That's more than anybody else. We waited for her to show and when she did..."

Maribel gripped Luke's hand harder.

"Ah, I get it," said Maribel. "You're going to play stupid. All the while you're slamming a gavel in your minds."

"I beg your pardon?"

"Oh please. As if you would."

"Maribel," Luke whispered. "Don't…"

"I don't expect any of you to care. Maybe you think I'm silly. Maybe you think I'm a bad woman. Good, fine, you go on imposing your own reality on how we live our lives. But blame me. Dara just wanted a chance and you slammed the door in her face."

Nancy Gildcrest, director of finance, cried out, "She showed up in her bra!"

At this, the General's eyes went wide, and he put a manila folder up to his mouth, hiding a smile.

"Was there head trauma in the accident?" That was Neil Thoreau from Human Resources.

Blushing, Derek massaged the bridge of his nose. "Was there, Mrs. *Rhodes*?"

Maribel took everybody in once more and basked in the silence. "Something happened that was out of Dara's control. That's all anybody knows. *I* believe her. Would it make sense for a sane and sober person to behave otherwise?" Maribel took a deep, quivering breath. Her hand on Luke's had become sweaty, cold. She felt this, too, and let go. "Don't hold any of this against my husband either—I didn't tell him I was coming here. Besides which, you don't pay him enough to be your moral equal. You've all just put our family through so much lately, and, and, that's it…I guess. I'm done venting. Sorry for the intrusion."

"I'm sorry," said the General, "it's none of my business, but I'm confused. Who is this woman to you?"

"My wife," said Dara calmly, before heading out of the room. The door shut and the air fell into a hard silence.

Even Luke had cringed when she said the word. "Thank you for listening," he mumbled and drifted out.

Outside, Maria had left only about an inch of daylight between her and Maribel. She was pointing at her as though disciplining a child. "If you don't leave right now, I'm going to be forced to call security. You can't just barge into a meeting."

"Really?"

Maria glowered.

"Don't worry, I'm going now," said Maribel.

"Good. Now move it!"

Maribel did not take orders well, and Luke could tell she wouldn't let the command slide. His wife looked the woman up and down in unchecked disgust. "Is this that cat in heat you always complain about?"

Luke closed his eyes, feeling like a wheelbarrow of bowling balls had cascaded over him.

Maria's eyes, heavy with mascara, narrowed. "What?"

Luke swallowed. "She's teasing. I never said that..."

"Who the hell do you people think you are?" Maria snapped and pointed at the stairway. "Get the fu—get out. Get out of my building."

"Oh it's *her* building now." Maribel simpered, turning a shoulder to Maria. "Fine, wouldn't want my eyes scratched out. Have a good one."

Luke contained his smirk as he followed her down to the lobby. Maribel walked ahead of him like a revenge-determined machine. Her phone rang, and she took it out, checked the screen, sighed, and put it to her ear.

"Hi Allie." She listened intently for a few seconds. "That was today? Oh, I'm sorry. I'll get there soon. Did the Sub hand out the music worksheets yet...? Yeah. How many are done? Just David. Okay. I'm on my way."

She hung up and glanced at Luke, a hint of shame surfacing in her face. "I broke. I've been dreaming about coming down here for a while. The interview made it impossible to stay away."

"Don't be sorry," he said quietly. For a moment, he wanted to pretend everything that happened just now hadn't, so he changed the subject. "What was that call about?"

"On certain days, Allie's husband brings his keyboard in and teaches the kids music. I forgot it was happening today."

"That the weird guy?"

"He's married to Allie, so there you go."

Luke chuckled despite everything and figured he couldn't avoid the obvious. "So, you okay?"

"He just creeps me out. He watches Allie like he doesn't trust her. Makes me trust her even less. I really need a different instructional aide."

"No, I didn't mean that. I meant are you okay with what happened to Dara?"

Maribel turned to him. "Was that not clear upstairs? No Luke, I'm not okay with it. And I don't feel too great about what they're doing to you either. This is all about me. I know it. If Johnny hadn't blabbed…"

He embraced her for a moment, but she broke away from him.

"I love you. I better get going. I'm sorry I just made this harder for you." She looked down, a thin sheen of tears rising. "I just can't let this stuff go on any longer. They're trying to break us."

"It'll all work out." He touched her face, his fingers caressing her chin. "It will."

Maribel smiled and hurried for the exit.

Drained, Luke climbed the stairs and returned to his office. In his breast pocket, he touched the envelope Maribel had given him. He'd planned on opening it at work on the day of their anniversary. If it was good news, it would be an ideal place to cheer him up. If it was bad news, well then, misery loved company.

Not for the first time and probably not for the last, he wondered: *does she love me the way she loves Dara?*

Out his window he spotted Maribel jogging to her car, fists penduluming back and forth. She wasn't moving like someone angry, more like someone at their wit's end.

She dropped inside her mini-cooper, looking so very tired.

Chapter 11

These dogs hated other dogs, and Man wasn't their best friend.

This was to say, in dumb-ass terms, that Lou and Jimmy were dead, and Johnny Cruz was next, if these slobbering pain-filled animals had their say. In the dark, it was difficult to distinguish the breeds; the light bulb at the top of the stairwell only painted their wet muzzles and eyes with a dearth of detail behind their plastic kennels. Breed didn't matter though. All moved with psychotic hunger, all bit at the grated kennel doors with a lunatic's flair for repetition, and all had the terminal haunting of the abused and the damned in their eyes.

Johnny had been instructed to kneel four feet from the cages (seven, that he could tell). The gun hadn't moved from the back of his head while the men questioned him. At times they sounded less like thugs than like concerned small-business owners. *Did some other yard like ours tip you off? Bullshit, what have our competitors said about our yard? You work for the city you say—so does the department of Water and Power have any clue about our operation?* Johnny couldn't answer any of that, and he supposed, unfortunately for him, the two eviscerated dead men on the floor hadn't either.

Over the last hour, Johnny's eyes had adjusted to the light. Against the far right wall, he made out two-tiered bleachers and a large chalk board. He could scarcely read the names written there, but each had a ratio next to it.

Puggy Panocha, 10:1
Ralphie-Boy, 3:7
Count, 23:1
St. Skeeter, 2:5

These fools had some brass balls keeping a dog-fighting ring so close to their storage place. If one operation attracted attention, both were screwed. Johnny was in no place to criticize, however, and reminded himself of this by glancing at the big pile of dog shit in front of Lou's dead face. One of the man's eyeballs had been ripped out, and a thin gray straw of vein lay limp outside the darkened hole. Good thing he didn't die staring at that pile of shit. Then again, Lou might have died *smelling it,* and he might have heard that congregation of blissfully feasting flies.

Their buzzing took Johnny back to the song—it was a lot like the song Dara had brought to the bar (*brought? No, it must have come on the juke when she showed up*).

The gun dropped away from Johnny's head but left a dull-feeling spot on his skin. Asshole Shitwad, the name Johnny'd given the thug during their time together, clucked his tongue obnoxiously several times at different pitches. "Should we take these bodies out somewhere?"

"What for?" replied Cockface.

"They might make the dogs sick, homey."

"Will you stop about the dogs? They aren't our concern right now. There's a fuck of a lotta work to get done today. This is already taking too long, and we got other guys, like this fatso here, showing up. Could be more, right?"

"Right."

"So we need to get those trailers loaded."

"I'll help you guys," Johnny chimed in.

"Shut up," Cockface warned.

Johnny took a risk. "Okay. I was here to help Lou and Jimmy— they told me this was their friend's yard. I didn't know about the copper until I got here. Look guys, it doesn't matter who I help. Shit, I'll help you load for nothing. Give me a chance."

"You said you were looking for your uncle's—"

"Lied, yeah. Yes, I did. I was scared. You'd do the same."

Cockface got close to his ear. His breath reeked of dehydration. "I wouldn't do the same. That's why I'm standing here, and you're about to have your dick pulled up through your throat."

Asshole Shitwad chuckled.

"What are you laughing about?" Cockface snapped. "Go up and release the locks on the cages."

"All of them?"

"Just Matrix and Sexy Man. No wait a minute—fuck it, let them all out."

"All of them? The Count, too?"

"Yeah, he'll enjoy tubby here."

"How do we get them back in their cages before the Count kills them all?"

"Let the Count's will be done." Cockface laughed. "Just make sure we bolt the plant doors so he doesn't come up into the yard while we're loading. That dog needs to live out the rest of its life down here."

"Naw—really? Come on, we've invested so much time in these fighters," Asshole Shitwad complained. "Can't we just light this guy up here? Over in a second, gives us more time, and we can move the animals to another location?"

"No more shots fired," Cockface said firmly. "We got lucky outside."

"Fine," Asshole Shitwad sighed. "But…all the dogs? Really?"

"Yeah. The world's full of fucking dogs, if you hadn't noticed. Now get going. I want to catch Round One at least before heading up to the yard."

"You guys need an extra set of hands," Johnny said. "I can lift two of those crates at a time."

Cockface walked around to the cages, giving Johnny a *gimme a fuckin' break* look. He kicked the first cage and evoked a growling, snapping discord from inside. One after another, he kicked the other cages, producing like results. At the last and largest cage, he stopped short and grinned. "We never disturb the Count."

The shapes in the cages twisted in the darkness, caged tornados of razors and hooks. *The song wants out.* Johnny had always figured he would die from a heart attack or maybe an accident on his bike. Getting shot outside a bar was up in the top ten. He'd been in some bar scuffles with several wiry son of a bitches who hadn't been all that impressed by his size. *The song wants free.* He'd still won, though. Except for a few childhood fights in the very fields that surrounded this old building, Johnny had always won his fights. *That's freedom, shitbird.* It was the only thing he could be proud about, besides doing right by Beltran and staying out of his life. He didn't know if it had been a big mistake. *How did that damn song go?* Doing the right thing was always harder, and as he kneeled there, awaiting execution, death by dog, he knew it must have been right, because he missed his kid right now.

"Can I call my boy? Say goodbye?" he asked.

Cockface dropped down on the top seat of the bleachers. Johnny could only see the points of his cheap-ass cowboy boots. "Even if I was that sentimental and drooling-retarded, I can't even get a signal from Verizon down here. You're SOL. Unless they got phones in hell for your three-ton ass."

The song was at the tip of his tongue (mind). How had it gone? *Bah-dee-bah-bah. Bah-dee-dee-bah-bah. Bah-dee-dee-bah-bah. Bah-dee-bah-bah.* It was a whisper and a shout, all at once. It was a coiled fist and an inviting palm, all together. Simultaneously, concurrently, in tandem, yes with no, it was a whip-crack in a slaughterhouse and a soundless buzz in empty space. The two contradictions would pull apart, just as Johnny got a grasp on the song, and then when he'd lose it, they would marry again, becoming a tangle of disorder stuck fast in his mind. He knew this wasn't the time to be thinking about the song. This was the time to form a plan.... As soon as those cages opened, he'd have to rush the bleachers. It was the only way. So what if he got shot? It was better than being torn apart...or at least, to be alive and feel the process. How could he haul himself over the block wall, though? He'd have to be quick enough to do that before the dogs even came out. That would mean...doing it right now.

Johnny turned around, and Cockface cleared his throat. "Na-ah, put your back to me."

He growled in frustration. "Give me a chance. I still got time left."

"Your time's up. Your chances are gone. You had one earlier, when you decided to come here." Cockface pulled a gun from the back of his pants. "The moment when you said, *Hey! I know what! I'm gonna steal someone else's shit today.*"

"That stuff isn't yours."

"That's a fine argument, from a five year old."

A creaking sound came from the wall. A bar turning over. Something releasing.

The locks.

"About fucking time," muttered Cockface.

Several of the cages rattled. Flicking sounds discharged in succession, seven for every cage. A spotted white-and-brown pit bull was the first dog out. It moved bowlegged to the perimeter of the ring, appearing almost to sulk, nub tail wagging friendly (no). A pair of Rottweillers padded out next, sniffing the ground, snickering and growling at each other. Another pit bull, solid brown, and wearing a padlock-chain necklace, trotted into the concrete circle, its red tongue hanging joyfully from its slobbery mug. One of its eyes was missing, and Johnny wondered if by some strike of fate this had been the dog to take Lou's eye. After that came a skittish German Shepherd with its fur cut from head to tail in a body-length Mohawk, and then behind it came a limping gray Doberman Pinscher. Most of the animals gravitated to the dead bodies, playfully snapping at flies and nuzzling the dead meat they'd created.

Johnny stared into the last cage. He could see the Count's hanging jowls and white eyes rimmed in orange-red. The droopy ears rested at the sides of those eyes, batwings not committed yet to flight. The music peeked through Johnny's mind once more, and one of the dog's ear fluttered. The Count cocked its head. Its eyes had a different fear in them, separate from the conditioned torture of these other animals. In a way, the concentrated look of apprehension reminded Johnny of how he'd felt at the bar, waiting for Dara to show up. *Storm's coming. A nightmare storm...*

"You like him?" asked Cockface. "He's a *Tosa Inu*. I looked it up. Japanese Mastiff. Black's a rare color for them, I guess. When we first picked him up from some rich bitch's backyard, he weighed like a buck-o-five, only half what he is now. Some of the dummies here used him as a bait dog. Filed his claws, taped his teeth—" Cockface grasped Johnny's wrist violently. "In only minutes the Count took the other dogs down and fucking choked them. You believe that? Shit. Fangs taped and he still found a way. Looked like he was sucking their blood. It's why we named him that—hey, Count, come on out buddy. Chop, chop. I gotta get to work. Fresh oinker out here."

The eyes waited there, unblinking.

Johnny swallowed, but there was no spit in his mouth. "Sounds like he's a good fighter. You should keep him."

"You're talking like my partner...anyway, I'm tired of going through trainers with him. Well, goddamn, I didn't waste all this time to talk dogs with you. Shit. You mutts are friggin' lazy. Motivation time." Cockface leaned over to something cone-shaped strapped to a beam.

Johnny jumped at the blast of an air horn. Four dogs collided in a tussle, and he backed away, careful not to make eye contact. Two pit bulls squared off at the side of the melee. The size of the ring shrank as the dogs spread out. They weren't coming after Johnny.

Yet.

The main mass of twisting brutality, wide eyes gleaming, jaws open, paws scraping the air, tumbled closer to him—Johnny moved sideways, and something sharp (a fang?)(a claw?) broke the skin on his left arm. He worked around the group. The brown-and-white pit bull lunged out of the pack. He put up his foot and pushed it back. The dog fell onto its haunches, consumed by the thrashing scrum.

Johnny moved to the other side of the ring. The Doberman's body rested near Jimmy's. In all his life, Johnny hadn't particularly liked dogs, but he'd never understood the barbarism of watching the animals tear each other up. Seeing it, being a part of it, made him hate Cockface more than he already did.

The mohawked German Shepherd limped out of the fight, heading toward him, gnashing its jaws. "Go away!" Johnny warned. "Back inside. Get!"

He gestured to the cages, thinking maybe the dog, knowing it was injured, would return. His pounding heart turned into a fist of ice.

The Count's cage was empty.

Johnny moved laterally past the German Shepherd and the growling horde, which had lost some of its energy but still looked like a viable murder machine. His eyes crossed as he attempted to make out individual animals. *Where is that Count?*

He would have seen him, a dog that big. No doubt.

Johnny peered into the stands.

Cockface wasn't sitting there anymore.

Johnny jumped onto the concrete rim of the fighting ring and awkwardly climbed over the chain link fence. One of the tines ripped a torso-long wound on his right side, and for a moment he thought one of the dogs had gotten him. Holding the stinging sensation in his side, Johnny struggled to catch his breath. He hadn't hopped a fence since he was a teenager. His vision went to dark spots and his head spun for a minute.

When his sight cleared the frenzy had died down some. More than a few dogs lay on the floor, bleeding. Johnny looked away and tried to find an exit from this hell hole. He noticed an open door in the chain link fence, the metal clasp broken in half. He shook his head at his own impulsiveness.

Wish I knew about that door before climbing that damn fence.

Johnny shut the door, though the dogs could easily get through if they tried. That was okay, as long as he was far gone by that time.

He walked down a dark stretch behind the bleachers and screwed his eyes shut for a second. *Didn't stop to think how that door got broken, did you dumbass?*

Cockface lay there, toes of his cowboy boots sticking up, his throat torn out, nearly decapitated. Johnny approached the body, too frightened to feel relief that his captor was dead. He bent down and retrieved the gun near the hand, which was shredded to the bone from defense wounds. The gun's handle still felt warm and sweaty.

Johnny glanced around. The music in his mind had grown in volume since he had left the ring. He was thinking about it more, dwelling on the melody, when he should have been concentrating on keeping his throat from being ripped out.

There were too many dark pockets in this place. Several dog fights continued on the other side of the bleachers, so he couldn't listen for movement. He inspected the gun. Safety was off. It was ready to fire. He didn't want to have to shoot anybody or anything, but he wasn't in a hurry to end up swimming in a blood puddle like the one at his feet. Across from the death scene, the floor rose into a cluttered hallway that was only made visible by a thin bar of light from an opening at the end. The light flickered, as though the door had recently been opened and shut.

Drawing a tremendous breath, Johnny raced up the ramp, gun pressed forward. Large formations emerged from the indistinct areas along the wall. Some were stacks of crates like those outside, and others were bundles of baled cardboard and plastic, stored there for ages. Between them, chasms of gloom broadened. Hiding places. Even a two-hundred-pound dog could hunker down between them. And Count, as Johnny recalled him, menacing and quiet in his cage, knew how to lie in wait.

Something cold and wet brushed his knuckles, and Johnny stepped back, gun pointed out, trembling in hand. He saw two eyes.

At first—but it was feeble light having fun with him, reflecting off the surface of two crushed soda cans.

Johnny quickened his pace. The door there was the swivel type he'd seen in restaurant kitchens. He hadn't noticed before, but it had a small glassine window. The window looked smudged, with a rusty-colored fluid in the shape of two oval nostrils. Johnny pushed the door open with his foot. The subtle florescent light of the small warehouse detailed the brown-red paw prints painting the sleek surface.

"Oh fuck..." Johnny whispered. The music jangled in his head. So close to being. A tickling whisper on his earlobe.

Across the warehouse teeming with crates, he saw a lift door with a chain just begging to be pulled. The air hung with the humid reek of fertilizer, of fresh soil and shit, a far from welcoming smell. Johnny moved out into the miserable enclosure, his lungs, already asthmatic, snapping shut like clam shells. He checked the ground for blood spatters, anything that would indicate where that dog had gone. He didn't see any signs.

Outside, he could hear the whirling sound of a forklift, and a subsequent banging as something heavy dropped into a truck. *Asshole Shitwad, you got no idea, do you?*

Johnny went to the chain and tugged at the lift gate.

A loud snort made his body lock in place.

Johnny turned and saw the Count, about ten feet away. Sitting, the dog came to the level of his chest. Its buggy, quietly insane eyes fixed on him...but there was something else. It was waiting for him to move. Johnny couldn't make out blood on its dark face, but the large jowls and snout were obscenely soaked with it.

"What do you want big boy?" Johnny asked.

The Count looked past him.

"You want out?" Johnny tugged at the gate and pulled it up halfway.

With a grunt, the Count took a few steps closer and sat again.

"Go on..." *Freedom. After all this abuse, you've earned it, fucker. I know how that is. For life to make you into something other people hate.* Johnny stepped up onto a crate and pointed the gun. "Get going," he ordered. "Don't want to shoot."

A door slammed outside, followed by the distant sound of cursing. Gravel crunched under approaching footsteps.

"What are you waiting for?" Johnny wiped sweat from his eyes. "Stupid! Go!"

The Count began to pant with a pseudo dog-smile.

His tail wagged fiercely.

It happened with a force that made Johnny's teeth grind. The dream song erupted inside his mind and burst into a series of falling notes, pounding beats, and swelling lyrics. It spilled into his ears. Into his heart. It reached out with all its invisible tendrils and leeched into reality. The violence of it made him drop the gun—he dipped to catch it and batted to the floor where it skidded to a stop near the dog's left paw.

"Aw fuck," Johnny whispered and jumped as an office door swung open. Two rows of sleek, powerful bull dogs ushered a naked man toward the lift door. He was bound at the hands by a tether that both dog's gripped in their jaws. The man writhed, in pain and full of hate. On its own, the lift door flew open, and sunlight washed out everything for a moment.

As Johnny's eyes adjusted to the light, he recognized the naked man's pasty face. It was Asshole Shitwad. Or a version of him beaten mercilessly for years and now turned completely feral. Outside, rather than a dumpy storage yard, a stone coliseum stretched, mostly empty, except for in the center, a mass of naked people tearing and clawing at each other. He saw a bloody hand lift up a detached jawbone, and he forced his eyes away.

The rows of bull dogs led their captive down the steps, toward the bloody chaos.

Johnny wanted to scream, but another scream quickly doubled over on it, rendering him silent. The Count took two strides, going up on his back legs, not quite standing erect, but walking like no dog should ever walk. His front paws also changed, became more humanlike. He held a scepter of human bones, a child's skull fixed to the top, and used it like a cane to support his demented gait. Johnny quaked so much he couldn't form a coherent thought.

The side of the Count's jowl lifted at Johnny, like a smirk of gratitude, and then he plodded into the arena, in a hurry to watch the next fighter enter the fray, canine eyes wide in delight, an emperor returned to his country.

Johnny jumped down from the crate and sidled up to the door. He checked behind him on the floor for the gun but it was nowhere to be found. Grinding his teeth, he turned back. The new arena had broken through the surrounding chain-link fence and had thrust many of the crates into the surrounding field, as well as tipping over the semi-truck the two men had arrived in. A frenzied maze of crates stood between him and his U-Haul, which he could see beyond a heap of crumbling stone and open containers of fertilizer. Johnny's vision blurred. He took off his glasses and at once saw everything clearly. Far beyond that, possibly miles away, he could see a great black curtain falling from the clouds to the ground.

"Holy shit." He stuffed the glasses into the pocket of his cargo shorts.

The Count would make him the next contestant down there. That had to be the point of this place. It might have been an odd thing to think otherwise, but he wagered that dogs in power could not be trusted. Another small intuition told Johnny he was too familiar with this area, with this neighborhood, and as long as he treaded in this land, the dogs would have their way. So he had to get to that U-Haul. He was certain that was the answer.

If he reached that big curtain, all this madness would end.

Chapter 12

Dara hoped tonight the kids weren't too wired.

She wanted to look forward to this evening out with Maribel and Luke. Since bursting through that black curtain in the board room, tense, ever-fidgeting and on-edge, she'd lived her life, and being around a bunch of hyperactive school kids sure didn't sound like a cure. Maribel counted on their support and so she didn't hesitate…it would just make things so much easier if Dara could explain everything to her and Luke, without sounding delusional and disturbed.

Luke had a phone conversation earlier with his friend Blake, and through all Luke's placations, it boiled down to this: the company had no intentions of hiring her now. That was just Blake's insight, but it was probably a good one. The bright side was that Luke's transfer to the satellite position for the San Francisco office would most likely move forward. He just needed to keep his head down and lay low during the Los Angeles proceedings.

If they could all eventually move up north…would the nightmares follow them?

It might have been foolishly optimistic, but one thing Dara could bank on now was having more control if she remembered the music again. The purple bug had given her that control—a *lucidity touchstone*, a term that became embedded in her mind, perhaps from the song itself. The nightmare—Lifemare—could still have its way with Dara and the world around her, but at least she knew that next time she'd be looking for a way out, she'd understand that reality had shifted, and wouldn't be drifting along, accepting everything like before.

Facing the vanity mirror, she licked her dry lips, and a troubling thought crossed her mind. *What if it'll be worse now that I know?*

Ignorance might have shielded her from the worst.

She went looking for her lime chapstick in her makeup bag, hoping that Maribel hadn't borrowed it and forgotten to put it back where it belonged.

Depression set in as she looked again in the mirror. She really didn't want to be around kids right now. Staying home, getting back to strategizing for her Orchish army in the Dragon God game that had long since gone stale; it was waiting for her, there on her hard drive, waiting to get her locked in and addicted again...

That's going backwards. You were supposed to get that job. Now, by some strange stroke of bizarre luck, if you do get it, you're going to be remembered as the woman who showed up with her boobs hanging out. It'd only be slightly worse than the high school locker room. "Double-Dee-Dee. Double-Dee-Dee. All that fat went to your chest—where's your ass?"

She considered how the nightmare incident would affect the rumors about them and Maribel. Poor Luke was going to have his hands fuller than they'd ever been.

"Jesus Christ," she whispered, giving up on her search. She checked her hair. It had no body at all, just silken, bleach-blonde bullshit. *I love your unicorn mane,* Maribel always told her. Dara smiled, but it instantly faded at the sound of Luke rummaging through the closet. He'd already tried on a few pairs of shoes, but his feet still ached badly from the burns. He'd been running in the street without shoes...those frogmen...what might have happened if they'd dragged Luke under like the rest of the people in the pool? Would the nightmare have ended when he did?

Dara shook her head fiercely, rejecting the idea of her husband dying.

If it wasn't going to be this job, she would instead figure out this Lifemare thing, bring it to Luke's attention, somehow.

Was it happening other places? Maybe they could both bring it to the world's attention?

A flaccid knock came at the front door.

"Can you get that, honey?" mumbled Luke. "I'm…I'm going to try these loafers again."

"Yeah, hon."

Dara moved down the hall, through the living room, to the front door. For probably the first time ever, she didn't dread the idea of it being Johnny Cruz. She'd like to ask him what he remembered from that bar. Never mind he'd behave like the whole thing somehow happened within the boundaries of real life; whatever he could supply would be more than she had now.

The door's hinges chirped as it swung open. Petunia Stedding stood on the porch in her drab yellow nightgown. Her eyes held Dara, wildly moving, but her body was perfectly still. A mountain bike lay in the grass behind her.

It took a moment for Dara to find any words. "Hello. How…how are you doing, Petunia? I'm so…" Dara put her hand to her chest, feeling all the emotion welling up. "I'm so sorry to hear what happened…we've been thinking about your parents all the time."

Petunia stared at her, through her. "I can see the curtain."

She couldn't mean…she was there, though.

"I know his whole life," said Petunia.

Dara swallowed and her spine stiffened. "Whose, dear?"

"Mr. Rhodes'. After I touched the ducky. I wasn't supposed to, but it made me come awake inside it, and after it ended, the song's been playing nonstop in my head. Pieces are missing—I'll never hear them, but Mr. Rhodes can." She tilted her head and her brow knitted. "You can hear it, too, can't you?"

"Petunia…"

"I don't want to hear the ballad anymore. It pushed a key inside me, but it doesn't fit like it would with Mr. Rhodes. The key twisted but there's nothing to unlock. I feel caught between both places right now—I don't belong here and I don't belong in the bad dream. I'm an alien invading a strange place…until the key is pulled out and put where it belongs. I don't want to hurt Mr. Rhodes. I think I should hurt myself."

"No," Dara said, beginning to step toward the teenager, but then she thought better of it. This was the part when the crazy girl plunged a knife between your ribs. "Don't hurt yourself. Is there a way to make this better? What can we do?"

A PT Cruiser quickly pulled into the driveway. The parking brake chirped and a door swung open.

"I want to be released," said Petunia. "Mr. Rhodes has to find his touchstone again."

Lucidity touchstone.

Someone came around the corner. Petunia's grandmother, out of breath, in her bathrobe with a long gray raincoat flowing over it. "God, has she done anything? I had a feeling she'd come here." The older woman rushed up and caught Petunia around her stomach and dragged her back.

"We were just talking," Dara told her.

"She's really, really upset."

"Get him to touch it," Petunia begged. "I don't want it inside my head anymore. I'll tear my brain out!"

"I'm terribly sorry about this. We have to collect her father's car keys and other things from his office at the plant, and I think the idea of going there just got the best of her. I can't let her out of my sight or I'd go alone. Tomorrow, we're on our way to the behavioral center, and we're getting help. Aren't we, Petunia? We're going to get you better. I'm so sorry, Mrs. Rhodes. Please understand."

"No, I understand."

Luke slowly limped up behind her.

"*We* understand," added Dara.

Petunia caught sight of him. "Mr. Rhodes! They aren't dreams! They're real! Mr. Rhodes you need to find that duck again!"

"Hush now," her grandmother told her, lightly putting a hand over her mouth. Petunia moved her face away with a growl.

"Please let us know if we can help," said Luke.

The old woman feebly nodded. "I'll come by later for her bike, if that's okay."

"No worries. I'll put it in the garage for whenever you're ready for it," said Luke with a faint smile.

Petunia was carefully put into the silver PT Cruiser. The grandmother locked the door for the short duration of walking around to the driver's side. After a moment, they were gone, and Dara was left on the porch with Luke.

Luke buttoned his shirt carefully. "She's so disturbed now. Poor thing. I feel like I should do more. I don't know what though."

"Do you remember a rubber ducky in the pool that day?" Dara asked.

He reared his head back abruptly, taken aback. He twisted his mouth to the side in thought. "I think there was one, yeah. A red one. Petunia mentioned it when she called for help that day."

"Have you ever touched it?"

Luke looked at her and simpered. "The duck? What are you talking about?"

"I think it's important."

He shook his head and hobbled back inside to the kitchen. "How could that be important? Damn, my feet hurt. I think some more aloe vera might do the trick."

"I've wanted to tell you...I don't know how to explain it though, not without you thinking I'm a nut."

"Is this about what happened at the interview?"

"Yes, but also what happened at the pool that day. The weird thing that happened to me, I think happened to you, too."

"You weren't there. How could you know?"

"It all feels the same. I think Johnny might be involved, too. I ran into him...before the interview."

"Weird."

"Right?"

"Yeah, I can't believe Johnny was up at that early, even on a work day."

"You should call him. See where he is. Just to make sure he's okay."

Luke snorted. "Never thought I'd hear that from you."

"He might be in trouble."

"When *isn't* he? I don't have time to get wrapped up in Johnny right now. We have a schedule to keep. We're going to be late for the music class, and Maribel needs our help more this year than ever." He opened the refrigerator and got a mini-can of Coke Zero.

"Call Johnny just to make sure. Please."

With a gentle sigh, Luke slid out his cell, found the number, and called. He waited, searching the ceiling. The light shone down on his upturned, handsome face, making him an image of a disinclined hero. "Not answering," he said and ended the call.

Dara leaned into the counter with a groan.

"I can go looking for him after Maribel's thing."

"Maybe you should skip. Go now."

Luke lifted his eyebrows. "Uh...no. Johnny's not top priority. You gals are."

Dara went silent as Luke popped the can and killed his soft drink in one tug. With a satisfied sigh, he tossed the can in the recycle bin. Stepping to meet her, he embraced her and kissed her neck. "You smell wonderful."

"Thanks," she answered quietly.

He gently pulled her face to his. They were nose to nose. "I promise to take care of everything when we get back. Whatever you want, I'll do it. Rescue Johnny. Touch a duck. Anything."

Dara burst out laughing. "Ass."

Luke grinned. "Better make ourselves scarce."

Despite the intense sunshine reflecting off the dirt-smudged windshield, the vibrant jazz on the radio, the icy rumble of the air conditioner, the trip across town completely exhausted Dara. Her husband drove like a man in a trance, occasionally breaking from it to wince at his scorched feet pressing the brake. She should have offered to drive—hadn't even thought about it.

The private elementary-school parking lot had no available spots. Seeing all these people cast a pall of dread over Dara's already sour mood. Luke wheeled out of the lot and pulled along the curb.

He studied her "You really don't want to be here, do you? Is this still about Johnny?"

"No. I'll be fine."

"I wanted to tell you, but I hoped you wouldn't be mad...."

"What?"

"That call from Blake was in response to Maribel. She went down there and chewed out the board of directors."

"Are you kidding?" Dara's face filled with hot blood. "Why'd she do that?"

Luke gripped the steering wheel hard and looked up. "Honestly? I think it's because she knew I couldn't."

It was Dara's turn to study him. "Neither of you have faith in me, do you?"

"That's not it."

"There are other jobs out there. Screw that job."

"We can't stand the idea of anybody humiliating you. Most people in that office are out to get all of us."

"I'm the one who showed up without a blouse."

"Can't wrap my mind around that yet," he said, shaking his head. "You must be leaving something out of the story. How do you lose your blouse?"

"I imagined putting it on. When I left the house, I wasn't in the right frame of…mind."

"How does that happen? Did you eat a mushroom or something? Jesus, Dara."

She scrubbed at her face, then stopped, fearing to smear her makeup every which way. "You won't understand. You *can't* understand. Not until…"

"I touch the duck?" The joke from last time wasn't in his face now. Deep concern had replaced it. "You really think the pool and the interview share something? How could they? You're starting to sound like Petunia, and that's freaking me the hell out. Dara, wait—"

She got out of the car. Luke hastily put up the sun shade and followed. The car's alarm beeped as he shambled up to her, grimacing. "Well, don't take me the wrong way. However it happened—I wish I could have been there. Stobecker probably crossed himself and fainted."

His nervous laugh elicited a smile from her. He took her hand as she stepped up on the sidewalk, and then, with her standing above him, he wrapped his arms around her tightly. She smoothed his thick dark brown hair and squeezed his neck. "As bad as that was…it changed something about me. I wish I could only be worried about my weight now."

That grin again, less bright, but trying. "Don't tell me you want *another* surgery."

"I love you so much, Luke."

"I love you too, honey."

She held him close to her chest for a moment. "You haven't been hearing music have you?"

"Have they begun?" Luke stepped up onto the sidewalk and started inside the small multi-purpose room.

That's not what I meant.

Dara trailed after him. Inside the small auditorium, a few Kindergarten classes, including Maribel's, ran around wildly with recorders and small bongo drums. Dara and Luke hadn't gotten far inside when a stressed-out Maribel approached, pushing a key into Luke's hands. "Can you go to my classroom and get my whistle?"

A Chinese boy nearly crashed into Maribel's leg. "Mrs. Rhodes, Mrs. Rhodes, Mrs. Rhodes."

"Yes, Victor?"

"Have you been to Puppet Town?"

"I know every inch of Puppet Town—that's our annual field trip."

"What's a field tip?"

"Go to your number along the wall, Victor. We're going to start soon."

Victor cracked a gap-toothed smile and rushed playfully back into the confusion, taking the longest route to the wall possible.

Maribel brushed errant strands of her chocolate hair from her eyes. "Where was I?"

"Your whistle?" Dara laughed.

"It's either in my desk or in the cabinets by the window—the key for those are in my desk. Luke, I need the bass drum. It's too awkward for me to carry. If you see Allie, tell her I need her right now, not next week. She's always fooling around with the equipment when I need her help."

"Sure," said Dara.

Luke touched Maribel's face. "Remain calm."

A flicker of disgust and Maribel returned to the chaos, asking kids to find their places.

"Sure you don't want to be a teacher?" Luke asked Dara.

"Ha-ha."

They walked outside and took the brutal hill leading up to the kindergarten room. From here they could see into San Bernardino, the bare brown mountains, the tapestry of freeways, streets, red-tiled rooftops and dull green treetops squeezed into every available spot between buildings. Dara gazed at the view, trying to sound less out of breath than she was, anticipating the fitness lecture she'd get from Luke. Her eyes caught sight of the immense shape standing out on the sun, highlighted by a sky with less haze and smog than usual. She halted and blinked.

Had the nightmare returned?

It didn't feel like it.

Reality had remained stable…so why was she seeing the black curtain out there?

"Do you see that? That curtain out there?"

Luke followed where she looked. "Hmmm. Yeah. Weird."

That was it; that was all; he was about to start walking away again.

"Wait—just 'weird?' That's all you're going to say? There's a friggin' curtain hanging from the sky, coming all the way down to the ground."

"It's very pretty. We better fetch those things before Maribel loses it."

Dara gave up and accompanied him to the room. If that wasn't the curtain to her nightmare, then whose nightmare was it?

Near the cabinets the teacher's aide, Allie Banks, was bent over, rummaging around. On seeing Luke and Dara, she locked the cabinet doors and returned the key to Maribel's desk. She gave them a cool stare and folded her arms. Allie had never hidden her disdain for them. She'd even gone to the principal and told him the relationship would be misunderstood by the children. It wasn't difficult for Maribel to win the principal back, however. He was a gay man, not in the closet, but increasingly private about his own life. So he viewed moral whistleblowers like Allie with the contempt they deserved. On top of that, Maribel had received *teacher of the district* the last two years now, and had come close to state recognition—she was the star of their school, and it was easy for the principal to wave off Allie's single-minded protests.

But they still had to deal with her.

"You guys can't be in here without an employee of the school," she stated.

Luke stepped inside the room. "You're in here, right? We need the whistle and the bass drum."

"I have to get going. I can't stick around."

"You're right," said Dara. "Maribel was looking for you."

Allie's eyes shifted. She had a narrow, puppy-like face, which wasn't ugly or even homely, yet wasn't allowed to be attractive with all her scowling. "Is it starting already?"

"Yep."

"Remember to lock the door, and be quick. Don't touch anything else."

"Yes, master," said Luke.

Allie snorted and hurried outside.

"What a pain in the ass. I'd take three Derek Stobeckers over one of her."

"Let's get that stuff."

Luke went to the corner to the bass drum. He removed a microphone stand to get to it. She watched him lift it easily. "Got it?"

"Cake," Luke replied, though his voice quavered.

Dara went through the desk's top drawers. No whistle. In the meantime, Luke balanced the drum on the student's table closest to the door. "You thought of opening Maribel's letter early?"

"Don't you dare," she replied.

"Just wondering." He chuckled. "What do you think it says?"

Dara took a deep breath. "Something good, I hope."

She found a small key next to some pencils. She took it, knelt, and opened the sliding cabinet doors behind her. She pushed a woman's hoodie out of the way. It must have been Allie's because Dara didn't recognize it as belonging to Maribel. A few piles of children's books had been stacked inside the cupboard. In the back, a couple of flyers from the Puppet Town amusement park and a plastic Jolly Green Giant leaned against a little diorama. Over the cellophane window on top rested a crayon drawing of a rocking horse, the word "marble" underneath. Dara moved it and her heart thudded in her chest.

"Oh my…holy shit," she whispered.

Inside the diorama sat three things, each with a label. A toy purple bug with DARA printed on masking tape below it. A red rubber duck, with LUKE underneath. An extremely wrinkled two-dollar bill. JOHNNY.

"What is it?" asked Luke.

"Come here." Dara put the diorama on top of the cupboard and removed the lid.

Luke peered over her shoulder. "Hey, a duck, what do you know?"

He picked it up. "That's a fine duck right there. Not really rubber though. Hard plastic."

"But is it the same kind from the pool?"

"If memory serves."

Dara watched his face. "Do you feel…different now?"

"Should I?"

It must not work outside of the Lifemare… She looked at the names. "Maribel doesn't print like this."

Two names at the top of the chalk board, one written by Maribel, and the other by Allie: Mrs. Rhodes and Mrs. Banks. The second had the same boxy quality to the letters.

"Our friend Allie had to have written that—what is this stuff? Some kind of Voodoo death box?" Luke tittered, but Dara didn't reply.

"Why would she include Johnny and not Maribel?"

"She's got the hots for Maribel. That's obvious."

"You're joking."

Luke shrugged. "Not really—"

"Allie's married."

"Oh well, then it's impossible." He smirked. Something lit in his eyes. "Allie did meet Johnny once. Don't you remember when we bumped into her at Shasta's? After she told him she was married, Johnny harassed her the whole night. He got pretty pissed when she said she wouldn't trade in a successful pianist for a turd farmer."

"That was pretty funny."

"Not to Johnny."

"Yeah, *where's your loyal hubbie right now? At home fingering a piano.*"

"He has a way with women," Luke replied dryly. "Now you got me worrying about him again. Come on, put that box away. I don't really *want* to know what it is, tell you the truth."

Dara covered up the diorama, returned it to where she found it, and located Maribel's whistle on top of a basket of well-used crayon nubs.

More questions. Few answers. Dara wanted to feel like she'd uncovered something just now, but she wasn't certain if it could explain anything. This puzzle had so many pieces to sort through, she'd not found the corners yet.

It left way too much to be desired.

Chorus:

Much of what he used to disbelieve, he'd discovered to be only partially true.

Gentle colors and friendly shapes gave the play-set its vibrancy. Normally, out there in the field all by itself, silly red-yellow-blue-and-green paints, it would be the first thing people noticed, but under this influence, it was cause for avoiding eye contact. They. Would. Know better than to look upon something to stir up the rot growing in their stomachs. He was behind this. All of Them, behind this.

A swing set extends from a pool of dark yellow poison where a red ducky floats. Studying the scene better, on his stomach in the swing, a naked green man with broccoli hair pendulums over the poison, lapping it up, holding it in, regurgitating back into the pool. In Their heart of hearts a klaxon would ring, *he's doing this to get better, whatever made him ill before, he's doing this to get better.* Pulling Their gaze away was certain. Certainly.

Save for the benched man… The tiny hairs in his ears flutter as he strains to hear. His ass stings from sitting on the wooden bench so long. From not blinking all this time, knife-points of cold tears sting the corners of his eyes. Below the peak of the play-set where nested rods of steel complicate the upper floor, and below the second level of plastic bubble windows, the psychotic face of a harlequin opens its bubble-gum maw wide enough to let children inside, and its beady candy-corn pupils evaluate the man. The oral passageway inside the harlequin's throat—has it always been thus?

A moment passes, and now this Abaddon stretches before him? How could that be? This song, this horrible, awful, forbidden song still can't drown out the plinking melody of the xylophone, nor can it rob him of the feral puppies eviscerating each other with all the jubilation infancy brings. A reply, just one, solitary, pitifully small reply, to all his cancerous questions brings his Ouroboros mind to the gagging point. Through the veils of tear, his vision blanches the scene of wildlings tumbling in the passageway, blood games melting the dark at its seams. Screeches; retches; gags; wails; his plaintive sounds betray his trance. Yes, yes. With Them, it is, it is.

"Do you…" he begins, shaking his head, coming through the fog a bit. "Hear me? Back there? If you could just make it quit happening, I could go and find help. What will it take? It can't end like this. I've had plans. We all had plans. Can't you just say something? Why won't you answer me goddamnit! Grunt or something. For Christ's sake! You better not let it get at me again. I don't…shit! I don't want to see it ever again. My body's breaking down and you don't even care. *Help me.*"

Verse 4: Invader

Chapter 13

Johnny hadn't moved for hours.

He'd managed to negotiate the scattered crates and massive dirt hills and circle the gladiator ring, but stumbled on an open area of crumbling, primeval sandstone blocks. If he set foot out there, the Count would spot him, as well as the gathering of Bone Men flanking the dog-thing like steadfast minions. Johnny hunkered down and stayed down, ultimately rethinking a mad rush to the U-Haul, which was only twenty feet away on a grade of up-turned gravel and dirt.

The Count had spared him initially, but with the gladiators dying in droves, Johnny wasn't so sure it would stay that way. For now, the dog was more interested in the spectacle in the ring—starving human beings ripping each other apart, fueled by the rage of feral survival and the gruesomeness of cruelty and abandonment. It was obvious in the snarling, drool-blood masked faces: the fight was necessary, not to continue to live, but to make others pay for the wretched lives they'd led. Leaning on his bone scepter, the Count, long dark jowls hanging, sunken flesh around his zombie eyes, watched with mouth parted in a smile of disbelief and unchecked marvel. He relished every eye plucked from the socket, every rope of intestine pulled from the abdomen, every death call and snarl of hungry homicide.

Johnny couldn't look at the dog anymore. The need to vomit in terror had come and gone, but seeing how that Thing was *loving* all this...he would turn his eyes across the brown field of Southern California dirt, rock, and weed, and in the distance, the rippling black curtain suspended from the sky. It wasn't unreachable. *Yes, I could make it.* The desert had never looked so inviting. At first he questioned driving the U-Haul through such an unforgiving landscape, but someone had replaced the tires with large tractor treads, well shined and onyx in the sunlight.

Hadn't noticed those before! No problem then.

He could cut across the ravine, and the sewer plant where he'd been suspended, wasn't that far at all.

I'm baaaack motherfuckers!

You're not anything, if you don't get up and move. You've been here so long, your ass has fallen asleep. Get to that U-Haul, dickhead.

Johnny squared his shoulders. Sweat dappled his back. With the number of gladiators thinning to only a few, this had to be done now. Before they found him.

"Oh, we know you're there," said voices in sync with the song.

The shadowy shapes of four Bone Men slid down the embankment, spears pointed at him.

Johnny threw his body forward and ran. He rounded the driver's side of the moving truck and ripped open the door. In his seat sat the man from the U-Haul store. A woman with tight brown curls sat next to him, looking worried.

"This is my truck," the man stated, looking forward. "You can't have it."

Johnny stepped up on the running board. "Move the hell over!"

"No," the man repeated. "My wife and I need this truck."

The Bone Men clucked their tongues as they flowed into a unified group moving toward Johnny.

Johnny pushed the man, but he wouldn't budge. "You son of a bitch! Move!"

The man shook his head fiercely. Thick saliva dangled from his mouth. Johnny yanked him out of the cabin by his collar and let him fall to the ground outside. The wife reached forward and grabbed the keys out of the ignition.

He lunged for her. "Give those back!"

A squeal, unnaturally sharp and agonized, made Johnny stop, poised just over her. The woman edged down in the seat and pushed the door lock down. Johnny hit the lock on his side and lowered his body. A sandaled foot connected with his face. The woman reared back, trying to kick him again. He caught her by the ankle. Her body twisted sideways.

"Fuckin' chill!" he whispered.

Through the windshield, a spear hoisted a body into the air. The wife squirmed. Johnny clamped his hand over her mouth. He could feel her tongue and teeth gnashing against his palm. The body of her husband jerked above them on the spear, flexing to right itself but having nowhere to go. Five more spears drove up into his body, stabbing repeatedly. Johnny saw the blood showering down. He closed his eyes, but he could hear it, torrential rain on the hood of the truck.

After a few seconds, the pitter and patter stopped. Johnny opened his eyes. The red-soaked body hung there in a sad upside-down U. Breathing heavy through her nose and trembling, the wife stared at her dead husband. Johnny took a chance and removed his hand. If she couldn't take that image as a hint to be quiet, then nothing would work.

"Give me the keys," he whispered. "Please."

She blinked and looked around the floor. A pounding outside made her start. Johnny tried to flatten his body even more. The woman found the keys. They rattled as she dragged them off the floor mat.

A metallic puncture sound, an ear-splitting *pop*! Warm mist sprayed Johnny's face. The spearhead exited the woman's neck and twisted around for good measure, then retreated, barbed ends tearing skin and gristle away, nearly severing the woman's head as it pulled back through the door.

Another spear plunged through on the passenger side, the edge of the spearhead slitting Johnny's jaw. Another spear came through, just over his head.

"Fuck this!" He scooted back, grabbed the handle, and pushed outside. The door struck a Bone Man in the face. He fell to one knee, using his spear to keep balance. Johnny dashed over a stony ridge, feet nearly slipping out from under him. He could hear things piercing the dirt all around him. His heart felt like a red-hot tea kettle about to explode. He kept on. Lungs catching flames. Bones creaking from his weight. He was going to collapse. It was over.

Johnny spared a glance over his shoulder. But there was nothing.

Just field.

Dirt.

Weeds.

Rocks.

No visible life.

It was a familiar landscape, not only because he'd grown up playing around here, but because Johnny understood the land. He commiserated with a place like this, with its unappealing, coarse exterior. Something had once been alive here.

He walked swiftly, keeping an eye out. At a distance he could see homes. Some of the houses had belonged to friends, and the windows glinted in the sun. The houses he'd never been inside had black curtains drawn over their panes and doors. Any of the curtains could get him *away* from whatever he was trying to escape. However, convincing strangers to let him inside their house, especially with him sweating and bleeding profusely, was probably out.

The large curtain would be the only way.

Spicy, unseen flowers perfumed the air. He knew the smell from lifetimes before. Calm. Nostalgic. Loving. It called to mind a time when Johnny Cruz still had the capability to behold life with a little hopeful wonder. Ever dubious, while winding down an old dirt-bike path, he enjoyed the scent, taking in a large breath through his nose. He didn't remember the stretch between the old neighborhood and the sewer plant having paths as wide and well-packed as these; he must have somehow missed that before.

Occasionally he would sidestep a dirt ramp. He thought of Beltran, how he'd always wanted to get him a bike when he got older. The week before he packed for Arizona, Johnny remembered taking him to these exact same dirt paths. Later that day he wanted to take Beltran on his Harley, give him a little fun, make a memory before they said adios. Shit, he'd just been trying to cheer the kid up, but instead of cutting loose and enjoying the ride, the boy had gotten all scared and whiney. The trip back home had been long, and Johnny remembered yelling at Beltran a few times to stop his sniveling. *So much for that.* But at least he'd known he'd made the right choice sending him back to Charles.

That's how Lisa would have wanted it.

"Lisa?"

Johnny froze. His mouth opened again, but no words shaped on his lips. He couldn't. With that scent of flowers in the air, with the vision before him, what words would he have used to express how he felt?

His ex-wife, who had gotten ill and died, stood on a nearby hill, alive as he remembered her in his best memories. She wore a white dress, but the sunlight cut through it and he could see her full, warm, wonderful figure within. He'd always loved her body. He gotten her some lingerie that she'd only worn once to make him happy, in spite of him trying to get her back into it a thousand times. It wasn't that she was self-conscious; she just thought that kind of stuff silly.

She couldn't really be here? Could she?

Yes. She was here now, no longer in the white dress, but in the sinful red and black mesh baby-doll lingerie, with thong. Johnny's body reacted at once. Lisa peered down and bit her lower lip sinfully. Someone else walked up behind her, in the exact same lingerie, but the fit was less tight, the hips more accentuated.

His first wife, Mandy. In one of her garter belts he could see a money note flapping there. He squinted into the sun…looked like a two-dollar bill.

"Oh my God…" he moaned, his pulse quickening. *It would be amazing if they…*

And they did.

Johnny watched as his two wives kissed, licked, and fondled each other. He went into a trance, silent splendor, awestruck, femalestruck, his body roaring with need. He never wanted this to end. The only thing better would be to have more—

"Come here," purred Mandy.

"Take off your pants," breathed Lisa.

Johnny did as commanded. His wives had sparkling murder in their eyes, and devil claws extending from bleeding cuticles, but he pushed those images away. *No.* That would not ruin this. He would enjoy his lovers for as long as he could. He would stay here with them until the end of time, if he had that long. Not just for their flesh, for their touch, for their love, for their wonderful, haunting, beautiful smell that made him feel alive again. He'd known it all along but hadn't taken the time to appreciate the truth.

Their musk smelled of those flowers.

Chapter 14

Near dusk, but the sewer plant swam in black.

Shasta's Bar and Grill was still closed after some food-poisoning incident, and the other dive bars were too far outside of town for Johnny to bother with. Luke had checked and he wasn't home either. The plant was the only place left in his sad life that Johnny'd even think of visiting. Still, Luke couldn't imagine his friend would show up here—this was, at best, a shot in the dark, and yet more than once on the drive home Dara had prodded him, "You sure you don't see anything weird over on that side of town? You think maybe that's where Johnny went?"

Hell if he knew. Luke did see the curtain spilling from the sky, but he didn't find it as remarkable as Dara did. When black curtains fell from the stratosphere, this was how they looked, right? Why was she so worked up about it?

Suspiciously, Maribel had been silent and moody during the trip home. She pled exhaustion and seemed to care even less about the curtain than Luke did. That made him feel better. Dara was just being Dara, which was to say, overreacting.

Her insistence got him to reconsidering the hard-line stance he'd taken earlier. Wives versus Friends. Johnny might need help, and Luke was the only person he could ever turn to.

When Maribel and Dara took a late afternoon nap together, he managed to slip off, hoping to resolve this before they woke. After twenty minutes of driving around, he realized he'd left his cell phone at the house. That was certain to piss them off.

He decided to make a quick stop at the plant and, if Johnny wasn't there, call the whole outing a wash. He'd made a couple wrong turns en route—that song had begun to scratch its claws into the back of his head again, and though he couldn't recall the rhythm, he sensed echoes of the notes rebounding off this part of town. It got more resonant as he neared the plant. A disgusting sensation absorbed him: he shouldn't be here; this wasn't his place; this wasn't his territory; *this wasn't his dream*. His fatigued eyes may have been working on him, but the air shimmered around the plant, all the way to the fields and the black curtain.

He looked around again.

Shimmered, it did.

Like diamonds bleeding golden silhouettes of the sun and stars. It was a field before him, a vertical mirage.

He drove through the mirage, and at once it disappeared. The atmosphere got heavier, and his mind relaxed, accepted every jagged shape, line, and fissure in the universe.

He slipped out of the Volt, shut the door, and walked the severely cracked sidewalk to the treatment plant's front office. Shadows cooked off the trailer and slipped down, splashing with hisses on the burnt brown grass outside. It had been a while since he'd stopped by here, probably since GeoGreen wrapped up the centrifuge and equalization tank project for the city. The structure housing the centrifuge and the new tank had to be the only modern construction onsite. Everything else was circa 1970 and every inch looked it. None of the administration buildings were kept up—the pair of simple rectangular military-style huts had slowly become warehouses for operators, sewer collection crews and mechanics. A series of trailers had been brought in at some point, probably when the city realized how much it would cost to retrofit the original buildings. Despite the smell and the crumbling infrastructure, Luke had always felt the sewer treatment plant had a homey, down-to-earth vibe, but it seemed *off* now, as if turning over a few stones would let loose something volatile.

Luke stepped up the iron steps to the trailer and took the door handle. Paused. He shouldn't be doing this. He involuntary gasped—*what if I remember the song right now, while it's already playing for someone else?*

Who was it playing for?

Hard to tell. But two layers of that hateful, splendid music? What would *that* do?

He didn't want to entertain that thought. He had to just concentrate, find Johnny, make sure he was okay, and then get the hell home for his scolding.

Right.

Like Petunia had said...he was an alien here, an invader of another's personal world.

The door swung open before Luke reached it.

Petunia's grandmother was there. Right there.

"Have you seen her?" the old woman asked, her eyes terror-drawn.

Luke shook his head.

"She came out here without telling me. Good God, we just needed to collect her dad's things and get out. I can't take this anymore."

Mouse Stedding...yes, he was gone. Because that's what frogmen do.

"She's going to do something horrible." The old woman clasped her hands to her face like an awful bone breathing apparatus.

"Don't worry. I'll get her back. Just stay here." Luke headed around the trailer, up the concrete stairs fixed inside the hill. They led to the headworks, the first place the city's sewage went to be treated. He could hear the mechanical bar-screen shuttering above, catching all the solid matter. This normally was the most awful-smelling place in the entire plant, but it smelled different today.

Flowers?

When he got to the top of the hill he took in a big breath; like roses and orange blossoms married. Luke actually enjoyed the scent for a moment. It reminded him of the perfume Johnny's wife Lisa used to wear sometimes. Poor woman died so young. The scent was a nice memory of her though.

Then Luke noticed the wastewater superintendent, Fabian Rove. On his knees, the man hunkered before the passing river of sewage, his head entirely submerged.

Luke hurried over to grab him around the stomach.

"Leave him be," said a cigarette-scarred voice.

The plant manager, Jack Portiere, leaned against a stanchion to the screener. His American Spirit filterless had jaundiced his hand. In fact, all his flesh had yellowed, including the whites of his eyes. It was a lot worse than Luke remembered.

Rove jerked his head up from the sewage and gasped. "Thought I saw it this time!"

Luke flinched in revulsion. Something that looked like spinach clung to Rove's jaw, and his face was speckled in pieces of brown.

Luke caught his gagging mouth. "Eh...saw what?"

"Alberto Cruz's heart. The fat fuck! Gonna use it to make a monster." Rove slammed his face back down and wiggled his body like a bear hunting for a trout, splashing sewage back and forth.

Jack Portiere chuckled dryly and took a deep drag of his cigarette. "Won't find Johnny's heart down there...I keep telling him. Nope. Johnny Cruz's heart is down in the field with those foxy ladies. They're playing with all his squishy parts right about now."

Luke shook off the obvious question. "Right. So, hey, have you seen a teenage girl around here?"

Portiere moved his head back. "Down by the new tank. Told her not to go. There's still construction equipment yonder."

"Why didn't you stop her?"

The man lifted an eyebrow that stretched the yellow flesh of his eyelid into a translucent film. "Not my job."

Luke didn't have time for this. Petunia and Johnny were both in trouble now. "This way? The scaffold still the best way to get down?"

The man blew out an unnaturally dense cloud of hazel smoke that surrounded his body, hiding everything about him save for the sparkling red cherry at the end of the cigarette. "So you choose to save the girl before the friend...the foxy ladies win, again. You are sooooo brave."

Whatever... Luke went to the galvanized scaffold and descended the first ramp. As he proceeded, the underground hiss of gravity-fed sewer pipes deafened him. The fire-escape-like scaffold was familiar; he'd gone up and down it for months. The descent felt endless now. Through the hissing came a loud banging, steel on steel.

The equalization tank holding nearly a million gallons of untreated sewage had a construction flaw in its secondary containment, and though it probably would be okay, Luke had cautioned the city. In case an earthquake struck, they should consider reinforcing the outer containment at very least. That had been so much pissing in the wind. The city was too happy to be at the finish line of a large project, so one of their engineers signed off on it.

It wasn't for Luke to question the client if they defined a big earthquake as a rare occurrence.

A track hoe, however, breaking through the side of the tank's containment wall, should have been equally rare. But halfway down the scaffold, Luke's stomach twisted.

Grover Franklin sat behind the controls of the track hoe, frantically throwing levers, prolific sweat running down his face.

"Franklin! What the hell! Ease off!" Luke yelled.

The pounding of the track hoe's bucket slamming into the wall drowned his words.

Sprays of sewage escaped through radiating cracks.

"Oh god..." Luke's feet thundered down another ramp. He had seen Grover use the machine in the sludge beds on more than one occasion and seemed to have a deft hand at its operation. Now the young guy acted possessed, out of control. What was with these people today?

Down another ramp, Luke spotted a small figure emerging from the gray shadow over the aerator basin.

"Petunia!" he screamed at the top of his lungs. "Go back up! Get out of there!"

The girl was sobbing. He could hear her, though she couldn't hear him. "Daddy!" she shouted. "Daddy! I know why this is happening now. Where's the curtain? Where's the fucking curtain?"

The track hoe stopped. Luke halted as well and let out a quivering breath. Grover Franklin, appearing to finally come to his senses, leaned out the side and looked down. "Hey! You're Mouse's daughter, aren't ya? Let me just stop this thing. One of these levers..."

The steel bucket bashed into the wall again and a steady stream of wastewater cascaded down the side. Several large cracks expanded from the impact. Luke flew around another ramp but somebody caught him from behind.

Female hands over his eyes.

Guess who? Love ya stud. Multiple pairs of arms cinched around him.

Bodies pressed against him. Some naked. Some clothed.

He fought to get through them. *We're all yours…men like you need more…Dara wasn't enough, was she? No. You cannot love. You cannot feel shame. Leave no cunt unfucked.*

"GET OFF ME!" Luke thrashed about. The nameless women brought him down. His chin struck the grated floor with a metallic *phwung!* They dog-piled over his body. He squirmed. They were suffocating him. In the background, above the intermittent banging of the track hoe bucket, he heard the swelling and buckling of the equalization tank's supports. It was giving out.

"Whose dream has come here today?" he heard Petunia say. "It doesn't sound like yours Mr. Rhodes? Who heard the song? Where are they? Somebody help me. It's burning through my mind."

Luke managed to pull partially free of the women and grabbed a support beam. He towed himself, bucking his body under the mass of weight. Making progress, he hauled him and them, and the force upon him somehow relented. Luke dragged himself out of the pile-up and dared to look over his shoulder. Behind him stood a four-foot-high hill of used condoms. He shook his head at the sight. Held his head, and marveled, grotesquely.

He stumbled up, sick to his stomach. His body felt hot and inappropriately sticky.

At that same moment, the track hoe bucket delivered a fatal blow to the containment wall. An unholy rainbow-arch downpour exploded from the top of the tank. Petunia's body was swept away in boiling brown seconds.

Luke blinked, not believing his eyes, but in a sense believing everything, maybe even acknowledging it as commonplace. Through the wastewater rainbow, frogmen slipped into the ever-growing pool of sewage below. Their wetsuits and air-tanks had the same pea-green color as the sewage. Luke watched as they dived in and swam about like abnormally fast human tadpoles.

From the filth and waste, a red toy duck surfaced, bobbing merrily. It traveled around the aerator basin on a swift current. Luke jumped down to an embankment and used a block wall to make his way to the other side of the aerator, where he hoped dry land still existed. On the other side, he saw a stream about three feet wide traveling down a culvert toward the street. He spotted the red duck as it skidded along a thin tributary that took it down an opposing road. He made it down to the sidewalk and hurried along.

"I shouldn't be here," he whispered to himself. The smell of rotten eggs, flowers, and shit made his stomach launch into his throat. He turned away from the wet-well, which had been left open and now overflowed.

A thrashing in the water got him looking again. An oblong glowing white cranium poked through the bubbling shell, brown fluid cascading over the sides. Huge charcoal eyes stared up at him. He couldn't move; he could only watch. The alien pulled itself up on the side of the pond and onto the scaffold.

"Pet-pet-petunia," he stuttered.

Sewage fell from its mouth. "Take back what is yours."

The alien rushed after him, long fingers wagging like a dying spider's legs. Luke thundered down the sidewalk. His blistered feet no longer hurt. He ran faster than he had since his high school days.

But the alien was already ahead of him, apparently hours ahead of him.

Across the concrete path back to the digesters, the alien grasped the face of a plant worker Luke had never met. The man convulsed, arms out, gray foam issuing from his mouth. The alien let go, and he fell to the ground, bursting into a mound of maggots.

"Mr. Rhodes," the alien called out, turning and leering at him.

"What do you want?"

The alien broke out running for him, large jelly-black bug eyes joyful to infect him.

Luke picked up a garbage can and heaved it at the thing.

He couldn't see the alien anymore.

Ran off?

Vanished?

His mind shifted gears with ease. The trash that spilled out of the can was more interesting now.

Next to a half-crumpled McDonald's coffee cup was his note from Maribel.

Luke picked it up. In this letter, yes, everything would be explained. How Maribel was leaving them. How she couldn't take it anymore. Living with a bad man like him. He would self-destruct without her. So would Dara. So would *they together*. The thought made his lungs seize up.

He had to see what it said.

The end of the envelope came apart in small shreds, one after the other. After a bit of cajoling, he got the thin slip of Maribel-scented paper out.

Unfolded it.

His eyes read the words, but not really. The letters reached into each other with thin veins traveling through the translucent paper. The words began to beat, steadily, then loudly, growing in size, the whole sight of it driving him insane.

It throbbed right out of his hand. He stepped forward to grab it, but it beat again and jumped like animated origami. Three bounds, and the piece of paper had made it across the street, Luke following it, feeling like a happy idiot, knowing that when at last he captured it, perhaps the pounding, beating words would finally make sense.

His hand poised over it, he dove—the letter blasted out from under his fingertips and zipped into a storm drain in the curb.

"Shit!"

He got down on his hands and knees. It was reachable; he just had to stick his arm through the bars and grab it. His arm went through, all the way to his shoulder. He searched down there on the dusty bottom of the drain, his fingers touching damp, dead leaves and rat droppings. Not feeling the letter, he pulled back to get another look.

There it was. Only now, in close proximity, so was the red rubber ducky.

"You again," he spluttered. "I should bring you home to Dara."

Luke swept his hand down there, hoping to get lucky. He turned his head, hoping that the alien wouldn't—

Across the street stood the creature, bleach white, with disproportionately elongated arms and wide telescope lenses for eyes. "You gave this to me," it said with Petunia's voice. "Take it all back."

Grover came bumbling up the way with a pile of manila folders. "Hiya, Mr. Rhodes! That was tricky getting around that spill. Hey, did you lose your wedding ring? Want some help?"

Luke tried to pull his arm out, but it was firmly jammed between the bars.

From behind, a white hand came down on Grover's head and locked there like a starving albino spider. Seizures overtook the man; his shirt opened, and his body split apart at the stomach, dropping red and black clusters from within that struck the ground in maggot confetti.

Luke turned away. His outstretched fingers brushed the rubber ducky.

That was all it took.

"I'm dreaming," he said and laughed. "I must have taken that nap with Dara and Maribel after. Oh, thank god!"

"You know now. But you aren't sleeping. You're really here." The alien stared at him with murderous stoicism. "I still have plenty of your song left inside me. I must share it with you."

Luke tugged to free his arm. "Petunia, get away!"

"This isn't your storm, Mr. Rhodes. You can't control it." The gummy white fingertips lengthened for him.

"Johnny!" he cried. It had to be. This was his friend's dream.

How in God's name was he in Johnny Cruz's dream? "Wake up man! Wake up!"

"Stupid...he isn't asleep either." The fingers clamped around his head. His eyes turned out to the dirt field beyond the plant, to the flowing black curtain. *It's the exit. Dara was on to something! Johnny has to go through!*

"Unless he dies before he reaches the curtain," the Petunia-alien answered his thoughts. "Then everybody here dies with him."

"Let me go."

"No, I don't want this connection anymore. The balladeer's lips will press into your ears from now on. If there is a *now on* for you."

Luke jerked again at his arm, but the alien's grip of his forehead tightened and dark electricity shot through to his spinal column to the base of his spirit.

At once Luke heard those foundations split and *crack*.

Chapter 15

Dara couldn't let this occur.

This was the final straw. Luke had taken a drive to look for Johnny and that was fine. Dummy forgot his phone, but fine. With all her constant prodding to get him to wake up to the nightmares, she'd put him on that path, after all. So that wasn't unexpected, but right behind him, out sneaks Maribel. No goodbye either. Dara was sick of this. She knew she and Luke didn't have the collective balls to confront their wife, and maybe they never would, but the woman was up to something. Ever since the music class, Maribel hadn't said much of anything. The moods. The letters. *What in the hell was going on?* Another point of consideration: it was pretty damned convenient that she started behaving funny once all these nightmares began coming to life.

Dara had to know more about this.

After losing her cell eight billion times, Maribel had a phone finder GPS set up, for which they all knew the password. It took a matter of moments on Google Maps and Dara found her. After that, calling a cab and giving an address, simple as that. The stalking part Dara had done well.

It was the discovering part she executed less gracefully. Through a combination block wall and wood-board fence she found Maribel with two strangers, a man and a woman, sitting under a yellow umbrella canopy at a patio table. The woman had her hand on Maribel's. So intensely did Dara react to this, that the scowl she wore spawned an immediate headache.

There had to be a reasonable excuse, but how could Dara ask without giving herself up? There had to be more evidence beyond snooping. This wasn't what it looked like. Dara couldn't have set herself up to be cheated on all over again.

Right?

"Are we going to wait a while?" the cabbie asked Dara.

Maribel stood from the table, idly laughing. She followed the other two through a side door near a glittering tropical pool.

What was going on inside that house? With every bizarre thing that was happening, the answer could be in Dara's reach...or the knowledge of something she'd never be prepared for.

The cabbie grunted his impatience and leaned his bald head back on the rest.

Dara resolved to just go home. There was too much going on right now and maybe she could discuss it with Luke—but he'd never *really* listen to her, would he? Because she was the one with time on her hands, the unemployed twit that would gin up all manners of controversies in the name of making herself the victim—that's what he'd inevitably think.

And Maribel would be beyond difficult to approach. If she didn't want to come clean, she would be the mother who dismissed the child. That was in her power and she would use her superiority. Why else would she have gone down and chewed out those people at GeoGreen? Only because she knew Dara wouldn't confront her about it.

Sometimes Dara was uncertain if she lived in the same world as her husband and wife. Their perspectives were so different, and yet, they were married, so they should have been a single mind with only one viewpoint. But it wasn't so. Reality was cloven in three for them and whether she undermined them by doing so, Maribel had always been the one to reconcile the pieces.

The cabbie cleared his throat and adjusted the meter, so she could see the red digits slowly climbing in price. It didn't matter. Dara was frozen in her thoughts of what might be happening in that house.

Early on she dreaded that Maribel only stayed because she was trapped by her love for Luke. That scenario was pleasant compared to what this might be: *Maribel might not want to be with either of us anymore.* She was tired of fighting their battles for them, tired of stroking their damaged egos, and tired of getting nothing substantial in return.

Dara could try to get information out of Maribel later. She could open her anniversary letter early. She could continue to hope the answers would make themselves known.

"Ma'am?"

"I'm getting out here," Dara replied.

After she paid, the cabbie reached through the window and handed her his business card.

"I shouldn't be long," she told him. "I'll give you a call."

The man nodded, gave her a two-fingered peace sign and drove off in a hurry.

Dara crossed the street to get out of view from the fence line, in case they returned outside. The house was a large, pre-economy-bust, middle-class luxury palace: a fountain in the front yard, in the side yard, one across from the pool (*fucking fountains everywhere!*) Who were these people? Maribel should have told them if she was visiting friends.

Maybe she had? Maybe she told Luke while Dara was passed out on the bed, but that hardly mattered now, because she couldn't call the big dork to find out, could she?

Dara crept over and caught sight of the massive double-door entryway. The impulse to knock came quickly and left quickly. There had never been a breach of trust between them before. *How would Maribel react to this?*

Dara sidled up against the fence. She could hear voices in the house. A figure drifted past the sheer white linen drapes looking out to the patio.

Surprisingly for an open neighborhood, the gate had no lock, just a latch. Dara wasn't sure if this was good fortune or bad.

Heart pounding, she lifted the latch and pushed the gate opened. She pressed against the house, shimmied over to the bat-wing doors leading to a salon. If she could just hear something that would give the situation away, she could leave. *Mention teaching. Mention that Maribel teaches one of your kids. Mention something that will free me from this foolishness.*

"We want you," the lady's voice rose from the hallway.

The tone couldn't be distinguished from outside. It didn't mean what it sounded like. Maribel was too loyal. She was incapable of infidelity, and even so, *she wasn't exclusive to threesomes for Pete's sake.* She wouldn't go out of her way to get into another complex arrangement. *There are a lot of impossible things happening right now. Maybe this is a nightmare?*

Dara shook her head. *No.* The music was not completely formed. Still present and ready to leap full bore into her mind, but not playing the entire song. Whatever nightmare had fallen on the other side of town had no effect here. She hoped Luke had stayed clear of it. Looking back, in her attempts to get him to understand, she'd perhaps mentioned that curtain too much. *Damnit! Why hadn't he taken his phone!*

Why am I here and not out looking for him?

She slipped through the bat-wing doors and saw herself in a mirror in the corner of the salon. Dara watched herself in disgust. *What am I, seventeen? Jealous? Suspicious? What are you doing here idiot?*

Then…

"…put it in me…cock!" Maribel said and a rustling sound, maybe amorous laughter followed.

Dara went to the open hallway. That couldn't have been what Maribel said. She had to have misheard her. Light blue shadows shifted on the walls. The pool's reflected light rippled there. More sounds of conversation. Light. Intimate. Emotional.

Cold-hot sensations surged across Dara's skin. *How could you do this to us Maribel? After all we fought for…*

She skulked into the hallway, again, promising to go only as far as she needed to hear proof. She didn't want to see anything. *Hell no. Not that.* In the other room, nobody was talking. The only sound was an oscillating fan. Dara passed a small dressing room. *These houses were incredible! How could anybody have ever afforded them?*

A door rattled shut, echoing through the house. Dara moved quickly. The hallway took two turns, one led into a vast kitchen and the other dead-ended at a large window hung with more white drapes. Footsteps snapped on the tile floor. The sound of a refrigerator door opening. Dara moved behind the drapes.

"That took a lot out of me," said the man with a tired sigh. "But it's what we wanted. Right?"

"I'm happy if you're happy."

"I'm happy."

A can popped open and the fridge shut.

"I'm going back out by the pool for a bit."

"She's with *us* now. We're not going to celebrate?"

"Later."

"You sure you're happy?"

A pause. "Of course I am. She's wonderful."

The woman came into the hallway, and through the semi-translucent curtains Dara watched her. She had a little smile on her worn but pretty face. Triumph glowed in that smile.

A car started up outside. From her vantage point Dara could see half of the front yard, the rest obscured by palm tree fronds. Out in the street, Maribel's mini-Cooper circled around and took off faster than the cabbie had.

Dara stared numbly. *Maribel left. Gone. And I'm still here. Shit!*

From outside came the sounds of splashing. The woman was swimming now. That was good. There might be a chance to slip out.

The man appeared in the hall. He was tall, well built, except for a slight gut. Coors Light in his hand, he whistled sweetly as he went into the salon.

Look's like I'm waiting here a while.

"Hon, I'm going to turn off the air and open the windows in the hall," he yelled.

Jesus Christ…

Dara fled into the hallway, through the kitchen—stopped midway at the large sliding-glass door overlooking the pool. The woman frolicked happily through the water, while the man stood there, slouching, watching her, sipping his beer.

Dara spotted another hall on the other side of a dividing wall. The wall ended in a large door with a chain on it. She went for it.

The sliding glass door *swooshed* on its rail.

An alcove with a grand piano became Dara's hiding place. She ducked underneath the large instrument and scooted to the wall as far as she could.

If he sits down and plays, I'm going to lose it!

She heard windows bumping in their frames, opening around the house, one by one. Some of them sounded far off, but she dared not emerge.

"Did you water all the plants out front?" the man called. Dara couldn't hear the woman's reply, but soon she saw the man's flipflopped feet snapping down the hall.

The chain rattled and the front door opened.

That rattling reminded Dara of a note in the song.

The Nightmare Ballad.

Dara could hear the balladeer singing now, giving her every note, depriving her of nothing. The atmosphere in the house changed from lighted angles to gritty shadows. She cowered at the small demonic profiles pulling themselves up and out of those slippery wells of anti-light. It wouldn't do any good to stay here and let them get her. This was happening. All of this.

On her knees, she edged to the hall. A black curtain had fallen over the front door, and of course it should, because she had never been to the front porch. But the man of the house was right outside....

Dara waited there, trying to figure out what to do, all while wheezing ghouls watched her from the wallpaper on the adjacent wall. Her eyes opened wider, trying to cancel them out through reason, but rather than clarity coming, everything dimmed.

The nightmare made the room a blur.

Chapter 16

The pain shot through Luke's back.

And through his heart. Through his mind. His consciousness. Soul. How long would this go on? Every major organ in his body had made itself known, crying out, "I'm weakening, I'm failing, stop this from happening!" But with Luke's every protest Petunia tightened her grip, and the painful despair had nearly blacked him out several times. Occasionally he would tug at his arm, but it was stuck between the storm drain bars.

He wanted to live, but flirtatious thoughts of embracing death strengthened the nightmare around him. It wanted him to give up. The dandelion orbs of luminosity cast from the plant's streetlights developed savage, eager eyes and radiant fangs. Shallow sewage puddles raced around in vortices that crackled with invisible electricity. Vast security railings around the headwork and aerator ponds stretched for the sky, the steel running together, lacing into a mesh, a web, that seethed with purple insects. Luke squinted to focus. They were a living version of the toy in the voodoo box that held his duck and Johnny's two dollar bill. *Lucidity touchstones…*

The duck had brought Luke's awareness of the dream, but it hadn't given him any control here. Now he had to feel the burden of the sinister yoke tied to Petunia. Feeling how terrible it was brought tears to Luke's eyes. Had he known back in the pool…had he known how the duck joined him to these living nightmares…he would have prevented her from touching it.

He should have tried harder to listen to Dara. It had just been natural to dismiss everything she told him.

It didn't want you to know.

Too late anyway. The pale, oblong forehead dotted with perspiration, the alien's shark-black eyes said it all; Petunia was getting her revenge now. Luke couldn't hold on much longer. He knew if he gave in and accepted death, the nightmare would eat him up.

For survival, his mind wandered.

Back on the scaffold, had those women who tackled me manifested because it was how I felt about myself? Or how Johnny felt about me? Grover had been a bumbling idiot with that track hoe and that had to have been Johnny's impression of the man, not the real actions of the man.

It wasn't all random. So how did these living hallucinations come to be? From my perceptions, or his?

Or from the singer of the song?

Or all of us?

It was getting darker, and draped behind the largest digester tank, the black curtain appeared to weaken in the gloom, almost to the point of invisibility.

How would Johnny find it to escape? He might be trapped in this nightmare until sun-up. Or he was dead, but the nightmare lived on.

No, don't think that way.

You'll never see him again.

No.

You'll never see Dara or Maribel again.

No.

"NO! GOD NO!"

Luke ripped his hand from between the bars, and bones twisted and shattered from his wrist to his elbow. Reflectively he used the injured hand to strike at the alien. His knuckles connected with her face, and Petunia reeled back in petrified shock, like something sealed in fluid at Hanger 18.

He hadn't even realized he'd brought the duck out in his mangled hand, and when he punched her, the toy made contact.

"More?" the alien asked in terrified wonder.

Her back arched at an extreme angle, she convulsed and cried out, then exploded into a column of gore. Luke covered his head, feeling blood and tissue swathe his neck and soak his shirt. The fecal smell tinged the air with a metallic tang.

Wiping bloody matter from his hair, Luke stole a glance at the nasty aftermath. Petunia's pastel yellow blouse and blue jeans had been reduced to clumps of fabric and string, the pieces hurled with her flesh and bones in a dramatic star formation that expanded from the spot she'd stood. Luke screwed his eyes shut and staggered to his feet.

He couldn't think of the girl, the real person, who had died right here. It would be too much. It would prevent him from moving on. He had to go and go now. He had to get out to that field and find Johnny.

His body felt dried out and cracked inside, like he was severely dehydrated. He shambled down a ramp to a chain-link gate off the service road. In the growing darkness, the weeds were talking to him, offering to poison his ankles if he got close enough. He hurried on through the dirt, avoiding the tumbleweeds that made scratchy pleas to skin him. For the most part, the field looked real, maybe as seen through a darker prism, but this was the field behind the wastewater treatment plant—he'd stood here when surveying the land for the centrifuge project. It looked the same, from the dirt clods to the dead yellow vegetation.

He stopped on the road and his breathe caught in his chest.

Johnny Cruz sprawled over a dirt hill, clawed to hell, blood cascading from his long black hair, down his temples, through his bandito mustache, and all over his t-shirt. He wasn't dead. He rested there, hands behind his head, long shorts pulled down to his ankles, watching two nude, bloody women sixty-nining each other.

Luke shook off the disturbing sight and ran down to meet him. "Johnny! Hey man get up! You have to!"

Johnny turned to him with bewildered eyes. "What are you doing here Luke?"

"Come on, quickly, to the curtain. This isn't real."

"Like hell it ain't! Fuck you Luke. You think I can't be happy too? Who the hell are you? What? You're the only man who can have two women? Ugly, fat pieces of shit like me don't get the same, is that right? You aren't better than me. Don't you dare make me sound jealous either! I've never been jealous. Not once! Back off! You *owe* this to me."

One woman lifted her face from the other's slick pubic mound, bloody thigh prints pressed into her cheeks like repulsive rouge. Luke gasped, despite knowing he could see anything here. It was Johnny's ex-wife Lisa—she was alive again, but something wasn't right in her eyes.

"Don't stop," whispered the other—Johnny's first wife, Mandy. She bent her leg. In the garter belt, hung a two-dollar bill.

"That's it!" Luke frantically tugged at his friend's pants, trying to untangle them from around his legs. "You have to—"

Johnny caught Luke's throat with astonishing power. His wet fingertips dug into Luke's skin. Luke tried to disengage him, but one hand was jacked up and the other wasn't enough.

"Goddamn you!" Johnny's mouth dripped with slobber. "God. Damn. You! Shit! You think you're some fuckin' hero? You're as afraid as I am. But I don't care if I die without an inspiring story. You want something triumphant, something valiant, and guess what? Sometimes things just end. There isn't anything heroic. No story. Just a punchline. That's it. Grim Reaper pulls you down and you're done. You're over. The End. No details. Glorious, good, bad or horrible. Just...done. Fuck you for coming here!"

With a disgusted sigh, Johnny released Luke's neck. He sank back and stared coldly.

"Johnny," coughed Luke. "You have to take that two-dollar bill. Take it...man."

"What for?"

"Take it!"

Mandy looked flighty. A demon's smile cut into her face. She leapt up about to run. Luke grabbed her foot with his bad hand and screamed out in pain. "Go on, Johnny! Take it, and I'll leave you alone. Promise."

"Is that all?" Johnny shook his head and reached over. Mandy thrashed to get away. "Settle down, baby. Don't worry. I'll give it back—"

She writhed to get away from him, but Johnny pinned her hip with his shoulder and pulled the two dollar-bill free.

The stupid grin on Johnny's face thinned, and he let the bill fall between his fingers. Mandy smirked as though it didn't mean anything and went down on Lisa, trying to draw his attention once again. At first Luke thought she'd succeeded, but the big man pulled up his shorts and zipped them closed. He looked over at Luke, almost in tears. "This isn't even real...is it? Are we on LSD?"

"We have to get to that curtain before we lose sight of it," said Luke.

With a sad glance at the moaning women, he nodded.

"I'm sorry."

The curtain drooped about twenty feet away, over a steep incline ending in what would have been a ravine if there was water around these parts. Saying nothing, Johnny stepped through the silken black folds, Luke at his side.

Johnny's silence didn't last long.

"Tell me what is going on!" He got so close he nearly bumped his belly into Luke. "That was a dream. Why am I not waking up? Why are we're really standing out here?"

"It's both," Luke explained. "At the same time. It happens when you hear all of the music...the ballad."

"Yeah," Johnny whispered. He ran a hand over his hair and then looked at the dried blood on his palm. "How did I snap out of it?"

"That two-dollar bill. It's your—"

"*Lucidity touchstone*?" Johnny asked, wincing in confusion. "Just popped into my head. I think the music put it there."

"Same thing has happened to me, and now Dara."

A screech made both men's backs go rigid. Down in the small valley, Mandy straddled a moldering corpse, her face inches above a rotted area that at one time had been a pelvis. She swiveled away and started vomiting and sobbing at the same time. After her fit of retching subsided, she threw herself away from the dead thing in the field, and Mandy screamed again.

Johnny put his hand to his mouth for a second. "How is Mandy really here? How was that not a dream? That *happened*? That *fucking* happened? Holy shitting motherfucking fuck!"

Waves of chills passed over Luke. "It must have brought her...both of them...here."

Johnny grabbed his long, wild hair in fistfuls and made like he was about to push them through his skull. His face was still clawed up, and blood doused the white neckline of his t-shirt.

Mandy came forward through the weeds, stumbling and crying, ridiculous in some black and red lingerie that didn't fit her and probably wouldn't have for some time now.

"Oh my God, Mandy—what, why are you here?"

Mandy, a squiggle of vomit dancing on her chin, found Johnny and seized him as her target. She ran forward and hammered him with her fists. "How did I get here you son of a bitch? *Did you drug me?* How the hell did I get here?" Her fists started slowing. "This is the desert... *This is where you live.* What scheme are you up to this time, Alberto Cruz? You better tell me right now!"

Johnny sought help from Luke. "I don't know what to tell her."

"We found you Mandy…" Luke said, trying not to make it come out as a question. "It must just be…one of those things?"

Mandy started to nod. Tears dried on her face as she clutched her half-naked body and contemplated something that seemed to become increasingly easy to understand. Finally she muttered with a sniffle, "Yeah I guess so."

Tears hung heavy in Johnny's eyes as he glanced at Luke. "Really?"

Luke shrugged. He really needed to get home to Dara and Maribel. They were probably worried out of their minds by now.

Johnny gently reached over and touched Mandy's hand. "I'll take you home, clean you up."

"No," Mandy barked at him. "It's not my home. I'm not going anywhere with you." Her dark eyes flitted to Luke. "Or you. Take me to my sister's house."

"Your sister's at the same house?"

"Mmmhmm," said Mandy, looking down at her torn lingerie. She glanced over to the corpse. "Oh my God. That isn't a real body is it? Who was that?"

"It's fake," Johnny responded dully, a *please-don't ask again* expression crossing his face.

"Sick-ass people." Mandy glanced over to the plant. "I need a jacket or something to wear."

"I've got something in my car," said Luke.

"Halleluiah. Is it far? I'm barefoot here. Where's it parked?"

Luke searched around. He was normally great with direction, even at night, but when it came to where he'd parked the Volt, just before stepping into Johnny's dream space, he couldn't say.

He'd honestly lost track.

Chorus:

People dream; Gods create.

Colors and shapes bewitch the play-set. Most often, it is easily seen, but through a nightmare, it's purposely overlooked. It. Is. A form of survival. He did this. Them too.

A rocking horse on a spring wobbles without a passenger. Practiced inspection reveals a painted word on the saddle: Whorse. Their spirit whispers, *ride it to dirty glory, whatever lathers you and makes you holy, ride it to dirty glory*. Turning from this sight is a must. Undoubtedly.

Not the sitting guy, though. Can't hear well. Can hardly move. Can't see a damn. But it's his tableau to admire. Under the play-set is a clown tunnel into the bowels of the earth. Was it there before? The perpetual song plays beneath a merry xylophone accompaniment and the raw laughter of children fighting from inside. No answers, many questions, his mind feels about to break. He sees troubling, yet suspiciously unreal images in the darkness of the tunnel. He gasps. Predictable. They all do that.

He implores, "Hear me now? Don't let it out. *Help!*"

Verse 5: Silence

Chapter 17

He walked in with the snout of a pig.

He sniffed the carpet, long pulls of air through each tremendous nostril. When she spotted the hooves for hands, Dara scooted back into the alcove under the piano. She couldn't remember how long she'd been stuck in this house, but up until now the nightmare hadn't found her. Hopes of hiding from it forever were all gone now. She couldn't escape through the back. There wasn't a black curtain that way, and besides that, there were frogmen in the pool. One of them had recently tried to drown a tomcat who'd wandered poolside. Somehow the soaking-wet animal had managed to slip out of the frogman's gloved grip, scramble up the side of the pool and up the fence, out of sight. Dara wasn't sure she'd be as lucky. She had to deal with this monster instead.

"I smell good slop," the man called down the hall. "They'll cook you down in their pot for days." He snorted and laughed. "Ah, good broth. The meat just floats off the bone."

Sniff. Sniff.

Silence.

I should have just run for it when the man was still in the front yard, Dara thought. She might have been able to deal with the real version of him outside the nightmare, but this…

"I want you sloppy on my face," he said merrily, "pieces of you up my nose, and ears to rot and savor for later. Where are you? Under my piano, no doubt."

She couldn't edge any closer to the wall. The snorts and sniffs continued. She tried to think of a way out, even imaginary ways. She envisioned a ladder descending from the ceiling or a hole opening up in the floor. This was her dream, goddamn it, why couldn't she control it?

"Because the dream's not all yours," a charred voice answered. "Calm your mind a minute, woman."

A Bone Man sat cross-legged in the hall, spear across his lap.

Dara changed position, just in case he tried to haul her out from her hiding spot. She met the man's gaze. The crazy blue-gray marbles that were his eyes stared up from skin as black as a dead universe.

"You've come to kill me," she said.

"I would instead enjoy taking you as our Queen and living out eternity in these lands, but you are no leader and I serve the Mare. Unhappy about that as I am, it is so."

"Why are you after me? My husband? Why is this happening?"

"All reins on the Mare's Horse must be severed, for otherwise, it cannot gallop across these lands forever making music. Time is short. You and the others will adapt, find ways to move and survive in our world. The Mare won't let that happen. It likes to drink your adrenaline too much."

"You don't need to do anything to the people in this house," said Dara. "Please don't hurt them. They aren't involved. I didn't know the music would come back so suddenly."

"It will only get worse."

"Can you stop it?"

The Bone Man ignored this and scratched at some dried blood on his fingernail. "The problem is, Dara," he said her name so delicately, almost kindly, "since you are tied to the Horse, you cannot die here unless you desire it. My people can help you though. Offering yourself will save you and us a lot of effort. The connection must be broken, the reins snapped in two, for you and the others are dragging the Horse down with all your weight."

Dara shook her head slowly. "I'm not just going to give up. On myself or the people here."

"We cannot control what happens to them." The Bone Man gently rested his spear on the ground. The feathers bound on the end looked prehistoric and sharp enough to slit a throat. "Even trying to control our world would be like changing the direction of the tides with your breath. You are a silly one...but the pig man was correct. *You will make fine soup for us.*"

Dara swallowed the dread rising in her throat. "What about my husband and wife? What happens to them?"

"As with you, we will kindly offer them the will to die. Your husband, sooner than later. He has a stronger connection now to the Horse. Its ballad is sweeter in his ears, than ever before."

"The Balladeer is the Horse? Not the Mare."

The Bone Man pulled himself forward on the carpet, closer. "You are learning. The Mare rides the Horse and its notes are like the splashing of hooves in a poisonous stream, are they not?"

Dara raised her voice, as though that would stop his advance. "You're saying the Balladeer is a vehicle."

Crawling toward her now, the Bone Man smiled, his jagged teeth dark grey and yellow. "The Mare makes all of this possible. Once it only rode through your minds, but now it rides through your world."

"Bullshit." Dara said this more to stall than anything else. All her experience with strategy games and she was at a loss to find a way out of here.

The Bone Man stopped his advance with a bewildered snarl. "The Mare has always been inside everyone. All of you!" His nose swelled and turned up, piggish. The body mutated, fingers gelling into hooves, skin bleaching and going pink, mud rising from new flesh stiff with ugly hair.

Dara balled her fist. "You won't touch my family!"

"Who? Your husband, the infidel? Or your wife, who now is the same?"

The pig thing lunged for her. Dara kicked but it pinned her ankle under a hoof. She grabbed for something to wield, to push it off, to pull, and her fingers grazed the wall, caught a handful of it, like gelatin.

"You can't escape! Give it up, prepare for real torment," the pig thing shouted.

Focus. Get yourself out of here. Take yourself home.

She reached through the wall and grasped the edge of a heavy object. Using it for her anchor, Dara pulled straight through the wall, feeling the hoof peel back a layer of her skin.

It worked.

She left that house.

How had she done it though?

Prone on their kitchen floor at home, her skin felt clammy and blistering. It was quiet and dark. Maribel's purse was on the counter. Luke's toolbox still sat near the pantry where a large hole led straight through the wall, a translucent sheet of plastic gently vibrating. Nothing seemed nightmarish, everything appeared as she'd left it earlier.

It was still happening, though. Spots danced at the far ends of her vision, telling her so. She'd not seen them before touching that purple bug, but now, with every Lifemare, the spots showed up. *Reality peeking in from the sides?*

"Maribel?" she called out.

A bubbling sound rose from the sink.

"Mari, are you home?"

Oh put it in me!

The plastic tarp rippled as a strong breeze passed.

"Luke? Anyone?" Dara's voice dropped. She was alone. Or being made to think so.

Another *blurp* came from the sink. Dara pulled herself up, the spots dancing fiercely in her peripheral vision. She used the side of the counter to brace herself. Down in the sink, curled in a fit of purple-blue flesh and suction cups, rested a dead octopus. Something constricted in Dara's chest. It was nonsense. She knew it was nonsense. Absurdity. Dream absurdity. So why was her blood pressure rising? A stabbing pain started at the bottom of her throat, the idea that a task needed to be completed, that life and death depended on that task, that if she didn't discover what it was and soon, everything dear to her would be lost.

Put it in me...

Cock.

"She's going to leave you both," a hatchet voice cut through her eardrums.

Dara spun around.

The kitchen was still empty. Just her and the dead octopus.

She looked out the window to the backyard. The black curtain fell behind a house catty-corner to theirs. She'd never been over there, for all the years she and Luke had lived here. That was strange but not completely surprising. Dara and the octopus had a lot in common, so many options for something to cling to and instead they were inert, rubbish, dead and unaccountable. She'd spent a lot of time in front of the computer, wasting her life on war games, never building a battle plan of her own. All those hours logged on social sites and not a real friend to show for it. That was where the anxiety stemmed from—this place, her home, was a trap, a pit of lethargy if given the chance. That's why she'd chosen this as her destination of escape.

Staying here would only make things worse. She'd have to hop that fence, get over to the neighbor's yard and through the curtain quickly before she gave up all hope and pulled the chair out to play computer games again.

In the living room, thin smoke drifted off the couches, the TV, and even the bricks in the fireplace. Nothing looked burnt, but everything was smoking.

A loud whirring kicked on and Dara jumped around, banging her toe on a leg of the coffee table. "Son of a...!"

She squinted, processing the impact, those spots in her vision doing the two-step with black flakes of pain.

The whirring echoed back and forth.

Hairdryer.

Maribel was taking an evening shower.

Made sense.

Dara turned to go to her, trying to explain to herself why Maribel would *need* to take an evening shower.

She wasn't there that long. Stop being an idiot. You misheard her. You had to. Maribel doesn't talk dirty like that.

Put it in me...oh that fucking cock!

Dara halted. She'd made it to the hallway and realized that the longer she lingered the more she was endangering Maribel. Just like those poor people she'd gone to visit. Would they be dead or, in the man's case, deformed, when this dream ended? What had the Bone Men done with them? Dara was responsible for bringing a nightmare into their house. She should have done something more to stop the Bone Men.

Now's the time. She headed for the slider and walked out onto their small patio.

The back fence didn't exist any longer. Instead, aquatic-looking blocks had been stacked fifteen feet high. In the center of each seaweed-encrusted Atlantean cube, a large bloodshot eye rolled around to look at her. Dara found an opening through the blocks, an entrance to the labyrinth. She made out the almost indistinguishable shape of the curtain against the night sky on the other side.

She stepped inside. The ground was muddy and smelled of kelp and dead fish. The salted air made her think of that day at the beach when she had met Maribel. So much darkness up until then, and finally she'd found light.

The eyes in the bricks followed her through every turn of the maze, keeping her in sight. She tried not to think about what they saw. What were they looking at? Her body? Or were they looking at her, thinking about how dumb she had to be? A woman with only retail experience. Worthless. Couldn't even handle the body God gave her. Cowardly. Couldn't approach Maribel and tell her everything that terrified her. Sad. Couldn't get it out of her head that one day she would lose Luke and Maribel, just like she'd lost her parents, just like she'd lost her uncle Sal.

I will survive, so that I can be made to suffer.

You don't have to suffer, a fluid sounding voice dripped inside her mind, *just let it end.*

With all of this pressing on her, the maze didn't seem that difficult. Though it was too dark to be sure, the curtain seemed to loom overhead now. She was getting closer. Maybe a couple more turns—

The opening before her closed as two blocks slammed together, the fronds of seaweed quivering, the eyes rolling around and going cross-eyed at the impact. Dara retreated the way she came, but two more blocks crashed together, trapping her in a small vestibule.

Nowhere to go.

Eyes all watching quietly.

A coarse hand snatched Dara's right wrist. Another enclosed her left. A Bone Man forced her to the muddy ground and put his sandaled foot onto her back. She cried out, but the foot pressed down, squeezing the air from her lungs.

The bubbling sound from earlier forced her to raise her eyes.

A large cauldron with several Bone Men standing around it.

One of them casually dropped the dead octopus into the pot. The other flared his wide nostrils, delighting in the scent.

"Bring her," ordered a Bone Man with bleeding eyes and swollen, infected cuts along the left side of his face.

"The pot is too small for her, and she will crawl out," said the Bone Man standing over her.

"Portion her, then," said bleeding eyes.

"Yes yes," sang her captor. The pressure on Dara's back was immense now as the Bone Man knelt on top of her. The silver edge of a long machete came into view. She squirmed and struggled to grasp the ground, make it pull away like dough or gelatin like at the house before, but those eyes were still on her, those damn, hateful eyes, and they stared through her, right into the doubt smothering her mind, lounging on it like she'd lounged on a couch, jobless, brainless, a leeching strumpet in the eyes of the do-gooders of the world. There was nothing else she could do. The blade was touching the flesh of her shoulder. It was sawing. Blood spilled from the stinging injury. Nerves severed. The machete rose up and hacked through the bone, splitting it cleanly—

Her right arm dropped off.

The Bone Man breathed heavily above her, exhausted from his work. He tossed her severed arm to the others manning the cauldron. They dropped it in with a heavy *glunk*. One put his spear into the broth to stir.

Dara was astonished at the small amount of blood running from her stump. She might have been in shock, for all she knew. It didn't matter; the Bone Man had begun work on her left arm, and it hurt worse than the right, and it gave him more difficulty to detach.

Through her shock, she realized she was sobbing deep belly-sobs. She didn't know what to think or do.

The Bone Man slid a hand into the back pocket of her jeans and withdrew something.

"Leave that alone!" she yelled through the blood taste in her mouth. Her tongue was bit to pieces.

Through a chorus of tittering, Maribel's letter ended up in the hands of the cook. Not pausing to consider, he ripped it into pieces and sprinkled it over the soup like a seasoning. A few minutes later, her left arm accompanied it.

More Bone Men gathered around the cauldron, leaving her laying there to bleed out, but Dara didn't feel completely incapacitated. She rolled over and put out a knee, pushed up, staggered and crashed into a block, the large eyelid of the block's eye blinking rapidly in surprise. She looked for another passage out.

There wasn't any.

She was still trapped in the maze, closed in on all sides. The vestibule seemed even smaller, and now a hundred Bone Men filled the space, clucking their tongues and beating madly on their war-painted chests. Their eyes and the eyes in the walls...

All of them on her, starving and big.

Chapter 18

Luke didn't think the world was ending.

But Johnny did. By the time they'd worked their way back to the treatment plant parking lot, a dozen police cars showered the area in arcs of red and blue haze. Several ambulances had arrived as well. Seeing his bloody face and shirt, a pair of response crew gravitated to Johnny, who promptly cussed them away. They went a few feet and stopped, discussing how to go about manhandling someone Johnny's size. Behind them approached a detective in a wrinkled, blue-collared shirt and black slacks. He had no tie on but looked like he had an invisible noose cutting off the circulation at his neck.

"Good evening. I'm Detective Edle. Just curious if any of you could help me out. Were you around when the alarms first went off?"

Johnny furrowed his brow. "Alarms?"

"Yes, several security alarms went off earlier when the equalization basin ruptured and the alien attacked. Some of the plant's systems had failed from the flooding. We came when no plant operator responded to our calls."

"We didn't hear the alarms," said Luke quietly. "You know about her—I mean, the Alien?"

"No worries. Its dead but yes, we know. We're reviewing the security cameras. They have most of the event recorded."

"Um, excuse me. I don't know about any of this. I don't know how I got here," Mandy added. "I'm from up north—I don't live here anymore. Can I have a ride to my sister's house?"

Edle evaluated Mandy in her nearly bursting, dirt-and-blood crusted lingerie. "You must have been abducted somehow. Does your sister live in this town?"

"Close by."

Edle looked over his shoulder. "Abrams?"

A handsome black police officer poked his head up from the other side of his squad car. "Yeah?"

"Have time to give her a lift home? It's nearby."

The flat look on the man's face said that he didn't have time, but he motioned Mandy over.

Johnny threw up his hands. "You're not going to ask her any questions? Just let her go off in her nightie. Like that?"

"Calm down," said the detective.

"What about all these dead bodies? Aren't you going to ask one of us about that? We're the only people left standing. So out with it. You cannot possibly be out here just for some stupid alarms at the plant."

Edle's mouth thinned, and he nodded. "I've never survived an alien attack, so I have no idea what you've gone through, but I would suggest you go home and get some rest. Have those cuts looked at first. Count yourselves lucky. One guy had his face forced under raw sewage and he's already showing signs of severe viral infection." Edle's head canted for a moment, and he stepped back, concerned. "The alien didn't give you those cuts, did it?"

"No..." Johnny glanced at Luke. "Is he for fuckin' real?"

"I think so."

"But I'm not dreaming anymore—we're not inside the dream, so why is this guy being such an asshole?"

"Hey!" Edle looked at them both, frowning. "Get on your way, both of you, before my good nature takes a detour."

"We're going." Luke grabbed Johnny under the forearm and pulled him toward the parking lot. They walked in stunned silence for a while, the sound of crickets buffering the air.

"You're not wearing your glasses," Luke said.

Johnny felt the pocket of his shorts. "Still got them. I just don't need them anymore. Not since...what happened. Jesus H Christ, what's this all about Luke? How did you know about that dollar bill? Or any of this shit for that matter?"

Luke stopped at his Volt, put his hands against the hood and leaned into it. Closed his eyes. "You, me, and Dara are the only people who know about these nightmare realities—Dara calls them Lifemares. We each have something in our dreams that brought us lucidity. Mine was a red ducky."

"Say what?"

"Dara's was a plastic toy bug. Yours was the two-dollar bill. We found those items in Maribel's classroom in a box. Her teacher's aide had written our name under each one of them."

"The ugly chick married to the composer guy?"

"The one you tried to talk into bed, yes."

Johnny put his hand over his forehead as though to squeeze the new information away. "So are they doing this? Is this like witchcraft?"

"I don't know. Who does? I know we have to get as far away from people as we can, before one of us remembers the music again. To tell you the truth, I feel like it could happen for me again at any moment."

"Holy shit." Johnny looked up to the dark sky. "I remember Dara brought one with her to the bar, and that's what happened back at the yard...with the dog...that was when the nightmare started, when I remembered the song...although that copper yard was pretty much a cocksucking nightmare from the start."

"What are you talking about?"

"Forget it. What about Maribel? Did she say anything about her assistant?"

"Allie? That woman's been trying to destroy her for quite a while. Don't you ever pay attention to anything I tell you?"

"No," said Johnny, thinking for a moment. "This is like Armageddon stuff...my wife, Luke...she was *alive* for fuck's sake."

"Only in the Lifemare."

Johnny didn't appear in favor of believing this and changed the subject. "Why are the cops being so stupid?"

"Nobody questions these things. Remember just before you touched that dollar bill? Remember your state of mind? Everything that happened to you was completely acceptable, as though the nightmare wanted us ignorant, marching along like idiots."

"To our deaths?"

"I think so. And if the outside world knew, that would bring attention to us—I don't think the Balladeer wants that."

"Balladeer? You mean Allie or her husband?"

"I don't *know*. Okay?"

Johnny tried to open the car door. "Get this open and take me home."

"You should come to my house. You're safer around us."

"No, no, fuck that and fuck you. I'm going to find my crappy work cell phone and I'm gonna call Beltran. I'm gonna tell him I love him one last time, and then I'm going to get fuckin' tanked."

"You're going to risk other people's lives?"

"Hell no!" He pointed to the door again.

Luke took out his keys and unlocked it. They both got inside.

"Well?"

"I'm going to buy a shit load of tequila and go rent a cabin. Stay clear of everybody."

"That's not a bad idea," said Luke, starting the car. "The cabin, I mean."

"You're not invited."

"Fine...try to find a cabin in a place you've never been before." Luke put on his seat belt. He realized as he did so that his hands were trembling like crazy. The music slowly uncoiled like a snake inside him.

"What difference does that make?"

"Remember the black curtain?"

"Sure. The exit. You have to go to a place you've never been before. I figured that part out when we crossed into that ravine in the field. I'd always been afraid to go down there as a kid. Someone told me once...." Johnny laughed dryly. "That a fucking crocodile lived down there."

"Good thing for you there was a place out there you'd never been before."

"Oh yeah, I'm *so* lucky."

For a few minutes, they drove down Palm Street, saying nothing. Just to break up the stinging silence, Luke asked, "So you're really calling your boy? At long last?"

Johnny lowered his chin to his chest and studied the dried tracks of blood over his hands. "It's the end of the world. I've got to make peace, right? As long as this music is buzzing in the back of our ears...we're living on borrowed time."

Luke pulled up to the shadowy façade of Johnny's house. "Well, call me too, if you decide to come with me and the girls. I still think all the lucid people should stick together."

"Thanks for asking. *No.*" Johnny got out and slammed the door.

"Take care of yourself," said Luke, and he watched his friend's lumbering shape disappear into the deepest shadows near the front door. Luke pulled away and headed for home. As much as he needed to see Dara and Maribel right now, he began to have second thoughts. The music was closer. He drummed his fingers on the steering wheel, mimicking the beat. The conversation with Johnny had helped him keep his thoughts off the ballad, but now it all came speeding to the forefront of his mind. Fragments of the sound chased each other, notes colliding with notes, rhythms starting and stopping, unusual instruments wheezing and howling and thudding. Petunia (*oh God that poor girl*) had done a number on him. Whatever connection he'd had with the Balladeer was tighter now. The song wiggled at the cusp of his memory.

With a plaintive animal whine, he turned on the stereo. It was the jazz station he listened to, but the saxophone was too smooth and his attention abated, the nightmare ballad cutting through. He hurriedly changed the channel to the preprogrammed hard-rock station Maribel and Dara loved.

Luke gradually let the car accelerate through the twilight-soaked suburb. He didn't know this song or the band. It was some form of heavy metal and he despised it, started to tune it out (the ballad inched forward), and then increased the volume to the max, power chords punching him from every side, thrashing the Bose speaker system, sweat popping up around his collar, his broken hand throbbing with the beat (the metal song, or the ballad?).

Luke switched on the air conditioner and set the fan to high. He shivered. His nose began to run with thin mucus. Things were unraveling again. The song was a whisper on his neck, jet-black lips about to kiss him there, remind him of the ballad's every refrain.

Johnny was right. He couldn't take this home with him. Luke had to get away. Far away from Dara and Maribel and anybody else who would be caught in this poisoned spider web. He pulled into a 7-11 where he'd seen a payphone. Gathering up some change from the center console, he said a silent prayer for the phone to still work. A couple of black teens huddled around the phone station, drinking sodas and making fun of one of their friend's shoes.

"Can I get in there?" Luke asked.

The teens gave him a sidelong glance, each equally indifferent, and their gathering shifted a few feet away. Luke popped in three quarters and picked up the cracked plastic phone. The dial tone stuttered a bit before it took on its normal meditative hum (sounded like something in the ballad). Luke bit his lip, hoping the pain would give him a head change. He couldn't remember Dara's number because she'd recently changed it, so he dialed Maribel. After two rings she picked up and spoke to him through a wall of static. Her phone was always cutting out, but she didn't want to bother changing services like Dara had. After a moment the static thinned.

"Luke," she said, "you there?"

"Yes, I hear you."

"Come home. Dara's trapped in a maze."

"A maze?"

"Yeah," Maribel answered, matter-of-factly. "Something smells good…something good is cooking."

Luke let the phone drop and ran for his car. He jumped inside, turned the ignition, and blasted the radio again. Now a DJ rattled on about winning Anthrax concert tickets. Luke pulled into the street and gunned it. Visibility in the neighborhood wasn't all that great, but a stop sign had to be coming up soon. The pepper trees lining the street became sparser, and he could see the moon poking out from the clouds. Moonlight lit a large black curtain cascading from the night sky. Luke tapped his brakes at the stop sign, nobody else was on the road, and the engine roared as he crushed his foot down on the gas pedal again.

He took a turn a little too wide and bumped the curb. The music on the radio set his teeth on edge but seemed to distract him from the nightmare ballad. He panicked at the thought of getting home. What happened if he brought his own nightmare into Dara's?

He couldn't worry about that right now. He just had to make sure the girls got through the curtain. Where had he left his headphones and iPod?

Popping open the glove box, he had a look. *No, of course, never there when I need it.* He slammed the little door shut, brought his eyes to the road, just as a massive dog stepped in front of him.

Luke slammed both feet on the brake, and the Volt shimmied left and right, the rear tires screeching. The dog, a mean-looking thing with large jowls, watched him with bloodshot eyes that said *I'm not afraid of you or your car.* The skid ended just a foot from impact.

Heart in his throat, Luke stared at the animal, blinking, unsure if the nightmare had penetrated his reality again…but no…in fact…

Slowly, he reached forward and turned off the radio.

Nothing.

The thoughts in his head were clean. The notes of the ballad no longer stained them. He watched the dog for a moment. It turned its massive head to the skyline, to where the curtain had been. Its tail stopped wagging.

The curtain had vanished completely.

Had Dara and Maribel gotten through?

That wouldn't change anything with me, though. At least, it hadn't back in the field with Johnny. Hell, even back on the day at the pool, stepping through the curtain hadn't taken the song away completely, like it was now.

The dog trotted off and disappeared into the trees.

Luke blew two red lights the rest of the way home. He roared into the driveway and jumped out of the car, running across the grass. The front door was open. He stormed through, looking left and right.

"Out here," Maribel called from the backyard.

Luke navigated around the coffee table and through the living-room sliding-glass door. His breath caught as he took in the devastation. Most of their fence had been crushed to pieces, and large impressions checkered their backyard and the backyards of several other houses, as though stone blocks had rested there. In a raised area between a series of impressions, Maribel hunkered next to Dara.

He charged over to them, almost twisting his ankle in one of the formations. His broken hand ached as he accidentally braced himself on it.

"Ambulance is on its way—it's her arms." Maribel caressed Dara's cheek.

Luke got on the other side of Dara. Her sleeves had been torn away. Some atrocity had been committed on her arms. The flesh looked burned and watery, the shoulders blue and yellow and black with bruising.

"Uh, fuck," Dara mumbled in pain.

"What happened? Can you tell me?" he asked.

"I don't understand, Luke," she said, tears dropping down fast around her dirt-smudged cheeks. "I don't understand."

"We're here. Don't worry. The music's stopped."

Maribel turned her head at this but said nothing.

"For you, too?" Dara almost tried to sit up and thought better of it. "They were breaking me...I was almost there. I almost wanted to...let them *do it*. Be done with it. Then I heard a buzzing sound, like an electric razor the size of a house, and then the nightmare stopped. I didn't leave through the curtain. Things just went back to normal."

Luke felt his own tears on his cheeks. "What did they do to you baby?"

"Took my arms and put them in..." Dara cringed and her face broke. "They were going to cook me."

"Who?"

"The Bone Men."

"The tribal people with spears?"

Dara nodded. "They cut them off. My arms reconnected somehow, when it ended. Not everything that happens can happen *completely*...I guess?"

Luke wiped away some tears with his wrist. "Maybe it's not all real."

"The deaths have been."

"The lesson from this," Maribel said, leaning over her with a goofy smile, "is don't get trapped in mazes!"

They both looked at her in awe. It was a very Maribel-thing to say, but absurd at the same time. She was still clueless. Would she have accepted finding Dara dead out here? The thought almost made Luke angry with her, but he shook the emotion away. It wouldn't do them any good.

The whine of an ambulance lifted in the distance. Dara shut her eyes to rest, and Luke touched her face.

"Why, Maribel, why?" she muttered.

Luke glanced at his other wife. "What's she talking about?"

Maribel shook her head. "Stay with her, I'm going to make sure the medics find their way back here."

"Okay," he said and looked down again at Dara.

Maribel kissed him on the temple, her chocolate locks caressing his face as she pulled away. "She'll be okay. We just have to watch where she wanders off to next time, right?"

"Right," Luke replied miserably.

She stood up, her knees softly popping. "I'll be back soon."

Luke wanted to hold Dara. The music had stopped but he had a feeling the true injuries had yet to really be revealed. The scarier, hypothetical part of this gripped his gut with a menace like no other.

For all this, there would be no mending.

Chapter 19

Johnny's head was blank.

Blanker than usual, he thought dryly. He'd decided to stay at his house for a bit, rather than book the cabin in Big Bear. Fuckin' thing was expensive, and it would have turned out to be for nothing, because he hadn't heard the ballad, not a single note since that awful night. His contingency plan was to get on the road if it came back—he wasn't an asshole—he knew that those people at the plant died because of the danger he brought. Now their faces went through his mind, from that young kid Grover all the way back to Mouse Stedding. Johnny hadn't liked those men, to their faces. Secretly though, the idea they'd been taken from this world, lives ended because of him, just about brought him to his knees. They weren't bad people. Some of them had even taken the time to try to know him, maybe understand him, too. He should have done the same in return. He'd always planned to, but so much time passed that he let it all go. Story of his life.

Sitting here, on his sofa, watching *Looney Tunes* marathons, it was all he could do to keep from slitting his wrists.

Then there was Mandy. His heart had so long been occupied with memories of Lisa that he'd forgotten about the Johnny Cruz before her. He was a younger man, full of hope about his new job at CRR Motorcycles. Goddamn immortal. He'd conquer the world with his babe by his side. The notion that he'd ever be reunited with her had to be the most farfetched thing from that nightmare, and *holy shit were there a lot to choose from*. He expected her reaction in seeing him—actually thought it'd be stronger, but she was as nightmare-drunk as those cops were—expected her to run screaming from him, in fact. Yet, in spite of knowing all that,

Johnny couldn't help feeling a twinge of pain by how she'd recoiled. They had been in love, too, once before. *Hadn't they?*

Daffy Duck got his face blown off. Johnny took a sip of warm Tecate and wiped a drop away from his mustache. From there he touched the scabs on his face and shifted around to feel the others across his chest, back, ass, and thighs. The head of his dick was raw. He couldn't remember where those came from and felt at peace with that particular amnesia. The different positions, the moans, the pain and pleasure, *those* he did remember, but not fondly. Several times he'd sat at his computer to jerk off to his favorite booty site, but all the naked bodies made his skin crawl.

The first night he'd gone to sleep, although he didn't hear the song anymore, he feared it would return while he was sleeping, or just before nodding off and then he'd be unable to defend himself. Just in case, he had his old shotgun, but no shells for it. Used all of them to blow away a manikin he'd found in the headworks at the sewer plant. That was a good day, and he had no regrets about using up the ammo until now.

Nothing happened the first night though.

The second night, he wondered if he'd have any normal nightmares and die of a heart attack, thinking them the real thing. Again, nothing happened. Some End of The World this turned out to be.

He wasn't convinced things were back to normal, even if his edginess had gone down a few notches. Now and again he checked his work phone. There were a couple messages from Luke. Mostly updates about Dara. He had sent a text late last night, warm and drunk as a horny skunk: GLAD SHES DOIN GOOD. That's about as good as it got from Johnny Cruz. You sure as hell weren't going to receive a "get well" bouquet.

Luke knew as much and likely didn't expect hugs and kisses. Still, that guy always gave him a chance. For a long time Johnny thought about giving the bike he was working on to Beltran. Maybe he'd give it to Luke instead. After all, his kid probably wouldn't accept anything from him.

He glanced at his phone once more.

"You sorry son of a bitch," he whispered. All this time, he was hoping he'd get a call back from Professor Charles Reinhardt. The douche probably wouldn't recognize the number, but Johnny hoped he might return the call, something like *Hey, were you trying to reach me the other night? Beltran's here. Would you like to talk to him?*

Johnny had let the phone ring a couple times that night before hanging up. It was pretty goddamn sad, too, because he actually felt accomplishment in waiting that long. He didn't want to answer to his son. He didn't want to hear what the eight year old had to say. Because he knew it couldn't be good. In that split second before cowardice got the best of him, Johnny had all his words planned out. "*I know you don't love me, kid. I appreciate that because you have every right. Just don't hate me, okay? Remember that we were once friends, you and I. We slow danced to Iron Maiden that one time in the living room and…we laughed so hard we almost wet ourselves. Didn't we? You can't hate somebody you laughed liked that with. Not totally. Right? But like I said, I understand and so, now, I've got to go. I love you and always will.*"

This is what really bugged the shit out of Johnny. Did he hang up because he was afraid to recite his speech? Or because he had hopes this wasn't the end of the world? Did he believe it was possible? What if this nightmare was some kind of glitch in the universe that had come and gone? Life would go on as it had before. No more get rich schemes. He'd find another city job, save some money, get his shop. Maybe when Beltran was eighteen, he'd get a wild-hair and move out to California to live with his old man. Crazier shit had happened.

Compulsively, Johnny stroked his bandito mustache and took the remote off the arm rest. Probably the first time the cartoon channel had been changed in days. He put on the news to clear his mind.

Stupid mistake.

A bug-eyed reporter, who could have been anything from Japanese to Hispanic to Italian for all Johnny fuckin' knew, gestured at the sewer plant with an open hand, pawing the air. The plant probably looked abandoned to someone who'd never seen it before. The reporter said in a meandering tone, "Petunia Stedding's father, George, and mother, Alice, had worked here until their recent tragic deaths at a community swimming pool, unfortunately overtaken by frogmen. Now, in a horrible chain of reaction from grief, Petunia was found floating in the plant's aerator ponds, *dead*. She'd been at the plant with her grandmother to collect some of her father's belongings…tragically also, the grandmother suffered a seizure and heart attack, possibly from the acute stress of witnessing Petunia jump in. Some people had suggested the Alien invader who killed the other plant workers also had a hand in Petunia's death, but there is no evidence to support thi—"

Johnny flipped the channel away and stopped when the picture of the old steel mill came on screen.

Another stupid mistake.

A blonde reporter spoke into the microphone as the wind tossed her hair over her face. "Strangely, the husband and wife, Michelle and Bruce Gamble, had recently rented another U-Haul trailer and yet were found dead near this one instead."

Shot of the U-Haul and various jagged spear-holes through its driver side door. Beyond it, the entire yard of crates looked to have been crushed under a single mighty foot. *Having a coliseum fall on top of you will do that.* In the background of the video, Johnny made out the shape of some of the coliseum's stonework against the mill, bits that had survived once the nightmare lifted. They had made it through. *What else had made it through?*

"Both died of internal injuries, indicating puncture wounds, but bizarrely there was no trauma to their skin, as though they were stabbed from within. In addition to these atrocious deaths, a ring of dog fighters, known as the Inland Mixx, were found brutalized nearby, at first thought of to be caused from an explosion, judging by the condition of the yard. However, early reports about the presence of fertilizer do not substantiate this since no ignition device was found on the premises. The injuries of the deceased are now being considered as animal inflicted."

Grainy photograph shot of a middle-aged man with bad teeth and an obvious chestnut-brown toupee to complement a dirty blonde mustache. "Edward Jacobs, a local Riverside oral surgeon, was found dead a few blocks away from the catastrophe at the storage yard. Detectives have confirmed for us that his injuries are indeed the cause of a dog attack. From the wounds to the neck and face, this would be a large dog—"

Click.

Black screen.

Johnny's hand hung suspended in the air, remote control pointed. He let it slip from his fingers and it hit the carpet. A moment later, he allowed his arm to fall to his lap. Enough time had passed. The music hadn't returned. If he heard a peep, there was still the cabin and enough money left on the Visa card. He couldn't rot in this house a moment longer.

Shasta's awaited. Where everybody didn't give three fucks what your name was, but still wanted a reminder other people in this world did exist; even if you were a waste of good oxygen, you could likely find someone worse off than you.

Johnny felt dizzy as he slid off the couch. He'd ordered three pizzas and had been living off those and lime-chili Ramen. It all burned in his stomach now, clashing with the Tecate. Disregarding the unpleasant sensation as best he could, he waddled to the garage, opened the door and flipped on the light. Rebuilding and modifying his bike had been the only thing keeping him from *becoming* a goddamn Warner Bros. cartoon these days. Since he already had most of the parts he needed, he'd made a lot of progress. He'd put off these mods for the last two years, buying the stuff, but being a lazy fuck about hunkering down and installing them. Last night on an internet forum he'd found an awesome tank lift and ignition/coil relocation. After he did that and farted around with the headlight a little more, the bike would be better than new.

But still not as unnaturally badass as that nightmare version had been.

For now, he didn't feel much like chancing some of his drunken welds from last night. It would be better to do a test run around the neighborhood later. That would mean taking the bus again. Whatever. Probably better not to drive drunk without a headlight anyway. All this nightmare shit was making an honest man of him.

Johnny took a quick shower. He didn't even do his usual routine, a disgusted once-over in the mirror of how fat he was. *Borrowed time, remember, shit bird. Freedom is death. Death is freedom. Just not as fun.* He had to chuckle at that. Did being a blubbery fuck even matter, though? Of course it didn't. Everybody would be dead soon. Fat or thin.

He did a piss-poor job of drying his long hair, which he typically put more effort into—chicks, when there *were* chicks, found his shiny Indian hair attractive, and from there, with enough drinks in them, just settled for the rest of Johnny Cruz. Maybe now that he had perfect vision and didn't have to wear those thick-as-shit eyeglasses, he might be able to work more magic than usual.

Yeah right. You wouldn't know what to do with them if that even did happen.

In his post-shower hastiness he left a wet stripe down his black KILLSWITCH ENGAGE t-shirt, but since it was still pretty much an inferno outdoors right now, he didn't worry about that because it'd probably be traded for sweat by the time he reached the bar. At least he had a freshly laundered (and, thank Christ, looser fitting) pair of cargo shorts to wear.

The bus didn't smell like ass. And that might have been a good thing, but it smelled like balls instead. No matter how you described it, the stuffy-fuckiness he had to breathe on the way to Shasta's did nothing to improve the bubble of *bleh* in his stomach.

Grease would be the only thing to help. He kept focused on that all the way to the bar.

"Loaded potato skins," he said, scooting in on the stool.

The bartender was new, an older man. His face looked as worn and creased as Johnny's soul felt.

"You from around here?" the man asked, writing his order on the tab.

"Uh yeah, I come here all the time."

"Really? Well I'm glad you're back. The place is under new ownership and we run a different show. Don't let nobody tell you otherwise."

Holy shit. So used to his habits, Johnny had come right back to the site of a nightmare. *You stupid son of a bitch!* What the hell had he been thinking? What if this set off another one?

Johnny began to rise out of his seat, panicking. The old man frowned and surveyed him. *Calm your ass down. There's no music. The ballad's gone. Chill fucker. Chill.*

Johnny pretended he was just getting comfortable. He did check the back booths for those Bone Men. Empty. Like the rest of the place.

"I don't believe in that stuff anyway," he told the man.

"What stuff?"

"The stuff that happened here."

The man lowered his voice and leaned into the bar. "Well, I'm sorry to bring up the bleak, but there's no sense in *not* talking about it. I don't know how it happened, but the poisonings are sadly true. At least, that's all the autopsies could point to. Most of our regulars died after some sort of day-long party, so it must have been minute doses taken over a long period. The bartenders died the same way, and Jim Clevates, the owner, wasn't even in the state so he knows nothing about it. The families of the customers are no help. They just figure it is what it is. Anyway, Jim's a friend, and I used to come to this pub when it was Lucky's."

"Yup, remember it then, too."

The man nodded and looked around in desperation. "I'd hate to see this place get shut down for good. I hope we can salvage the name and keep going."

Johnny swallowed and shook his head. "I'm sorry."

"Me, too." The man's voice rose. He glanced around, a man surveying the spoiled landscape of a sacred area. "Me, too."

"Well, I'm here."

A calm smile entered the man's face. "That you are. Tell your friends."

"I'll tell them," said Johnny, with a smile of his own.

A few wannabe bikers shambled in, leather squeaking and heavy feet clomping. "A squirrel trying to get a butt-fuck," said one with a shaved head to a cadaverous man with slicked back red hair.

This man chuckled politely but obviously didn't find the joke funny.

"Hi, guys," said the bartender. "Menus?"

"Nah. How much are your pitchers of Bud?"

"On special. Seven bucks."

The red-haired whistled.

"Just two glasses," said the shaved head.

"You sure? That'd be six bucks. Pitcher holds about four and half pints. Better deal."

"I said two glasses, old timer."

"You're the boss."

"You know it. Hey, put on the TV. Isn't there a game on?"

"Don't think so, but here." The bartender picked up the remote, and an old tube TV flickered on over the row of Scotch. He looked back at Johnny. "You decide yet?"

I sure as fuck don't want a glass of Time or Death.

They're the same drink…

"I'll have a pitcher of Tecate with those skins."

"Sounds good."

"Tecate?" the red haired guy piped up. "Mexican piss water, how can you stand that stuff?"

Johnny ignored the bait and watched the TV. It was the news station he'd been watching earlier. And the hits kept coming.

"Authorities have now identified the body in the foothills near the treatment plant as that of Lisa Gwendolyn Reinhardt, a Flagstaff woman who once lived in the area with her son. Reinhardt had succumbed to diabetes several years ago and was buried in Arizona, where her family still lives today. The grave site at the Calvary Cemetery has not been disturbed, leading some to believe her body was never actually buried there and an investigation with the cemetery is underway. Her husband, Charles Reinhardt, a professor at the University of Flagstaff, openly shunned the media in the past during a school protest, and has again not made himself available for interview."

That's good Charlie, thought Johnny. *Keep those reporters away from my Beltran. He doesn't need those assholes reminding him his mommy is gone…and especially not that she resurfaced, like this.*

The bartender set down his pitcher and a glass. Johnny quietly thanked him and expertly poured one. Then drank it down by half.

"Thirsty man," said the red-haired biker.

"Somewhat," answered Johnny.

"What's up, brother? How'd you get so tore up? Cecil, check out his face and arms. What's that look like to you?"

Johnny grunted. "You guys knock it off. Leave me be. I know what you're doing."

"Oh, he knows. He's got us all figured out. Mister... Mister...help me out, Cecil."

"Shit, man," said shaved head. "Mister Cat Scratch fever. What the fuck *did* happen to you, big boy?"

Johnny looked over his glass. "Give it a rest."

The guy raised his tattooed hands. "It's all good brother. It's all good. Just bustin' your berries."

"Bet his old woman did up his face like that!" said the red-haired asshole.

Shaved head's mouth opened for a nice, wide laugh, just as Johnny's pitcher of beer shattered in his face. Johnny jumped up and dove into both men, taking the stools down with them amid shards of glass and beer suds. Events suddenly ran together: he was punching one of them in the face; he couldn't tell who at first because of the blood; driving his fist down; the stinging bruising breaking madness in his knuckles feeling so wonderfully wondrous and again and over and once more; and he was being kicked in the side and punched in the head, and oh it was the shaved haired guy he was punching; how great because Johnny didn't like his asshole smile or his asshole face.

Then something split across the back of his head and the lights went out.

Opening one eye was terribly difficult.

The world appeared in a thin slice and dropped to nothing.

Johnny did this probably fifty times before the slice widened.

He could see the bars and the corridor. He'd been here before. The Riverside drunk tank down at the station. At least he was alone, and the cell was clean. His head throbbed under an ace bandage wound tightly around his head. He heard something click down the hall...but it wasn't in the hall; rather, this sound was, in his head. Faint, but undeniable.

Softly, the ballad had returned. Not loud enough to recall yet, and maybe easy to ignore, but knowing that it was back made him close his eyes again. Tears broke around his clenched, throbbing eyelids. He'd hoped this was over, but he'd never believed it was. He hated being right. What a day this was turning out to be...he took a deep breath through his nose to calm himself. His stomach coiled. Cleanliness was obviously deceiving to the eye.

This cell was rank.

Chapter 20

Luke hoped all his good dreams were still pending.

He could use some good dreams, but sleep and wakefulness were dreamless places and he had to be thankful for that. The ballad, once gone, was faint now; and from his brief conversation with Dara last night and a "Nope" text from Johnny, it seemed that Luke was the only one who could still hear it. At least he had some idea now how loud the music had to be in order to "remember" it. If it got too close to his mind again, he'd have to get the hell away from his family and the rest of the world.

For now, Dara needed him and Maribel to see her through her hospital stay. The doctors had found identical injuries to her supraspinatus and subscapularis muscles on both shoulders, as though precise incisions had cut through the muscles and the force had driven the humeri out of joint. They'd never seen anything like that, since there had been no external damage; it was as if a knife had cut her from inside instead of outside.

Luke only had a slight fracture to his scaphoid, but in the nightmare he had felt like every bone in his hand had been reduced to meal. The swelling of his thumb and the bruising around his wrist was minimal although he'd seen a blackened mass of dying flesh while inside the nightmare. This might have instilled hope that these twists of reality could not enforce all the horrors they promised, but Dara had made him think up another, darker theory about these sorted outcomes.

We have to want it...the Bone Men would grant us that desire. To die. To end this.

Dara told him she'd been getting pretty close in the backyard. Accepting it, hoping for death, might have been a way out of the agony. Thank God the balladeer had stopped singing at that moment. Luke didn't want to even think about how close a call that'd been.

On a hunch that Johnny'd given him, he asked Maribel about Allie's weirdo husband. Turns out he'd been conducting orchestras for a ballet in Los Angeles for the past three days. She'd recorded one that was televised on the Arts channel. Luke watched as much of the man's stolid performance as his attention span would allow before disavowing all his previous suspicions.

Allie though.

She was still not off the hook.

Luke went to the fridge to get the water pitcher. He drank an entire cup of water and tried to fight off the trembling in his muscles. He supposed he should call his work. LA had officially dropped the contract and would be suing the company to recover monies for the fines accrued by the State and Federal government. But that wasn't all. The head administrative secretary, Maria, had filed some kind of suit against Luke and the company. Sexual harassment, or something equally outrageous. They were also trying to pin the tank rupture at the sewer plant on him, saying he had signed off on the final design. He'd already called the CEO and offered his verbal resignation, but the board wanted to have a cordial sit-down to discuss the details of his departure. Luke still had to call back to schedule it, but so far he'd considered just forgetting it. With the music growing in his mind, it wasn't safe to go about life as usual anymore.

He needed to talk to Maribel, who was still an innocent in all this, but had no idea how to broach the bizarre subject. Now he understood what Dara had gone through with him earlier. He found himself dialing the hospital and asking for her room.

"Hi," Dara rasped. "You coming down here soon? It's boring."

"I'm hearing the music again."

She went silent.

"Did you hear me?"

"Yeah. What are we going to do?"

"It's still really faint, but I'm going to drive…somewhere, if it gets louder."

She whispered, "Great...just goddamn..."

"Are you hearing it?"

"I'm so high right now, I have no idea. These drugs are killer."

"Well, call me if anything changes."

"Luke?"

"Yeah, hon?"

"I have to tell you about the other day."

"You don't."

"No—I do. See, the nightmare didn't start at the house."

"No?"

"I followed Maribel to someone's house."

Luke swallowed. Immediately his throat felt lined with sandpaper. "Whose house?"

"I've never met them before. They don't look like anybody from her school. Maybe they are, though."

"Why would you follow her?"

"You know why."

There Dara went again. Getting jealous. Getting suspicious. She'd been correct the last time, though.

"I heard her say something." A loud exhalation came through the phone. "This is stupid. I know there are other things going on. Let's not worry about it. Sorry to even...just forget it."

"What did she say? How did you hear her?"

"Look," Dara said. "I was...nearby."

"What are you getting at? Did you see Maribel with someone else or not?"

"I think she's with another couple. I *strongly* think so."

"How are you *strongly* sure? Maybe it was part of the Lifemare. People were acting unusual at the treatment plant too."

"It wasn't the Lifemare. I followed her, right before it started. It could have been nothing, but why hasn't she ever mentioned those people to us?"

"It doesn't sound like you're *strongly* certain, then."

"Stop harping on that. I don't have much to go on, but I thought I heard some things said that were…sexual. She called them earlier when I was sleeping. She didn't know I was listening."

"What did they talk about?"

"I think just about what happened later that day. They lived through the nightmare somehow."

"You glad?"

"Of course, I'm glad," she snapped.

Luke put his hand to his forehead. He had cold sweats. "Maybe that's what our letters are about. Do you still have yours?"

"The Bone Men…I don't have it anymore."

"Shit, I lost mine too. Well, this is dumb, we just have to ask her."

"I'm so scared, Luke. She's still living life like nothing has changed. If she isn't doing anything wrong with these people, she'll hate me and how can I take that? If she is screwing around…does that mean we're over? Are we going to lose her? Because of me? I don't think I can take that on top of everything else."

Luke looked down at his empty glass, watched the condensation on the sides bead down. He absently brushed his thumb through it. "We have to face it, either way."

"No, we should let this go for now."

"Let it *go*?" He heard his voice grow louder.

"We have to figure out the nightmare thing first."

"Yeah, right."

"Maribel seems to be stuck right in the middle of that, too."

"You mean Allie's diorama box?"

"No, I was thinking about the other stuff in that cupboard. There was a picture of a horse with the word MARBLE under it."

"Uh-huh. So?"

"The Bone Man told me about something called the Mare. I looked it up on my phone this morning. It's a mythical creature, the maker of nightmares. It rides on the chests of people and gives them bad dreams. This Mare thing is using the Balladeer as its transport. I've been thinking about that drawing of the horse. Do you think that was some kind of sign? The ink is so bled together on the page now that the word *Marble* could have once read 'Maribel.' We didn't take a close look at it because we were too interested in the touchstones."

"Are you implying what I think?"

"I've heard Mari trying to sing the ballad in the shower twice this week."

"She hears the song, too, that's obvious, but that doesn't mean anything. We see her every day and she's not singing. This balladeer sings non-stop—"

"The singing could all be internal. How do you know, Luke?"

He didn't. He really didn't. And his silence gave him away.

"What if she doesn't know she's being used by this Mare thing? Maybe this isn't on purpose."

A vein in Luke's temple throbbed. "Maybe it is," he replied darkly. "She might have stopped the song the other day when she found you in the backyard."

"Still...there's Allie. She wrote our names under the items on the diorama."

"How do we find out?"

Dara let out a quiet groan. "We'll burn that bridge later, I guess."

"Hey, I love you. We'll make sense of this somehow."

She didn't sound convincing. "Love you, too. Yeah."

Maribel or Allie.

The balladeer.

"Talk to you a little later."

"Visit, if you can."

"I'll try."

"Good."

Allie or Maribel.

The balladeer.

Could they both be behind this?

Luke ended his call and put the phone away. One of his wives, a piece of his own heart, could be doing all of this. Causing pain and death. Traumatizing reality's makeup. Unknowing of her puppeteer and its dark plans for their family.

If this was true, what was it intending?

Chorus:

Dreams are soft reality, and space and time are hard reality, and this is highlighted by the scene before him: the play-set distinguishes everything in the spectrum and twists into every geometrical configuration, attracting people from the small parking lot across the grassy field, people who are not nightmare-riddled, for if they are, the ultimate desire is to look away, and He, They, can be at peace for a moment, not notice the tar pits of lifeblood that seep up through the sand where toy buckets and plastic shovels lay discarded, to where one might bend on a knee to gaze at the small discolored hands that, while maimed at the wrists, still hold the handles of said shovels, nor perhaps the grotesque vermillion contents of the buckets, because all of this sends a teeth-breaking current into the soul, making Them call out, *we are playing and laying in the hungry sand, whatever tastes better, flesh or marrow, playing and laying in the hungry sand*; wheeling away from the scene is inevitable, and foreseeable—except for the man hunched over on the bench, who struggles to hear, move and see what's occurring in the fun-tunnel, clown face mad with merriment, engorged lips stressed up and down, throat open wide, and the man has to wonder if such a diabolical opening in the mouth had always been present, and the xylophone music and the animal-people killing each other from inside the tunnel are strident even over the nightmare ballad, and answers are scarce, questions impregnate all things, the man's mental state is in tatters, and though he won't believe his eyes, bestial acts play out inside the tunnel and imprint them forever on his lenses; shouting, calling out, he awakens for a split second, which is so obvious, for They all do the same, and despite this, he begs, "This is progress! Your voice lowered. Something got through to you. Maybe you can get some food and water for me? I'm dying, sitting here all this time. Don't you care? Can you listen to my voice for just a minute? Concentrate. I need you to stop singing the song, like you just did a moment ago—you sing even when you sleep, so this is not a small thing. We can win! Just try. We can help each other. *Fix this.*"

Verse 6: Childcare

Chapter 21

Maribel had to be brave and upfront with her loves.

She wasn't getting any younger, and her husband and wife's interest in raising a child had gone from tenuous to nonexistent in the past year. Not being the kind of person to press her needs on others, Maribel had kept quiet about it for too long, and now the bubble was about to burst. It wasn't that she entirely blamed Dara and Luke, not after rumors started making rounds at GeoGreen, and then the fallout of that horrible interview and her subsequent overreaction.

The path they'd chosen, being a trio, wasn't easy to accept in many social circles. Nevertheless, Maribel embraced it even more; she liked the idea of leading a pair of reluctant soldiers to victory against oppressors. You only have one life. You only have one chance to be bold in your happiness. Nobody suffered for their joy, as far as she could see, so the rest of the world could go to hell.

Maribel had given Luke and Dara all the reassurances they needed to be at peace with themselves. Now, she needed them to come through for her in the same way. How could she ask for that, though? Voicing it would make it a mandate, and she didn't want to pressure them. Happiness was exploring, learning, becoming something more. She had never given birth. A couple pregnancy scares in her early twenties was the extent of her experience. She *taught* children, for crying out loud. She'd even studied midwifery right after college. There was a whole part of her that yearned to see the most important thing her body could produce. Life.

She'd made as many hints as she could and that wasn't getting through to them. Clearly, Luke and Dara weren't ready for the next step. In the past, a younger Maribel might have dropped them at the first sign of mutiny, but she'd left a parade of worthy souls in her wake doing just that very thing. This marriage was no farce. It was damned sacred to her, *because it had to be*—it was the last chance to prove the relationship wasn't a fanciful experiment but the real deal. If they weren't going to be torn apart from outside forces, she'd be damned if she'd do any of the world's dirty work.

No. She couldn't steamroll over the wishes of her loves. For a change, Maribel had to be strategic to achieve her goal, not breaking down doors and yelling at board members (for starters). She'd grown moody about the whole thing, though, not knowing how to approach the subject. If she could artificially have someone else's child—not being unfaithful in the process—she would have the experience and they could all be happy. And maybe, this was her ultimate hope, maybe Dara and Luke would be more comfortable with starting a family of their own, having gone through a proxy version. Sort of a trial run.

Opportunities didn't always fall into your lap like this. She had had a chance discussion one day with a substitute teacher, Kelly McKesson, who couldn't deliver due to cervical issues and had been on the lookout for a surrogate mother. Maribel had been so excited she had almost rushed home that night to tell Dara and Luke. Good thing she hadn't—good thing she thought it through first. Had her spouses told her "no," that would have made her need to defy them, because she couldn't stand being controlled. That was her flaw and she accepted it. Therefore, she needed to work around that jagged point as best she could. Levelheaded and mildly calculating, she got clear of all that drama by writing the letters, each separately crafted to cater to each personality. It was methodical, but the stakes were high here.

Now she'd wished she hadn't made it an anniversary letter. The anxiety of what they would say had her on edge, and the prospect of losing the McKessons to someone else made her paranoid enough to drive over there and tell them that she just needed to get the "OK" from her family. Kelly's husband Robert had thrown her a curve, though.

"What if your family doesn't want you to? You'll lose all connection to the child. That's pretty jarring. It's no small thing you're planning to do here."

After blathering like an imbecile for a moment, Maribel had assured him with a nervous laugh, "They'll say yes. They better!"

"Will you be scared?" asked Kelly.

"Oh I've helped with six natural births, four of which were water births. I know some different scenarios to expect."

"Actually…" Kelly winced. "I meant with the embryo transfer. The entire process puts your body through some hoops."

Once again, Maribel had been caught off guard, but she recovered more quickly this time.

"I'm not squeamish at all. Ready, set, *put it in me, Doc!*"

She'd been awarded a laugh then, and finally started feeling better about her plans.

Then Dara and that maze.

(*There'd been a maze in the backyard? Yes?*)

Of course there'd been a maze, and the Bone Men had tried to cook Dara.

(*Aren't you afraid about that? Terrified for Dara?*)

It was to be expected. Just like the fragmented music that kept trying to surface in her mind. Maybe this wasn't a good time to take a large step. Things had to calm down. Luke and Dara had to heal from their injuries.

And what? How long would that take?

The McKessons called her the day after Dara was admitted to the hospital. Evidently, right after Maribel left, there had been a major disturbance at their house. Kelly almost drowned in their pool, and Robert nearly got crushed when a wall near the piano crumbled to pieces. Some kind of site-specific earthquake or something. Understandably shook up by what happened, they seemed a bit leery about the baby plans. Hopefully after the letters were opened and Dara and Luke had their say, Maribel could deliver some good news to the couple.

Maribel put a stack of workbooks in the cupboard. She'd been selfish about this baby thing, sneaking around, writing letters. Tonight, she had to just be out with it and see where they stood. It would break her heart if they told her no...

Calm down. They haven't said anything yet. Give them a chance. At break, call Dara and check in on her. Her health comes before all this.

The music drifted closer. She almost heard the complete song. Where had she heard it before? It was familiar, yet unique.

Allie walked past her, heels clucking quickly, hatefully. Maribel couldn't wait until the woman got relocated. What a pain in the butt she'd been. Opening the cupboard, the woman knelt and started pulling things out.

Maribel sighed. "Looking for something?"

"Why do we still have this diorama project?" Allie asked, pretending not to hear the question. "Is this like your little shrine to the *one who got away*?"

"You don't know what you're talking about."

"These are your students, not your children. You should be their teacher, not their mother. It would help them."

Maribel let another pile of workbooks fall with a loud snap on top of the others. "And why would I listen to you?"

"I thought you would, for a change."

"Can we *not* begin our day like this? Please. Let's just do our work."

"You should throw this diorama away," said Allie decisively. "It's unhealthy to keep it here. Pathetic too."

"I like keepsakes. But fine, do whatever you want with it."

Allie stood and set the cardboard box on a desk. She stared down at it, one fist planted in her hip. "I wish others could see what I see, when I look at you."

Maribel put fists into her hips. "Do I need to call the AP in here?"

Allie shrugged, snatched the diorama off the desk and strode off. She went into the quad between classrooms, and most likely would stay there, sulking, until the kids got their snacks.

Maribel supposed she'd have to put all the worksheets out on the tables herself. *Oh well. All pays the same.* Every page she took off the stack swished…gentle, breathlike, exhaling, beating…

The rhythm came all at once.

A stunning ballad filled her mind, just as her first student tapped at the door. Weird that she'd had such a difficult time recalling the song before. The balladeer sang in a magnificent range, from bass to tenor to alto to soprano and beyond. Drums pounded. Symbols crashed. A story emerged for the first and last time. A newborn and dying-old story.

Maribel didn't like the song, but was in awe of it, as she opened the door to the smiling faces of her kids standing outside, already consumed by the infernal heat from the sun.

They all wore the same black shirts.

Wore the same white shorts.

The same tennis shoes.

Same bodies.

Faces.

Same smiles.

The same cyanide eyes.

Bowed, backs with the same crooked posture.

They moved the same ambling, out-of-control, out-of-their-mind way.

Shadow-beings with torn-out faces, who must have been their parents, shuffled back to rusted contraptions that must have been automobiles.

The children rushed inside the room, and Maribel gasped and retreated to a corner, watching them pass, the odor of sour milk wafting by.

No matter if the Kindergarteners had turned into other *things*, she had to keep control of them and control of the class. That was her job. She was good at it. She had to keep being good at it.

"Class, you have to get in a circle on the carpet." Her voice was hoarse, unconvincing. "Class?" She tried to find the usual troublemakers, but the children's new features all resembled the same haggard creature with the face of every bad student she'd ever had.

They ran around, tackling each other, punching each other, laughing and kicking each other. Maribel chased them but could never arrive in time to stop any of the misbehavior.

"Allie, can you come help me please?" she shouted.

Maribel waited, but the door to the quad didn't budge.

"Allie!"

Frantic, she took out her cell phone. She normally never called home during class, but if Allie was going to be a jerk all day, maybe Luke could drop by. Sometimes the kids settled down when he showed up with lunch. After she dialed, she looked up...all the kids were hiding under the tables.

Giggling.

Smacking their lips.

Whispering.

"Luke?"

He'd picked up but didn't say anything. Finally, "Yeah Maribel?"

"What's up with you?"

"Nothing."

"Hey, I need you to stop by the school real quick. These kids are really insane today—"

"Really...I just wanted to soak my hand in the bath. It still hurts, don't you remember?"

She flinched and straightened. "Of course I remember...sorry."

He sighed. "I spoke to Dara."

His voice was small, like something coming from another lifetime; she couldn't appreciate his morose tone, though she could slightly detect it. "Is Dara okay? Is there any news?"

"It's not about that. What was in those letters, Maribel? There's too much going on right now to play games."

"We can discuss this tonight."

A quivering breath escaped through the phone. "Did you go see someone the other day?"

Maribel watched one child break away from a huddle under a table. He leapt on the wall, one hand over the other, and with animal grace began climbing to the ceiling. A scream lay at the back of Maribel's throat but her shock overcame it. "You're not allowed to climb the walls!" she at last cried. She hung up on Luke and dropped the phone back in her pocket.

Stretched on her tiptoes, she reached for the child. Like an overgrown rodent, he sped around the ceiling.

"You're going to fall! Get down...uh..." She tried to match the squealing child's face with a name and could pull nothing up from her music-filled mind.

At a rising clatter Maribel turned. Twenty other children had climbed the walls, with the remainder trailing after them. She ran to those children closest to her, never able to reach any of them.

Allie walked in, carrying a small video camera. The red recording light was on. She was filming.

"Thank God. Allie! Help me! Don't you see the kids?" Maribel stepped up on a desk. "We have to get them down from there."

"This is my Truth Camera." Allie's voice was husky, almost aroused. "I can see you, Maribel. *The real you.*"

"Stop fucking around and help me!"

The children, like roaches skittering above, broke out in a chorus: *she said fuck, she said fuck, she said fuck, she said fuck, she said fuck, she said fuck, she said fuck, she said...FUCK!*

Maribel captured one child by the arm. He or she wouldn't budge. Maribel pulled harder and the kid began to cry: "I'm telling my parents."

"I'm telling the school," another cackled.

You'll be fired and fired and fired and fired and fired.

"You left David in the car, didn't you?" one kid said and the others went *ewww*.

Allie stood there, breathing heavily as she filmed. Her hand slid down her pants.

Maribel hopped off the table. A sick feeling wrenched through her. She usually helped a fellow teacher, Mrs. Gable, with her nephew David in the morning. Gable was a nice lady but terribly forgetful. She relied on Maribel to help her get David out of his car seat and walked to preschool.

Through the window, she could see Gable's car.

The only car in the parking lot.

The sun blared on the glass.

Maribel forgot about everything and flew outside. Allie followed her, moaning, the camera trained on her.

Immediately Maribel was by the car. David was inside, in his car seat, unconscious, asleep, dead. The doors were locked. She kicked at the driver's window. *Go get Gable from her classroom.*

The school had changed. There were no doors or windows. Maribel yelled something incomprehensible, an animal word, and turned back to the car.

High above, Allie leaned over a branch on a sycamore tree, trying to get a better shot with her video camera.

It was getting hotter. The California sun changed from yellow to white.

Beyond the magnifying car windows, David's flesh brightened to lobster red.

"Help me!" Maribel banged on the car. "Please! Help!"

Sweat poured off her as the sun roared overhead. Maribel tried to think up a plan. Nothing came.

Panic lifted through her, a scattering of mad doves.

Chapter 22

Nothing sobered you up like a jail.

Johnny had, unfortunately, discovered this a few times before, although never with this insistent, nagging collection of broken chords and staccato rhythms fighting at the edge of his mind. The ballad wanted through. It was almost needy in its persistence. He wished it would just suddenly go away again. He'd rather not be confined to a cell when a nightmare showed up.

His cellmate Roberto turned on his side. "Fuckin' concrete hurts my back."

"S'why I'm standing," Johnny replied and leaned his forehead against the cold bars.

"You see any of those *cochinos* out there?"

"Nah, they're off on donut break."

"Bitches."

"Well," said Johnny drearily, "we *were* shitfaced."

"Just doin' their jobs, right. Could have just drove us home, yeah? My buddy had this cool cop take him home one time. Some pricks have all the luck."

"What bar did they get you at?"

"Aye man, I wasn't even at a damn bar. Fuckin' *Food For Less*. Got in a fight with a checker."

"That's pretty damned funny."

Roberto's mouth twisted a moment. "Not really. The guy didn't deserve it."

Johnny went quiet. The ballad flexed against his skull like a new muscle expanding from cerebral tendons.

"Where were you at? A bar?" asked Roberto. He slid on the sticky concrete bench and sat upright. His wife beater had yellow sweat stains complemented by a spattering of orange vomit designs on the side. His bony face looked cheerless and wan.

"Shasta's."

"Holy shit. You went to that place? Is that where—?"

"Poisonings. Yes. I heard."

Roberto accepted his curtness. "Cool place though?"

"Been going there a while."

"You look pretty messed up. No offense."

"Yeah, I guess I do."

Roberto stared down at his split knuckles. "My guy didn't fight back."

"No?"

Roberto snorted and leaned forward, bowed his head into his hands. "Fuckin' head is pounding. Wonder if these cops would give me a painkiller?"

"Don't hold your breath."

"I'd like to tell that checker I'm sorry, but I think he'll probably press charges."

"Why'd you do it?"

Roberto shrugged. "I'd been to the store about five...no four...uh, fuck, I don't remember. I'd been drinking all day, kept going back for another forty of Old E."

"Damn."

"It was around the third time I noticed he was looking at me...reminded me how my mother used to look at me. She worried a lot. Pretty nice lady, *mi madre*. She uh...she killed herself over a boyfriend who cheated on her."

"Sorry to hear that."

"She didn't do much for anybody...she did care about me though. Fuck, I don't want to depress myself. I'll shut up now."

"Maybe you should."

Roberto massaged the back of his tattooed neck, while Johnny concentrated on the white bricks in the room, taking in their size and shape, counting them, anything to distract his mind from the music puzzle quickening toward completion in his mind.

"Yeah but that checker. Older guy. Maybe sixty. He looked like he could have been my mom's brother. All that worrying, those heavy hound dog eyes. I knew what he was thinking. He was thinking he was helping me kill myself, every bottle he sold me. I couldn't take him looking at me like that. He finally did say some shit, said I should hold off or something like that. I got in his face. He didn't like that and pushed me. Made me fall on my ass. I got up and beat the fuck out of him. Then I threw up on the bagger who pulled me off him."

"That's a very pretty story. In a shitty kind of way."

Roberto's incensed eyes rose from his hands. "Think I don't know that?"

Johnny folded his arms. "You tell me, guy."

"I consider myself a nice man. I don't bother anybody. I'm not asking for anybody to care about me. You know?"

"Not really."

Leaning back again, Roberto clicked his teeth nervously for a second. "Why hasn't anybody come looking for you in here?"

"I've got people," said Johnny.

"Lucky you. I can tell you wanna criticize me. Go ahead, dude, give it your best."

"I ain't fuckin' criticizing nobody. I will give some advice though."

"What's that?"

"Buy enough beer the first time. Five trips? That's stupid."

Roberto laughed. "There's always more trips, dude. Always."

They were quiet for a few minutes. Roberto lifted his butt cheek up and let out a fart that trilled like a toy ray-gun. He chuckled and waved a hand before his nose. "Ah man, my apologies. Smells like a bag of *chicarones* in here."

Johnny tried to ignore him, although the smell was formidable.

A young police officer with an auburn crew cut walked down the cellblock toward them.

"Can I make my call now?" Johnny asked.

The cop raised a finger for *one moment*, turned a corner, and vanished down another hall.

"I'm running away from my mom. I think that's it. That's why I keep screwing up," Roberto said to himself. "Everybody's running from something. It's natural. It's easy. We're all cowards."

Johnny stared at him. "Stop sharing. I'm not interested in your philosophy or problems. This isn't a fuckin' confessional in here. They put us here because we're both Mexican and that's the only goddamn reason. I have nothing else in common with you. I don't want to have anything else in common with you."

"Well, excuse me."

Johnny went back to the bars and looked out the window across the hallway. A black curtain dropped from the sky.

"Shit..." he whispered.

The music hadn't come together in his mind yet. It was for someone else.

"Hey!" he yelled and went to the bars. "Hey! Officers! Hey! I want my call! Please let me make my call. Hey!"

He kicked at the bars but no sound, not even a vibration, came from the impact. "Officers!" he called again.

The cop from earlier strolled up to the bars. Everything about his face suggested exhaustion, his blond hair even sagging limply at the temples. He sighed out his nose. "What's all the hollering about?"

"I really need to make my phone call, sir. I think my friend might be in danger."

The cop smirked. "How would you know, big guy?"

Johnny impatiently pressed his lips together, drawing a blank.

"Oh I see. I need to drop everything I'm doing so the drunk with the premonition can make his phone call. Is there anything else I can fetch for you?"

"It's not like that. *Please.*"

"I think you need a little more time to cook."

"No!"

"What about me?" asked Roberto.

The cop just laughed and turned away.

"More people will be in danger if you don't let me call," Johnny shouted.

The cop looked over his shoulder and grinned, his teeth an entwined nest of fangs.

Johnny started back; the ballad, formed and completed, beautiful death, soared to a mind-splitting volume. He retreated from the bars until his back hit the wall.

Roberto sat in the same position, not noticing anything. He was too still, almost looked inhuman, one of those automated androids in an amusement park ride that lost power. Through the searing symphony, Johnny could hear the man's individual breaths. The sound gave him goose bumps.

"Listen close. Believe me. Okay? This is a dream," he explained to his cellmate.

Roberto's eyes opened, and a skeptical expression bent his mouth. "Oh, how I wish it were."

"Whatever happens, just do what I say."

"I'm through talking to you, dude."

"If we work together, we can get out of here."

"Oh, brother," said Roberto. "Stay away from me *pendejo*, got it?"

Johnny spotted something next to the concrete slab. The worn two-dollar bill had been folded in half sideways, but it was undeniably the same bill he'd touched to gain awareness before.

Lucidity Touchstones.

"What are you looking at?" Roberto followed his gaze. "How the hell did this get here?"

Johnny plucked the bill off the ground. The object's magic must have been used up, because he felt nothing holding it now. He examined it. Nothing seemed different about it, other than the general weirdness of two-dollar bills.

With remarkable swiftness, Roberto snatched the money from his hand. "Lemme see."

"Wait!" Johnny cried.

Roberto screeched and doubled over, dropping the bill. He held his stomach and ground his teeth.

"What's happening?" Johnny asked him.

"We are in a DREAM," Roberto glanced at him with blood-red eyes. "Your dream, you bastard…I don't want it inside me. Why did you let it get inside of me?"

"Get away."

Horns sprouted from the man's forehead and his skin boiled red. "I'm a dollar devil now, and I'm giving you back your Hell."

A barbed tail thumped on the floor behind him.

"Listen to me."

Roberto's mouth parted and a forked tongue slid out. "You're looking like my mother…I don't need your sympathy."

Johnny's next words were cut off as the Devil collided with him. He was on the floor, the fiery face above him screaming and sulfurous. A clawed hand caught his throat and squeezed with ruthless supremacy. Roberto's burden from the two-dollar bill flooded into Johnny. More of the ballad's song invigorated the already lively rendition bursting through his consciousness. He was closer to the

Balladeer now, could almost feel the words of the song brushed on his ear lobes with soft lips.

But the song faded as he fought to breathe.

Maybe he wanted this.

Death, or life?

What way was easier?

Freedom, shitbird.

Run away from it all.

Sometimes there is no heroism. No courageous last stand.

Sometimes things just end.

He squirmed, and the Devil rocked back and forth excitedly, an infernal parasite on his chest. Johnny had always had fights. Some easy. Some hard. Some brutal. No matter what happened, Johnny always thought about the story he'd tell later, usually to Luke. He wanted to make it an engaging story, because really, next to his fab work, his fighting and drinking stories were the only thing that made him worth shit to anybody. A fight with the Devil would have qualified as a real keeper. But with these sick, burning fingers digging powerfully into his throat, the hard knee going deep, crushing his stomach and guts, the pain and hatred cast a web over his thoughts and all conclusions but one caught in its stickiness. It was simple truth, something he didn't want to embrace, but he had to.

Sometimes there is no valor. No details. No dramatic crescendo.

Sometimes things just end.

It was plain now.

Johnny would not live to tell Luke this tale.

Chapter 23

Luke took a bath to ease his body, the whole time gritting his teeth.
Ballad-borne, the Frogmen lost little time and pulled him
underneath.

Chapter 24

For the boy's sake, Maribel could not fail.

But every way she tried to break into the car led to further disillusionment. She'd found the crossing guard's heavy folding chair near the sidewalk and bludgeoned the car windows with its sturdy steel legs. The glass didn't even crack. Then she found a brick near the flower garden under the window of the 1st grade classroom and launched it at the driver's window. The brick shattered to red dust.

David moved inside the car like a deaf mute in distress. She couldn't speak to the child. He made plaintive mumbling sounds and groped around the seats and dashboard. His skin had turned dark red, almost devil red, but it fluxed back and forth. Sometimes she thought she could see smoke rising off his flesh, and his crying was getting more intense and agonized; and then other times he looked like he was getting better.

How could he be getting better? It's over a hundred degrees out here. It's probably over two hundred in there.

A pit spread across Maribel's stomach. She wasn't going to get the child out. David would die. One of her students, under her watch, would suffer heat stroke, dehydration, and death.

Her heart felt like an industrial bellows about to pop all its rivets and explode with hellish fury. Sweat stung her eyes as she rounded the back wheel to look for a spare key, perhaps on one of those magnet things. Stooping near the trunk, she found a large yellow handle with the stenciled word EMERGENCY above it and to the side showed a stick figure picture of a child trapped in a car. Her mind rationalized it immediately. *All automobiles have these, just for this type of thing. How stupid of me to forget.*

She pulled the handle. Not only did the trunk open, but the rear half of the car folded back, thousands of individual pistons pushing the panels of steel rearward and coupling them with others. The back seat lowered with a hydraulic hiss and David hopped out. He no longer had red skin, but he did sport a pair of long horns.

Demonic or not, the child did not appear evil. He regarded her just as he would have in the classroom during a project. "Mrs. Rhodes, I want those pineapple ice creams."

"Oh, David, we can't go to Puppet Town right now. We have to get back to class."

"Why?" he whined. His horns disappeared. He was just a regular little boy now.

"Where'd your horns go?"

"Someone borrowed them."

"Oh."

"So can we? Can we go get an ice cream? Pretty please?"

"I said no. Now come on, we have to go back to the classroom. Move along, okay?"

"Why can't we go, real quick?"

Maribel bit her lip for a moment, stymieing her impatience. "For one thing, David, we'd have to drive there."

"Na-ah, they have a new spot."

He ran toward the empty street.

"David, get back here!"

Maribel chased after him, but her strides softened as she saw Puppet Town's main entrance across the street. *Wow, it wasn't as far as I thought. Why did I always dread driving to this place? It's always been here.*

"Wait, David. We'll get the ice cream, but you have to stay with me."

"Okay." The boy groaned. He slowed and put his little hands in his jeans pockets.

Maribel walked with him to the clown-tunnel entrance. She glanced over her shoulder to see if anybody had come out of the school, but the building was no longer there. The real estate office across the street from Puppet Town was in its place. *Well, sure, I remember that being there.*

Somehow, she and David must have found a short cut across town. Looking back at the amusement park, she noticed a large black curtain over the beer garden in the back. It was probably the only place in the park she'd never visited, since she'd always been with her class. A few feet away, near the mouth of the tunnel, sat a Jolly Green Giant doll. The doll looked so familiar it gave her pause. Where had she seen it before? Her mind raced but came up short. She stepped over to the doll, her tennis shoes somehow echoing throughout the parking lot. *Where were all the people? This place should already be packed by this time of day.*

Maribel had bent to retrieve the doll when a harsh wail rose from the tunnel.

David was gone.

She hurried into the darkness, through the obscenely wide mouth of the clown. The tunnel smelled as it always did, like water stagnant since the 1950s. Once she crossed over the threshold, she found David hunkering near a fountain. Spouts of water shot from it, suspended in the air with luminescent purple bugs splashing up through the jets. It was a pretty effect, and Maribel might have thought to examine it further if David hadn't been in distress.

She knelt next to the boy. Above the ticket booths, flags made to look like 2 dollar bills rippled fiercely, despite the lack of heavy winds today. "What's wrong? Don't you want the ice cream?"

"I'm not allowed here!" he shouted into her face.

Maribel leaned back from the child. "David, we don't yell."

"Kiss my ass!" He hissed, jumped to his feet, and took off running for the exit.

Shaking her head, Maribel went to get him, deciding it was better that he was out of the park again and they could go back to the classroom.

But the clown tunnel's mouth clamped shut in a satisfied grin.

Maribel rushed over and tried to pry the iron lips apart. Not only did they not move, they felt welded closed, as though the mouth had been built in that hideous smirk. On the other side of the wall, David's shoes pounded the concrete as he ran.

Discordant whistles came from the Puppet Safari ride on the edge of the courtyard. Through the exaggerated African jungle, she made out the forms of a tribe of men, their skin supernaturally black and full of bloody bone piercings. Two carried a long spit with four human bodies charred in grisly positions, the wooden shaft inserted through their mouths and protruding out their asses.

Before they could see her, Maribel fled, holding a hand to her mouth, trying not to puke. She ran into Gracie's Greek Coliseum, where puppet shows usually went on regularly all day. The marble stands were empty though and a scaffold stood in the center of the dirt combat circle. A dark gray horse hung by the neck from a series of ropes, tied off tautly at the corners of the wooden structure. A roasting pan beneath it caught blood as it plinked down from cuts in its flesh.

She shuddered and stepped back.

Words carved into the side of a horse: MURDER ME AND IT CANNOT WIN.

Maribel wanted to scream but she was afraid it would alert the Bone Men. Even the sound of her own breathing might bring them back, so she struggled not to go dizzy from the small breaths she took. It was quiet in the arena, but the ballad still penetrated her mind. The dead horse joined in the song. The creak of the rope. A rustling of wind through the matted mane.

Melodically, blood dripped from the coarse tail.

Chorus:

Dreams. Reality. Human. Divinity. Shapes. Colors. Play-set. Noticeable. Not now. They make the world unaware. Monkey bars. Dripping spinal fluid. Closer. Looks. Sharp, thorny spinal columns grow from the sand. Bone garden. Heart-attack. Exclaims, *the bones are used for building new people, whatever otherwise God might tell you, the bones are used for building new people*. They turn. Right on cue.

All but one. Man. Bench. Listens. Waits. Watches. Clown face tunnel. When? Bad song. Can't. Bury. Xylophone. Dark massacre there. Mind. Broken. Answers. No. Questions. All. Eyes. Shadows. Entrails. Cries. Yep. Sure enough. *Human*.

"Hear? Me?" he asks. "Don't. Let. It. Out. *Save. Me*."

Verse 7: In Dash Display

Chapter 25

The ballad fired into her mind like a gun.

Dara had known it was coming, but like always, she had no idea exactly when the song would build to completion. She was due to leave the hospital tomorrow, now that the burns on her arms had started to heal with no signs of infection. The nurses went longer between visits. She took advantage of this and started working her right arm out of its sling. The left shoulder looked more bruised and hurt, so she let that arm remain in the sling. One arm was better than none. Next she had to go about the nasty, tiresome process of unwrapping the bandages and taking the excruciating IV out of her wrist. The machine let out a digital alarm. Pushing a button with a bell icon shut off the sound.

She put on the sky-blue terry bathrobe Maribel had brought her and went into the bathroom to wait for the ballad.

It took a little less than an hour before the nightmare fell upon her. The entire time Dara concentrated. *When I open that door, I'll be in the parking lot downstairs. Luke's Volt will be there.*

She tried to envision the new location, push her imagination to the limits, but when it was time and she grabbed the handle to open the door, it led to the Emergency Room. Nurses and doctors milled about the area, all wearing black scrubs and black face masks. Their eyes stared at her like cold lead.

Dara slunk out of the bathroom and made for the hallway to the main lobby. More people in black scrubs stood in the unlit hall. They watched her pass. They whispered to each other, "Chop off her tits. Chop 'em off. Chop 'em. Chop. Chop. Suck the fat out. Slurp!"

A door banged open, and Kyle Turner—a memory from high school—jumped out with a meat cleaver. His face took a beastly shape as he howled and sang, "Double Dee Dee. Double Dara. Why won't you rub them in my face, you slut!"

The cleaver imbedded in the wall behind her. Kyle lunged, his freakish long blond hair flowing back like a golden cape. He looked like the young man she remembered, but his features were twisted and also resembled...

No...

Luke?

The resemblance passed as soon as it arrived. Now Kyle looked like a devil or demon, distorted and snarling, bitter with rage. A clawed hand grabbed her breast, and the thumb rubbed her nipple. Putrid breath blew in her face. "Those are good eaten tits right there. Soup time!"

Dara kicked the back of the monster's knee and swept it off its feet. It struck the ground with a tremendous snapping sound.

She ran through gatherings of the dark-clad nurses and doctors, her free arm throbbing. She rested it over her sling. A few more steps and it slid off the side. The shoulder bone grated at the site of the break. Dara fought off a yelp and plowed through the front doors of the hospital.

The Volt sat in the parking lot, just as she'd envisioned it. She'd made it happen. The dream could be manipulated, even if she didn't have complete control.

The doors were open and the keys were in the ignition. She got in and surveyed the sky. Four curtains hung in different areas. She could not distinguish hers from the others... Who had manifested *the fourth* curtain?

Dara had never been great at judging distance, and with the nightmare still influencing her, the atmosphere contracted at the far ends of her peripheral vision. The street across from the Rec Center was still up-earthed from Luke's nightmare, so she couldn't drive through that way. She would have to exit her curtain first, the one that dropped in the barrio side of town, a place Johnny had once told her and Maribel to avoid. Funny...not only was the ghetto not scary to her in the least at this point, but had become a sanctuary.

All it took was hopping on the freeway and she could be there in fifteen minutes.

She turned over the ignition. The speedometer looked different. Instead of the normal display, a digital clock counted down minutes and seconds. It judged Time instead of speed.

As the car pulled forward, the numbers raced. She braked and the pace of the descending numbers slowed. Something didn't feel right...what would happen when the timer went to zero?

She tried the doors.

Of course; locked.

She tried the auto locks and the manual locks. None of them moved.

Her arms hurt. This was going to be a tough drive. She pushed gently on the brake and, with a grimace, leaned over to shift the car into park. Instead of stopping, the wheels squealed and the car shot off, jumping a curb and screeching onto the main street. She headed to the freeway, flying around other cars in maniacal swerves. Numbers on the timer dropped so quickly that their intervals couldn't be rightly distinguished on the display. Several drivers laid on their horns and others rapid fired them. As the Volt went through a red light, a semi truck raced at her. Dara ducked down in her seat and clenched her eyes closed.

She felt the impact and the car spun around twice, the force throwing her against the driver's door. The semi drove on, pushing the Volt against an embankment near the freeway onramp. A terrible trembling hum vibrated deep in the tires. Dara grabbed the wheel in one hand and reefed on it, bones grinding in her broken shoulder. She stomped on the gas pedal. With a steel scream, the car dislodged from the semi's grill and flew up the embankment. The distant foothills lifted in the windshield, disappeared for a moment, only the sun and the cloudless sky looking back at her. Her teeth glanced off each other and she bit her lip just as the car landed. Hundreds of cars were braking and fishtailing on the freeway; she couldn't see them; she could hear them; she could picture the drivers' wide-eyed, tight faces, *Oh shit* forming on their lips as they tried not to hit her.

A small green Sedan skidded into her, but the impact pushed her in the right direction. The Volt's engine thundered, reborn. Green-gray smoke wormed its way out of apertures in the dash. The timer had reached less than eight minutes and quickly worked down to six, to four, to three.

The curtain draped over a high convenience-store sign off the freeway. She tried to direct her movement there, but the car veered toward the sheer drop-off before the exit. The brake wouldn't work. She pulled at the parking brake and though it came up, nothing happened.

In the rear-view mirror, her parents gazed at her, motionless in their church clothes, still young and alive.

"You're going with us now," her father told her softly.

Her mother nodded. "Make it up to us, Dee. Do something right for a change."

Dara cast her burning eyes away and then looked back once more. She had to. She had to see them again. How beautiful they were. Jesus Christ, she missed them *so* much!

Two Bone Men had replaced her parents. Their lips peeled back, showing jagged brown teeth. "They want it? Do *you* want it?"

Dara whipped back and searched the dash. She punched the odometer button, not expecting much. The car tilted away from the cliff and began to slow. After a minute, it stopped. Cars blazing blue fire whipped past her, their skeleton drivers indifferent.

The timer counted down to 10, 9, 8, 7...

At least the Bone Men weren't in the back seat anymore.

Dara tried the doors again but they were still not giving. Feebly she slammed her shoulder into the driver's side, felt something loosen inside her arm and spike through the muscle.

Her cry sounded like it came from another woman—someone in desperate need of help who wouldn't get any.

She sobbed and thought of Luke and Maribel...it wasn't fair she'd gotten this far only to end up trapped again.

Maybe this countdown wasn't to an explosion?

Smoke plumed out of the vents, fiercely now, and filled the cabin.

Through the haze, the radio came on. "Give up, Dara," said a staticky voice. "The pain will never stop. Luke's already dead. Why not join him?"

She saw the dash number changing into a 1.

Chapter 26

Billions of pieces thrown everywhere.

Dara watched the explosion in slow motion, abject from the destruction, subject only to the pain. Her body fragmented like a porcelain doll—she realized immediately that an actual explosion would have ripped her apart in seconds. So what was the purpose here? Breaking away into glittering bits and parts, no lungs to fill with air and scream, but the pain was unbearable. All of her nerves ripped at once, re-formed and ripped once more, an atrocious process leading to the most staggering pain imaginable. Her parts were twisted between the flying scraps of metal, plastic and rubber, but her mind was intact, hovering over it all, possibly with billions of invisible connecting strands to each part and particle of what she once was. At her thought, the pieces moved about, the roar of agony was silent in the gradual expanding chaos of fire and meat. She tethered her arm closer, along with the muscle groups that made up her neck. Bones calcified and reformed, went into every appropriate socket. She reached out with her mind to rebuild her face…and then she paused.

What opportunity had come to her right now?

Death.

My Luke is dead.

You can't believe that.

You WON'T believe that.

Everything ached and twisted and hurt, but that would go on only as long as she remained part of the explosion. She didn't have to. Just this once, she could use the pain to rebuild herself, and not only that, she could become someone else. A better person. Somebody Luke and Maribel could be proud of. A real woman.

With a better, less selfish heart. An inbred sense of duty that would never let parents drive off alone to their death. The kind of person who would take every opportunity when it arrived. She hadn't told her Uncle Sal how much he meant to her, but this new woman would have. Luke would stop being critical of her laziness around the house, and he would appreciate everything she did. Maribel could finally lean on somebody else's shoulder for a change and not have to endure her hardships on her own.

The new body came together. It felt perfect. Right. Smoke inundated her, but Dara kept working, pulling, fastening, melting, twisting, weaving, tightening, growing! The pain was staggering— this could only be done once, she only had this one chance.

With a cough, she recognized that she'd re-formed completely. It seemed to have happened quickly and yet had taken a thousand years. Her arms still showed the burns, but the broken bones in her shoulders had fused.

Through the mess of smoke, she could see that even the Volt had been repaired. Dara shuffled to it, happy, but remembering the raging pain of the moments before. She examined her hands, her body, her silken blonde hair.

It was all the same. She was just Dara again. This body, this mind, it was the only blueprint she knew. Her vision drowned in tears. She'd wanted a way out so badly. For a moment she grabbed her face and buried her fingernails into the flesh.

Get a grip. Get moving. Don't waste this.

It's already wasted.

She pulled her fingers away from her eyes.

Porcupine cars and Dragon trucks roared by quickly, the drivers sitting in the monsters' eyes, their own faces demonic, buckled flesh.

Terror crept over her. Suffering through that pain again...was something she would not do. Especially now that she knew there was no changing who she was. If that happened at all, even a moment of it, she feared that giving up and wishing for death would be the only recourse.

Dara froze as a face appeared in the smoke. The Bone Man's eyes and nose protruded just enough to be seen. The bone through his nose flexed as he spoke. "Your mind disfavors you. *Please*. Allow me to ruin your thoughts so you won't come back again." The gleam of a hatchet shimmered through the smoke. Dara turned away, her legs prickling with pins and needles. "The Horse needs to lighten its yoke. Release yourself for the good of the world."

She ran on the glass-littered freeway. Out of the corner of her eye, she saw the Bone Man, hatchet raised over his head. He closed the gap quickly and his heavy breathing grew intense. A battle cry rang out. A motorcycle engine roared.

Dara fell to the ground.

The Bone Man dropped his hatchet and flew back from the impact as Johnny turned his Harley into a side skid that he stopped with his foot.

"Johnny?" Dara yelled in disbelief.

His face, t-shirt and shorts were covered in dried blood but his sly smile belied his appearance. "Never thought you'd want to see me, eh?"

"You're right," she said, getting up and climbing onto the back of the motorcycle. She wrapped her arms around him and gave him a grateful squeeze. "Get me out of this dream."

"Yah-fucking-yes, ma'am." He revved the bike and took off.

"Look out!" Dara saw the Bone Man dash at them, hands outstretched. He grabbed her midsection and held tight.

Johnny glanced back as the motorcycle wobbled. "What the shit?"

Dara dug her fingernails into the Bone Man's wrists. The crazed monster had steadied himself on the running board, perched like a crane.

"We're going through!"

Looking ahead, Dara tried to figure out where they were. But she didn't know. She'd never been to this side of town. The black curtain unfurled in front of them. A moment later, they burst through, throwing its silken folds every which way.

Dara was in a daze when Johnny stopped the bike just outside the convenience store. He put out the kick stand and slid off. "Now somebody is gonna get fucked up!"

The Bone Man staggered backwards, looking in terror at the new world around him. His skin was a normal shade of brown now, more human looking. His eyes were not cauldrons of ink, but shallow pools of gray, full of lucidity.

Johnny didn't stop to ruminate on the Bone Man's changes. He hurried over, lifting his big fist, about to club the man. Like a flash, the Bone Man drew a knife from a feathered sheath on his leg. Johnny halted and took a step back. "Fuckin' pussy! Put that shit down."

The Bone Man spoke in a dialect that carried rage and panic.

"Where is the Balladeer?" Dara slid off the motorcycle and was almost overcome with dizziness. "The Balladeer, the one you call the Horse? Tell us how to find the Horse."

Eyes widening, the man took another step back. He looked to the distance, to one of the other black curtains.

"You spoke English before. Tell us. We can help you, if you help us."

The Bone Man crept back further.

"I'm going to run your ass over—"

"Johnny! I'm handling this."

The Bone Man glanced at them and then took off, sprinting into an alley. He was twice as fast as Johnny could even dream of moving and Dara, no athlete herself, would not come close to matching his speed.

Johnny lowered his arms and shook his head. "Great handling job, Dara."

She scrubbed at her face. "Shit."

"Whatever. Fuck that guy. Let's just focus on Luke and that other curtain—could that be Maribel?"

Nodding, Dara looked to the rippling black shape in the far distance. "But why would she be on that side of town? She was at her classroom."

"We better check there first then. If it's not her, I don't care to jump into another one of these things for some asshole I don't know."

"How did you find me, Johnny?"

"I was off looking for you guys. I'd just busted out of my own curtain—you should see these new mods on my bike—I rode it through the curtain and they actually still work here and *there*. I don't get it, but that's what's happened. I think if you take something through the curtain, you bring a version of it into this world."

"Like that Bone Man?"

Johnny shrugged. "Aside from running like a mother fucker, he looked pretty weak."

"We need to get to the others."

"Agreed. Which way?"

She didn't want to choose between her husband and wife. Luke was at home, and Maribel should have been at school.

"There's something you should know, too," said Johnny.

"What?"

"The song is much closer now for me. We could have another one fall down on us soon. It might be better to split up. I don't think we want to see what happens in a double-nightmare."

"Maybe they'll cancel each other out?"

"Or maybe it will do all sorts of great or fucked up things, but we don't want to experiment."

"Right." She felt sick. "I need some clothes, and we know Luke's in one right now. Maribel isn't for sure."

"Yep."

"We'll just chance it. Let's both go to the house. It's safer if we stick together."

"I'm not kidding about it being close," warned Johnny. "This song is about to come together again. I can hear it clearly now. We won't have long. Could be in an hour, could be five, but it's coming."

"We just have to do it. Okay?"

He gestured to the motorcycle. They both got on.

Dara sighed. "Thank you for coming for me."

Johnny started the bike and his shoulders dropped a little as he tried to calm himself.

"How do you feel about the plan?" she asked.

He glanced at her for a moment and then laughed.

"Like I'm taking a very dumb dare."

Chapter 27

Johnny had earned this new improved Hog.

As proud of his new mods as he was, the ride was altogether different, unnatural. It didn't move like a 900-pound bike. It didn't move like a crotch rocket either—*shit, it moved like a feather in a cyclone*. He kept checking himself to see if the nightmare had come back, that this wasn't some twisted version of reality. Last time, caught in Dara's nightmare, the new parts had disintegrated inside the bike when she left the curtain. Game Over. This time, he'd taken it through and it had survived. Permanent. Not going anywhere. Johnny's heart leapt when he looked down at the gas gauge and found an infinity symbol.

At a stoplight he traced his finger along the ∞.

"Hot damn," he breathed. This was the first good thing to come of this madness. It was too good to be true. It couldn't last. Could it?

The song had almost come together now. What if it just kept quickening, iterations coming one after another? He'd have to keep finding new places, new curtains. Going into Luke's neighborhood was a mistake. These were well-traveled roads for all of them. Who knew how close another curtain might be?

"Has it come back again?" Dara asked.

"No, but anytime now."

Entering other people's nightmares seemed easier than conducting your own, although each was unpredictable.

Johnny's thoughts returned to the jail. Just as he had been about to slip away, his cellmate Roberto had loosened his grip and, with sulfurous breath, told him, "No-no, you have to want to go shit-ass. It's time to have fun." The devil lifted up a five-inch claw. "I'm going to ram this through the hole in your dick so far I'll be able to pop your heart open."

Johnny's cock—still recovering from whatever trauma his amorous wives had put it through—twitched at the recollection. He'd kept little Johnny safe this time, though. He'd reached out in a panic, grabbed the devil's horns, thought about how good it would feel to rip them off, and *fucking did it*! He tore the horns out of Roberto's head, and left two holes, like he had struck some kind of biological well, the source of the human race itself. It was gory, disgusting, and satisfying as all shit.

Johnny had used the horns to pry open the bars to the cell and defend himself on the way out of the police station. The cops had turned into some ghoulish things with bare skulls for heads and tumor-spotted hands that leaked Time and Death from their ruptured surfaces. He had been praying to find one of the cop's motorcycles outside the madhouse. He had found something better. His own bike...but one from some kind of Flash Gordon Shrooming fantasy. It pretty much looked like his Hog, *but goddamn*.

"There it is. You can see the dream boundary right there."

Johnny snapped to attention at Dara's voice. He did indeed see where the trees began to darken and the houses looked bent, pulled by an unseen force.

"Why here? Luke's been on his own street."

"It has to be a radius. You got caught up in my dream while you were at Shasta's, right?"

"Yeah. That's only a couple of miles from here."

"It must move with us, extending only so far."

"Then that means the curtain could move, too."

Dara nodded.

Johnny pulled up to the curb at the boundary of the nightmare.

Dara stared at the dim area stretching before them. She took a deep breath and shifted to get off the bike. Johnny put out his hand and laid it over her arm. "God, I don't think I'm ready to go into another one."

"Maybe you shouldn't, then."

"No, I'm okay. He's my husband. I have to."

"I know you want to go…but only a couple notes are missing."

She sighed. "You're really that close?"

"I think so. Like I said, it's getting closer."

"But we don't know when it will happen. Just because it's almost there doesn't mean anything. It's unpredictable."

"And sudden. It's too risky, Dara. Let me go in first. See if I can't get Luke out."

"Sit here in a bathrobe and wait?"

"Just for twenty minutes—half an hour." Johnny pinched his eyes shut for a second, the song nearly coming to fruition. "I'll leave my keys in case you need to use the bike."

Dara pressed her lips together. She couldn't look him in the eyes. He studied her a bit. She was one of the prettiest women he'd ever had the pleasure of knowing, but he'd never said as much. That was Luke's fucking job. Still, maybe he should have told her something to make her feel better.

The stress in her brow indicated she must have been feeling what Johnny was—that all their good luck was about to dry up.

She patted his knee. "I was wrong about you, Johnny."

Damn, he'd jinxed himself thinking about comforting her. He looked down at the bike, uncertain what she wanted him to say. His mouth opened and shut a few times, almost involuntarily.

"Cat got your tongue? What were you going to tell me?"

"That I liked your boobs a lot better before the surgery."

"You weren't going to say that."

He half-smiled, got off the bike, fighting the ballad internally as it closed in on his brain. He swallowed. His throat was paper dry. A beer would be lovely right about now. He looked at Dara, who still sat as she normally did, arms folded over her chest, white-blonde hair hiding most of her face.

He started, "If I don't…"

Her long-lashed hazel eyes lifted and held him.

"Just make sure, if you can…call my kid one day, let him know he means a lot to me."

"No, no, none of that," she said resolutely and checked the clock on the bike. "Now get going. Half an hour starts now."

Putting up a hand in farewell, Johnny slipped into the nightmare side of the street. A hot-cold flash went through his body and his guts dropped. He kept walking so as not to alarm Dara, but he couldn't help quickening his pace. The boundaries of the nightmare might change once he arrived, so having Dara hang back would be all for nothing if it worked that way.

We've all lost our damned minds. That's the root cause. Mass insanity.

Johnny walked up to the Rhodeses' house and opened the front door. At once he heard falling water, like a pipe had broken in the walls. The living room looked untouched, and except for some construction in the kitchen, there didn't seem to be anything going on there, either.

"Hey dumbfuck!" Johnny called out. His words played with the music in his head *du-du-muh-muh-fu-fu-kuh-kuh.*

He climbed the stairs. His knees hurt but not as much as usual. This experience had played hell with his eating and drinking schedule, and he must have lost about twenty pounds. *Hell of a diet plan. Do not recommend.*

The roiling water grew louder as he approached the bathroom. A bass thump came from the other side of the door. He halted. The carpet was wet.

"Luke?" he hollered. "You in there? I'm checking on you, man. Put your magic wand away."

Johnny twisted the handle. It was locked. Luke always locked doors. It was normally irritating but right now it was damn infuriating.

"Luke!" he yelled. "I'm breaking the door if you don't open up."

The music agreed, *oh-oh-oh pen-pen-pen uh-uh-ppppuh.*

Taking a big breath, Johnny took a step back and mafia-stomped the knob. The door warped, and a west-east crack split the wood. Another kick blasted it open, the cheap knob almost popping out the other side. The sounds coupled with the frantic, growing rhythm of the nightmare ballad.

A caution sign, that looked to have fallen, rested against the wall. That must have been the thud he'd heard.

DANGER!!! FROGMEN!!!

The dark figure of a scuba diver swimming underneath.

Johnny stepped over the sign and peered into the tub. The surface of the water was murky and pond scum had collected on the sides. Through hazy green, Johnny saw that the way led into a vertical cavern below the house's foundation, maybe sixty or seventy feet down.

Being a shitty swimmer, Johnny wasn't about to swim down. He'd have to return outside and follow the boundaries of this nightmare, and maybe he could find where this tunnel ended up.

That would have been his plan if the ballad hadn't exploded in his mind like all the fireworks in the world.

The atmosphere closed in on him, became cold, dark, bubble-filled. He struggled to see, to move, barbed hands clutched his throat, injecting painful venom—it wanted him to succumb, to wish for death. *Where the hell am I? What the hell is happening?*

He never jumped into the tub, yet he was in the watery tunnel now, fighting with something in a charcoal-gray scuba suit, air tanks, fins, and all. But this thing wasn't human. It didn't move like a person, and that poison on its hands—it had to be Time and Death.

Water filled both of his lungs, but he lived anyway. Pain made him concentrate on *accepting* the fate of drowning: *how much Time (pain) do you want before dying?* His body quaked with so much torment that the answer was easy—no, it couldn't be easy. There were other people in his life, people that depended on him.

Me? But he was no longer Johnny Cruz.

Me? But he was no long Luke Rhodes.

Aluke was both.

The two nightmares had merged them into one being. So while the fear of water and drowning consumed one part of his thoughts, new-found strength in Johnny's large arms empowered the other part. He reached around and grabbed the wicked thing by its neck and twisted hard. Underwater, the snap didn't sound devastating.

But it was.

Aluke watched as the scuba diver drifted up, arms floating to the sides. The air tanks bumped hollowly against the cavern ceiling. Before swimming away he glanced up at his tormentor one last time.

The scuba mask fitted over the face of a frog.

Chapter 28

Safety was rare.

Maribel had forgotten how it felt. She'd made it out of the *Puppet Inferno*, which was like a haunted hell-house for older kids. Demons lived there now. She'd seen them doing things to each other…didn't want to think about it again. She was just glad not to have attracted their attention. Then there was *Puppet Deep* where scuba-diving puppets and fake sharks swam—thankfully, it wasn't as populated as she remembered from her outings with the kids. She found an alley between *Puppet Deep* and the food court, where a black curtain spilled from the sky. She'd made her way to it when growling glass monsters came rushing out of gift-shop windows. Their footsteps sounded like mirrors shattering, again and again. After running nearly to exhaustion, she'd lost them and ended up in the same alley where she started.

She was about to move when lips pressed into her neck.

Maribel turned and drew her hand back.

Allie stood there, rosy-cheeked, video camera still in hand. "I have so much good footage of you. I'm learning so much. I want to show you."

"How did you get in here?"

"*I will follow you,*" Allie sang the oldie song, swaying her hips disturbingly.

"Keep your voice down. Jesus! What is your problem, anyway?"

With a petulant sniff, Allie thoughtfully clicked the video camera on. "My problem? I tell you what my problem is. My husband wants you, Maribel. He's going to leave me. I'm not a *liberal* woman like yourself, see."

"Are you kidding?"

"He doesn't think I can fuck a woman." Allie took a deep breath and unbuttoned the top button of her green blouse. "I can fuck a woman."

"You're…confused."

"No I'm ready. Let's add this to the rest of the tape. It's great stuff. I'm learning to be worldly like the Rhodeses."

A deep snarl came from the alleyway. Allie's head jerked and her eyes widened. "You sent it here to kill me?"

"Get in here, before it sees you." Maribel sank into the darkness in front of the men's bathroom.

Allie screamed and charged down the alley. She shrieked as a jumble of glass flesh lunged at her. Maribel winced, imagining the woman being torn apart, but Allie staggered sideways, just as a potted tree toppled in the beast's swiping paw.

Allie sprinted through the black curtain, camera in hand like a runner's baton. The curtain swished to the side as she broke through it.

Another growl, but it was from afar. The beast had gone elsewhere and could be heard gutting Frogmen on the other side of *Puppet Deep*.

Maribel emerged from her hiding spot and ran for the curtain. It would be nice to leave this crazy place. She certainly wasn't bringing the children back here. This place had become really dangerous, what with demons and frog people and beasts. *It just wouldn't do*, her mind told her.

Someone walked through the curtain from the other side. At first Maribel thought it was Allie again, but it clearly wasn't. This man was a Bone Man, his brown skin darkened to a perverted tone, beyond deepest night. Bones protruded everywhere.

Maribel slid against a wall, hoping he'd go past her.

The Bone Man peered up at the black curtain as though it was something he'd never dreamed of seeing before. He took the fabric in his hands, feeling it between his fingers and then, unexpectedly, wrenched it. The curtain tore away in shreds, falling around his feet and disappearing in puffs of black smoke as it struck the ground. With one last mighty tug, he pulled down the rest of it, and the tattered curtain fell from the sky and, as it connected with the earth, a great column of gray-black smoke lifted.

Dozens more Bone Men emerged from the shadows. Maribel stepped back. She wondered where to go, now that the curtain was gone. A tall Bone Man approached the other, nodding.

"It is good to be back in my own place. Out there, my heartbeat made strange music," the Bone Man told the tall man. "But I feel real again, and now we can all last forever."

"How did you take down the curtain, brother?"

The Bone Man shrugged and raised his arms. "I am from both places now. This was the only way. We have our own land now."

Just then a craggy hand fell on Maribel's shoulder. A Bone Man hauled her forward, bringing her through the hooting mass of warriors.

"And do you see? At long last, we have a Queen to abuse us," said the newcomer with a laugh, zeal sparkling in his savage eyes.

Everybody dropped to their knees and put their spears at their sides. They bowed their heads in supplication to Maribel. Even the man who had brought her over to the crowd fell back, chin pressed to his chest, spear pointed down.

"We will serve you," they cried in unison.

Maribel couldn't think what to say. Her eyes continued to search for a way out of Puppet Town, but there was nothing.

The newcomer lifted his head and gazed at her with his knowing eyes. "I will help you rule this place. Enslave the frog people to bring us fresh fish from the lowest points of the coldest seas. Ensnare the demons to use for sport in the arena, use their hides for clothing and roofs for our homes. That is only the beginning to this place. There is so much here to *rule*!"

"I don't want to rule anything. Let me out of here!" Maribel shouted. "I want outside. There are people who will come looking for me soon."

"Nobody will find us here, my Queen," said the newcomer with a grin. "Nobody."

The tribe hurrahed.

"Not even The Mare."

Chorus:

Has this Godhead song always been audible? Nobody knows. *It's bloody, whatever it is, it's bloody.* But, then *it's a way to have fun, whatever anybody else may say, it's a way to have fun.* You see, *he's doing this to get better, whatever made him ill before, he's doing this to get better.* Therefore you must *ride it to dirty glory, whatever lathers you and makes you holy, ride it to dirty glory.* Too many questions while I'm *playing and laying in the hungry sand, whatever tastes better flesh or marrow, playing and laying in the hungry sand.* People do not create people. Bodies do. Flesh does. Bones, yes, *the bones are used for building new people, whatever otherwise God might tell you, the bones are used for building new people.*

He implores the very heart of the clown tunnel, *"Stop singing."*

Verse 8: All for One

Chapter 29

It was a bizarre view of Hell.

Aluke Rhoduz examined the offices of GeoGreen Motorcycles Inc, still half-submerged in the cold water of the passage that split the ground in the lobby. Aluke climbed onto the marble floor. His teeth chattered. He tried to rub his arms to warm up. Behind a bronze statue of a motorcycle popping a wheel over surging flames, a crisp, clean waterfall dribbled down a sheet of diamond plate on the wall. The water ran down the plate, across the floor, and into the passage to the tunnel.

Aluke had worked for this clean-technology motorcycle-engine company his entire adult life. He'd gotten the job just after marrying Dara Mackenzie, who left him for another man a few years later. His second wife, Maribel Wilson, had passed away from complications with diabetes not long ago. Their son, William, had gone to live with Maribel's grandmother.

If Luke Rhodes and Alberto "Johnny" Cruz had separate thoughts on these new details, none of them surfaced. They knew that they were in a nightmare and needed to escape, but as far as being Aluke—that was who they were.

He walked, shoes soggy with water, to the waterfall. His rippled reflection in the diamond plate stared back, tired eyes and perfect movie-star hair belonging to Luke Rhodes and pudgy bronze face and bandito mustache belonging to Johnny Cruz. Aluke was not quite as large as Johnny, but probably flirted with morbid obesity.

None of this felt right, and Aluke hurried to the exit to search the horizon for a curtain.

"What?" he breathed.

Across the freeway stretched the black curtain, a broad stroke of nothing in space. Two others rippled, but these were a disconcerting blood red.

"We are inside out, outside in," said a voice on the staircase.

A man who might have been Luke's friend Blake Jackson, and who also might have also been Johnny's co-worker Grover Franklin, staggered down the stairs, bracing himself while he devoured a long strip of bloody meat from his forearm. His darker skin had paled to Irish white, yet his short cropped African hair remained; his close set eyes looked to belong to Grover and his other strong, handsome facial features were most definitely Blake's. The abomination's licked blood from his lips and hissed like a snake having an orgasm. His eyes fixed on Aluke as it reached the final stair.

"Where's that dead concubine of yours?" He glanced down at the bloody mess of ripped fabric and exposed biology in his crotch. "I might have rammed her good and hard, had I not been so goddamned HUNGRY!"

The hybrid charged Aluke, who, too stunned to think, backed against the cold, glass double doors. He had crossed only half the distance when a figure hurled from the shadows and began feeding on the his neck, taking both to the ground. Between tremendous chunks of muscle tissue and gagging slurps, the attacker chanted, "get in me, marry, marry, marry, get in me, all in one, one in all, get in me. All for one. We'll be MARRIED now! One. One. One. One." It lifted its head a moment and Aluke recognized it as the merging of Maria, the secretary, and Lou, the copper thief.

Aluke couldn't open the door. Needed to try the other pair of doors across the room.

Something struck him bodily—everywhere, every cell, every particle.

Not something.

Somebody.

And he was changed for it.

Suddenly.

Different.

One.

Of many parts.

Dara had merged with him. She must have entered the nightmare and recalled the ballad also.

Now they were all together. Alberto Cruz, Luke and Dara Rhodes.

Alukara.

A man wearing Crusaders' armor jogged noisily up and started hacking with a broadsword at the struggling pair of hybrid cannibals. The crusader chanted something in Latin, growing more impassioned with every gushing wound he created.

Alukara tried to leave—the broadsword touched her chest.

The warrior stood before her. As surreal as the nightmare was, its grip and hold on the sword were steady and too realistic. The point of the sword stung from its tip down to her heart.

"Do the interview," said the crusader. Only his burning eyes, visible through his steel visor, indicated his humanity. Just the eyes. Calculating orbs of judgment. They belonged to both Stobecker and Dara's father.

"I don't want to do the interview."

Blood welled through Alukara's *Killswitch Engage* baby doll t-shirt. "Don't...please."

A metallic laugh from a metallic face.

"Dara wasn't enough for Luke, was she?" the crusader asked.

"No," said Alukara, lips trembling.

"Luke wasn't enough for Dara, was he?"

Alukara swallowed. The word was less than a whisper. "No."

"And Beltran wasn't enough, either. That's why you let him go. After you pushed your son to the ground and screamed at him to *go to fucking bed already*, that's when you knew what a piece of sewage you really were? Isn't that right?"

"Right."

"You are blighted animals willing to spread your contagion over this good land. You have no place here." The crusader lifted the sword, eyes burning with ecstasy. "Interview over!"

Alukara ducked, felt the sword swish through the air inches above her head. She staggered forward and ran.

The crusader's loud plate armor clanked. "I condemn you for eternal sin! Unclean, intoxicated, bigamist, slug! For you, love is only a hole to crawl into. You have sullied your marriage and damned your souls to a dark, roasting pit! I shall cleave all your lusty parts from your filthy union and litter the ground with your bones!"

Alukara shifted, in a daze. The sword came at her, she bent out of its path. The momentum caused the crusader to lose ground and fall sideways to the floor.

She went on through the massive lobby and burst through the exit. She'd always wanted to work in that place. She had a mechanical engineering degree and had made something of a name for herself in local bike competitions, but she'd been in a cocoon for the past ten years while her partner Maribel supported her. Alukara didn't know how long that would last, now that she was certain there was no job for her again; and with these nightmares, who knew if she'd live to make Maribel proud of her.

Maribel…where was she?

There was a single black curtain across a sea of whirling graph papers. A boat waited there. Alukara lumbered toward it. She was fat and disgusting. God she needed a drink, or a good run or swim, maybe just a few hours playing on the computer. They didn't seem to go hand in hand, but she desired them all.

Beyond the black curtain, three burgundy curtains swayed. She didn't want to take a chance with those—she knew that the black curtain would get her out of this strange land. Stepping in the boat, she almost lost balance as it swept slowly through the papers. Beneath the freeway underpass, the papers flowed like a raging river toward the black curtain. A force from beyond was helping facilitate this.

The boat bumped against a curb near a Jamaican Jerk Chicken restaurant. The black curtain dropped in front of its door. Alukara lost no time and bolted through.

Then!

Like they'd all been struck with lightning, Johnny and Luke and Dara staggered three different ways and collapsed just over the threshold.

The room cloyed with the tangy aroma of chicken. A man with his dreadlocks tied up glanced uneasily over the front counter.

"What're you doin', you t'ree?"

Johnny shook his head and pushed up on a fist. Luke helped Dara from the floor.

"We're drunk," Johnny said absently.

"Go'on out din." The man snorted and dropped a pan of fresh chicken in a steamer tray.

Luke shook out his bad hand, having fallen on it. Dara wrinkled her forehead and closed her eyes. "What was that?"

"Pretty fucked," Johnny commented.

Luke held Dara for a moment. "Don't want to do that again. At least the music seems a bit disconnected now. How about for you?"

Dara and Johnny nodded.

"What were those red curtains?" Dara asked.

Johnny yanked open the door. "All I know is I don't like it. This shit is just getting shittier. I've got confusion on top of my confusion."

"Here, here," Luke replied.

"That stuff...that the knight said." Dara looked from Johnny to Luke. "It was just trying to get to us, right. That was part of the nightmare."

"It wasn't true," Luke replied flatly.

"You never pushed Beltran down like it said. That never happened, right?" she asked Johnny.

Johnny took a deep breath and sniffed. "We need to get out of here before that guy loses it."

"Go'on wich ya if ya aren't eatin'," the man behind counter said with a scowl.

They followed Johnny outside. The blare of distant sirens and the whipping wind greeted them. Burnt graph papers blew in small dust devils up and down the empty street.

"So you aren't going to comment, I take it?" Luke prodded Johnny.

"Drop it, man—I probably killed an innocent man tonight, okay? He was just a drunk, and now he's probably lying in cell right now, bleeding out from his head, and it's because of me, all because I brought that nightmare with me to jail."

"He might be alive. Sometimes people live," Dara said quietly. "I discovered some that did."

"That makes me feel a whole fucking lot better, thank you. I'll just hope from now on that all the shit does not slide downhill."

"I'm just saying it's possible."

"I'm not going back to jail to look for him."

"Then why are you bringing it up?"

"Lay the fuck off Dara!"

"Knock it off, both of you," Luke snapped. "We're alive. I was begging to die when you came looking for me. Now I'm alive. Standing here. Breathing. Let me just enjoy it for one goddamn minute."

They turned away from each other. Luke rubbed his eyes for a moment, trying to think.

"You want to know if what the knight said was true? After being the same person for a bit, we all know each other a lot better now," Johnny said. He glanced at Dara. "So no more obvious questions. You know the answer. You deal with your own shit how you want to, but for me, there's enough going on right now not to add being delusional on top of it."

Dara changed the subject. "None of us have ever eaten here then, I take it?"

Luke and Johnny exchanged glances and shook their heads.

"The curtain fell at the place where none of us have been."

Johnny examined his *Killswitch Engage* t-shirt. "That makes sense, since we were…one person. But what about those red ones?"

Luke strained his eyes. "I don't see *any* curtains now."

"What happened to the fourth black curtain? You said it might have belonged to Maribel. Luke's right. I don't see it anywhere."

Luke took Dara's hand, and something dropped, heavy and sour in his gut.

What had happened to Maribel?

Chapter 30

The classroom was clean.

Luke had only seen it this way at the start of the year when Maribel set everything up. It turned out that class had never been in session. He and Dara had spoken briefly to the principal, who matter-of-factly informed them that all the students had been redistributed to other classrooms since the teacher had not arrived or answered phone calls. One child, David, who had been unaccounted for, was picked up in the parking lot of a real-estate office downtown. Severely dehydrated and sunburned, the boy claimed he'd wanted to visit Puppet Town. His parents had taken off work and had him now. They told the school he had a habit of taking buses into the city and had run off before, so it didn't surprise them. It didn't sound like they were blaming Maribel or the school.

"Thank God," he added.

After the principal returned to his office, Dara and Luke sat on the children's desks, stoned by the stillness of the room. Luke had never imagined how much Dara hated herself, not until becoming her. She must be sorting through all his psychoses right now, too—at least she'd understand the guilt he'd had for being unfaithful to her—but then she might have also realized that some things she constantly pointed out, her teeth, her breasts, her nose, had actually become objects of disdain for him as well. He couldn't help it; she'd *made* him not like parts of her. He hoped she'd also gleaned that from their experience. Things would never be the same between them. He still loved her, though, and prayed that she still loved him, for better or for insane.

He watched her, the silence finally getting to him. "Johnny's Harley's pretty nuts, now."

"Pretty nuts," she agreed. "It's amazing what you can take with you out of a nightmare."

Luke craned his neck to the ceiling and rolled his head a little. His muscles were jacked up. His hand still hurt. The soles of his feet still felt crisp from burning. He was a wreck. He continued to roll his head until he spotted grimy handprints on the ceiling's drop tiles. It might have been an odd sight at one time, but with the music alive and well in his mind, he didn't bother reacting at first. There were bigger things to do. They had to find Maribel so they could get the hell out of this city.

Johnny was busy packing things and getting the RV ready. The Nightmare Harley could easily fit three riders, possibly four if you counted Johnny as two people, but they wouldn't be able to live in the motorcycle up in the mountains.

Johnny Cruz...

He and Dara understood Johnny quite a bit better now. He had many more issues from his past that he'd not worked through, but they were coming to the surface, sure enough. This ordeal with the Lifemares had forced him to deal with his demons.

Luke shuddered at the thought of demons. Those people back at his job, eating each other—after what Johnny said, his conscience got the better of him and he had called GeoGreen to ask about survivors.

The motorcycle company no longer listed him as an employee, though, and he found himself whispering, "I'd just applied not long ago. My name is *Alukara*. I'm...following up."

Dara had leaned over him during the call, consuming every word.

The company remembered her (them), but said they would have to get back to her because they were experiencing major plumbing problems in their lobby. A giant sink-hole had opened to a subterranean river that stretched across Riverside into Moreno Valley.

After hanging up, Dara folded her arms over her chest and closed her eyes. Her body trembled. "The company didn't change back. What will the Lifemares leave behind next time?"

"I don't know."

"These things are going to fuck up the world."

Luke snorted derisively. "We won't be around to care."

Dara glared at him.

"What?"

She shook her head and pushed off the desk. A squeak broke the silence. Dara's eyes searched Luke.

"Wasn't me."

He scanned the room a moment, then heard it again.

The large closet just beyond the story-time rug.

They both got up and walked over. Luke reached out, hesitated, and then grabbed the handle.

Tucked inside the closet, bony knees to her chest and a video camera poised before her blue-lit face, sat Allie. Her swollen, tear-soaked eyes turned to them. Fleshy shapes bobbed on the camera's viewscreen.

"I love my husband," she told them.

Dara ripped the camera out of her hand.

"No!" Allie screamed. "You have to let me keep that!"

Luke watched the screen with Dara, and his gorge began to rise. A sweaty, naked, moaning Maribel stretched over the classroom tables. One tall white guy was sticking her in the mouth with his long, curved erection, while a black guy penetrated her ass. Breasts swaying under her, a woman that looked like Allie hovered above Maribel and dipped two fingers in her vagina.

Dara almost dropped the camera as Allie lunged for it. Luke caught the woman and shoved her against the closed closet door. "Where is she?"

"This isn't her," said Dara, her voice intense. "It's NOT."

A quaking smile broke over Allie's face. "She doesn't love you anymore. You two are old news. Didn't you get the memos?"

"Tell us where she went."

Allie tried to move, and Luke put his hand on her throat. At first he thought Dara would tell him to stop, or shove his hand away, but instead she leaned forward and got in the woman's face. "Tell us, or you'll be sorry. I promise."

Fear surfaced in Allie's eyes. "She got a new job. She's moved on. She doesn't love any of us. She doesn't love anyone. But she will be loved wherever she goes. That's how Maribel operates."

"Where?" Luke asked sharply, dismissing all the other bullshit.

"Where she belongs."

Dara's brow furrowed, and she shook her head angrily.

"What are you talking about, Allie?" Luke pressed.

"She is the new Queen."

Chapter 31

His tools littered the floor.

Dara didn't like looking at the mess but was in no mood to aggravate Luke's foul attitude since watching that video yesterday. They'd not said a word about it to Johnny, because he would have wanted to see it for himself. As it was, they'd watched it a few times, growing number with every viewing. Though they couldn't agree on very much right now, she and Luke decided they didn't want to take the camera with them to the mountains. Allie hadn't provided them with anything except that "Queen" nonsense, but they both wondered if it meant something sexual and therefore horrible.

Luke struggled underneath the bar stool. The loose leg had finally come out, and he was wasting his time trying to thread it into the stripped socket. After another failure he pushed the useless stool away, its remaining two legs sticking awkwardly in the air.

"I need to just glue the fucking thing," he said.

"There are enough folding chairs in the RV. I told you to forget about it."

"And I told you I won't leave a broken chair for us to come home to!" He reached for the stool again, then got up resignedly to fetch some glue.

Dara tapped her cell phone. After deciding against calling Maribel for the thirty-seventh time, she brought up a medieval role-playing game she'd recently downloaded. The suit of armor on the title screen reminded her of the crusader back in the lobby…back when they were Alukara.

She shut off the phone.

Luke knows everything about me now. Probably knows I didn't want to ever come back to him after meeting Maribel. Maribel had incorrectly thought that Dara wasn't ready to leave him completely, and the rest was history. True, she'd fallen back in love with Luke, but Maribel had given their relationship an energy it had lacked before.

Now look at us. Our battery's been removed.

Where was she? There had been another curtain. Had that been Maribel's, and had she escaped?

Her husband shuffled across the carpet and dropped down on the tile, knees first, a bottle of glue in each hand. He bent over the two legged stool.

"What happened to her, Luke?" Dara asked softly.

"You saw."

"I can't believe the video."

"You won't believe that...but you saw her go to those other people's house."

"But in her classroom? That's crazy. She cared too much about her job. She respected kids to much to do something like that."

"Maybe she isn't who we think she is."

"How can you say that?"

"Easy." He raked his forearm over his nose and sniffed. "After all this...whatever it is, I can say just about anything."

"What about that fourth curtain?"

"Your curtain disappeared once, too, remember?"

"That was when the music stopped for everyone, though."

"Yeah," Luke breathed and considered the glues for a moment.

The music *hadn't* stopped this time. The ballad was as close as it had ever been, but the notes had been rattled around something fierce for everyone. For Luke and Johnny, it could come at any moment, but a day had passed since their last recall.

"I don't think either one of these will work on galvanized steel." Luke inspected the back of each bottle.

"Just leave it."

His face went red. "I just want to fix it. All right? Do you have an issue with that? You aren't the only thing in this universe that needs fixing."

"Oh fuck you." She went into the kitchen, though she had no idea for what. She was far from feeling like eating or drinking. So alone, so utterly and completely alone, she hated that her first impulse was to go back to Luke with tears in her eyes. At first her mental state didn't register with him. Then, almost out of irritation, he dropped a screw driver and stood up to hold her.

"That stuff on the camera. Is it real? Or something manufactured from the dream?"

"I don't know," he said into her hair. "And it doesn't matter, anyway."

She pulled back from him to look him in the eyes. "Why not?"

His left eyelid twitched as he considered her a moment. "It happened. Just like GeoGreen isn't an engineering firm anymore. This stuff is real now. She was with *those people*. Whether she wanted to be…or not."

"Those people might not have even been real. I had my arms cut off and boiled—I healed myself after being blown into atoms. Anything is possible."

"Exactly, Dara. So Maribel might not even remember us anymore. Don't you get it? Do you think I'm so miserable because I'm just a worthless asshole? No… I'm miserable because it's all changed. Our lives can never be put back the way they were."

"Oh come on, how can you be jealous when you know—?"

"It's not jealousy I'm talking about…she's gone, goddamn it anyway. I don't think she's coming back, either. Do you?"

That was a loaded question. "We have to find her."

Luke shook his head and leaned into the counter.

Johnny bustled through the front door with a plaid sleeping bag under his arm. He was really slimming down these days. It wasn't surprising since none of them wanted to eat much. "Is it okay if I take this one?"

"Yeah," Luke said.

Sensing something amiss, Johnny would have normally hit the road, but he too had a better understanding of them now. He dropped the sleeping bag at his feet and walked over. "I'm thirsty," he announced. "Got anything in the fridge?"

"Just lemonade."

"Good enough." He poured himself a glass. The sound of his glugging was obnoxious.

"So," he said, coming out of the kitchen, wiping his mouth on the sleeve of his *Entombed* t-shirt, "are you two really broken up about that video?"

They turned to him at the same time, and he chuckled. "Guess that's a yes."

"How do you know about it?"

"I stayed here last night, remember? I heard you guys watching it. I figured it was important."

"It's nothing," said Dara.

"I know," said Johnny, "because I copied it and watched it on my lap top."

"How?" Luke straightened, the color leaching from his face.

"There's a little port in the side—"

"I know how you copied it, dumbass, but why?"

Johnny's face stiffened as though to say, *what's the big deal?* "I figured we were pretty tight after yesterday—not that we weren't before."

"Not that tight."

Johnny cocked his head to the side. "I know you guys are worried about Maribel. But that video isn't anything I'd be concerned about. She wasn't being hurt or anything."

"That's hardly why we were bothered by it, Johnny," said Dara, shaking her head.

"What am I missing then? It's a shit video for one—bunch of static and jumps, and for two, Maribel is chasing around some of her students in the classroom. They look pretty wild and the camera's moving around like crazy, but I watched the whole thing, and I don't see what the big friggin' deal is. The rest is white noise and ant races."

Dara narrowed her eyes at Luke, who suddenly looked paralyzed. "You must have copied the wrong video," he said.

"That was the only one on there. Lap top is in the RV. It's fully charged. You can see for yourself. So your video is different than mine?"

Luke shook his head. "Forget it."

"I should have watched it on the viewfinder. Damn."

"Leave the camera alone okay. It's...look, ours has Maribel...*with* other people." Dara could feel Luke's eyes drill into her back, but she didn't care.

"Oh," Johnny said, trying not to overreact. "Oh! Two different versions then. How the hell does that happen?"

"That's the question of the hour."

Johnny leaned against the kitchen door jamb. He looked focused for a change, but she could tell that part of that was him fighting the ballad in his head. Luke also had that flighty look about him. He went over to the bar and hopped up to sit. "It's possible she was caught in

Benjamin Kane Ethridge

one of the Lifemares…okay, Dara? I'm willing to give you that. But she hasn't come back home. The curtain is gone, so—"

"So we just give up on her?"

"Let me finish." He tried to be calm but it wasn't working. His nostrils flared several times and he licked his lips. "Back in that tunnel, in the water, with that frogman trying to kill me…I was in so much pain. My lungs hurt so much. I wanted air, but I began to want death more. I know what you went through Dara—with the bomb."

"I didn't even—"

"Doesn't matter. I know you wanted to give it all up. You were a part of me yesterday, remember? Just like you, Johnny. I know how you were going to let your wives rip you apart that night outside the plant. You'd do it again, only this time, there would be no hesitation."

"Why are you saying this shit?" asked Johnny, stone-faced.

"Because I'm there too—this thing has worn us. We won't be able to fight it much longer. The next time we're faced with such pain, we'll ask for the end. And that will be that. We have no idea when the ballad will come together again—what if it comes just before we fall asleep, like it did to you, Dara? The forest is plenty big, and it'll let us by, give us options for a time, but for how long? The ballad wasn't even that loud during my bath and then suddenly—I'm pulled down into that tunnel. How can we even hope to predict these things?"

Johnny's bandito mustache made his frown look deeper.

"What is it?" asked Dara.

"There's this dog I met."

Luke's eyebrows rose. "A dog?"

"Yeah, a mean-ass dog with a big fuckin' head."

"And?"

Johnny shook away a memory. "I think the dog actually liked the nightmare."

"Weird…what's your point?"

"The dog knew when it was coming, like it had intuition or something. It got all excited and everything. It probably could have come after me and ripped me to shit, but it waited for the nightmare to fall. It got to wagging its tail. It was *happy as hell*. I don't know where the dog is now…but if we can find it, we could use it up in the mountains, like an alarm system. If it gets excited in the same way, we know we better find somewhere new."

Dara wasn't certain she followed him. "This is a mean dog, right?"

"Yeah, but like I said, it didn't really care about me. Shit, I think it wanted to be part of the nightmare. It got off on it."

"This dog was from the nightmare?"

"No, not at first. I just think he's one fucked-up animal, to tell you the truth. His owner called him The Count."

"Wonderful," said Luke. "Sounds like just the kind of problem we need to keep around us."

"It's no crazier than anything else," Dara said. "We should use whatever we can. How do we find it though?"

"It's somewhere in the old neighborhood, that's all I know."

"Was it like a mastiff?" Luke asked.

Johnny shrugged. "Maybe. Black coat. Bloodshot eyes."

Luke nodded. "I had a feeling. I know that dog. I almost hit it with my car. I was in the old neighborhood. I got the feeling this dog was headed toward the curtain. Maybe it was trailing the nightmare."

"Likely, I guess."

"So it's possible we could lure it with one, then maybe catch it, muzzle it. Just hope we don't get our asses chewed off in the process."

"No guarantees there, but getting a heads-up on these nightmares might be worth it."

"We can head out sometime today, then."

Johnny nodded. "Let's do it."

Dara spoke up, "Should I come, too?"

"Somebody should stay here in case Maribel shows."

A knock echoed through the house and everybody froze.

Someone was at the door.

Chapter 32

Rapt, Allie peered down at the screen.

"I don't understand," she murmured. "This wasn't what I recorded that day in the classroom. Can I keep this?"

Dara and Luke watched her for more of a reaction, but, rosy-cheeked as she was, the woman was fairly hypnotized.

"Can I? Despite John's explicit demand that I stay away from your family and go with him to his next rehearsal, I instead came here to return things I took, to come clean and ask forgiveness, even after *you* assaulted *me*. Where's your good-faith effort?"

"You can't tell us what happened to Maribel? The video on the camera itself…we don't trust it."

Allie grinned. "She offered herself and became Queen. That's how it is. What is so difficult to understand?"

Luke triple-inhaled, blew out a big sigh, and sat back on the couch.

"You said you brought some of Maribel's personal affects you stole."

Allie snapped to attention. "I'd like to exchange them for the camera."

"Go to hell, Allie."

"Well, can I keep this video file at least? Just in case there's something encrypted or—"

"Go to hell, Allie."

Allie reached into her oversized purse and brought out the diorama. "I took a liking to this because of how fond of it she was. A day barely passed that she didn't mention him coming back, so she could be a mommy. But women like her can't be moms. With her values, Maribel should not be left around children."

"Coming back? Who?"

"Beltran."

Luke leaped from the couch. "Beltran? When was he in Maribel's class?"

"The week before he left for Arizona. Don't you remember?" Dara folded her arms and chewed her lip for a moment, looking back. "We were trying to convince Johnny to let him stay with us."

"I thought he only visited her class once."

"Everyday...that last week. You were busy, with the Los Angeles project just getting started. So this is Beltran's diorama?"

Allie brought out the Jolly Green Giant doll. "Yes. These were *people objects.* You had to draw a picture or choose an object that reminded you of a person in your family. He chose these, and I wrote your names for him—Beltran couldn't write very well then. He didn't want me to put 'Dad' for Johnny, so I wrote out his name instead. He gave this doll to Maribel because he couldn't really think of anything to assign to her. He wanted the doll inside the diorama, too, but it was too big." On the other side of the Jolly Green Giant doll was a strip of masking tape with the word MARIBEL on it.

"That's where I saw that little plastic bug," said Dara, snapping her fingers. "I gave Beltran a quarter, and he got it out of a machine at Puppet Town."

Luke lit up. "I played a shooting game with him that day. Little red duckies went by on a conveyor, and the man gave us one that fell off. I forgot about that."

Johnny walked in and put a mini-cooler down. He swung his ponytail back over his shoulder and vented his t-shirt sleeves, one at a time, to cool off his armpits. "Sumbitch...when will winter get here? What are you assholes gawking about? Are we going after The Count or what? Daylight would be nicer."

"Come here, Johnny," said Dara.

Johnny did as he was told, though was reluctant when he saw the items on the couch. His dark eyes went to Allie. "What's this junk doing here?"

Allie rolled her eyes and turned away from him.

Luke nodded to Johnny. "Do you remember going to Puppet Town with Beltran?"

With an uncomfortable roll of his shoulders, Johnny considered this, then shrugged. "I suppose it was around the time he left."

Dara picked up the two-dollar bill. "Remember anything?"

Johnny's eyes widened. "Yeah...uh, Beltran wanted to spend some silver dollars and a two-dollar bill there. I wouldn't let him because they were rare. He brought the two-dollar bill anyway. I got mad at first, but then I let him buy a cotton candy with it. The cotton candy lady gave it back to him, just being nice, I guess. Don't know why I couldn't remember that until now."

"I don't think it wanted us to," Luke answered quietly.

Allie pulled out the picture of the horse. "This was part of Maribel's little shrine too. Beltran sent this in the mail from Arizona. She had a funny discussion with him on the phone about 'the Mare riding on the horse.' She tried to explain that a mare *is* a horse, but he wouldn't back down. The Mare will ride on the horse's back."

"Maribel spoke to my kid?"

Allie's beady eyes turned to Johnny now. "Beltran called her a few times. She always said that everybody would come out to Arizona and visit some time. It's been a long time though since they last spoke."

Johnny to Luke, "Did you know about this?"

"I recall her mentioning talking to him once."

Dara nodded. "Yeah, it wasn't often."

Silence fell in the room for a moment, then Luke tapped Allie's shoulder. "Is there anything else?"

She shook her head.

"Then you can leave."

"But I've given this stuff—"

"Get the hell out."

The woman didn't seem to believe it, but after a moment, she collected her purse and stormed out the front door, slamming it behind her.

Johnny looked terrified as Dara and Luke closed in on him. "You spoke to Beltran recently, right?"

"Man, I'd already slammed three shots. I called his step-dad, Charles, but I hung up after a couple rings. Just couldn't do it. Yeah, I'm almost sure of it."

"Christ," said Dara. "That was the night the music stopped. You need to call Charles again, Johnny. Right now."

"I'm not getting Beltran involved in this shit."

"He might already be in danger..."

Johnny ran his palms over his long black hair and gripped his pony tail. Slowly, he took out his cell phone and wandered into the den. He dialed a number and waited.

The music swelled in Luke's mind. He and Dara stood there, breathless.

Shoulders dropping, Johnny must have heard someone pick up on the other end. "Beltran...it's...it's your dad. I was calling to see how you were, son. I, uh, I miss you."

The nightmare ballad halted in Luke's head, sharp dark notes burning to dust.

Johnny dropped the phone and backed up against the wall. His face pinched and terror overtook him. All the color drained from him.

"It's him, Luke. Oh my fucking God, he was singing the ballad! He's the one who's been singing to us this whole time. I can hear it in his voice. My baby boy! Why? Why is it him? Help me, *please*."

Dara and Luke stared, feeble, no words to offer, just madness, insanity. Johnny let out a primeval sound and tore at his hair.

"What do I do? What does this mean?"

Chorus:

Charles Reinhardt was a man of science but had determined that God *did* make living things in his own image. The act of dreaming, for instance, was a restrained, simpler version of God's power to create. We create on a neurological plane; so compelling are our imagined structures that we believe everything we're dreaming. God creates on the plane of time and space, and He also believes the output of his dreams, *luckily for us*. Our acceptance was inherited from divine origins. God creates substance and proclaims it real, or "good," as religion might explain.

Things were no longer good, however. The evil that had once perverted our dreams had wiggled its way outside the network of human thought and into the universe. It now had access to the thoughts of God, or what we call reality.

The result, simply put: God was having nightmares. Maybe for the first time ever.

Charles knew how God felt. For a long time Charles had stared at the Foxglenn playground, all its colors, all its shapes, so merry and yet so frightening, all so human. It'd be impossible to miss such an elaborate play-set in this park of lush grass and lovely white sand pits. A place like Flagstaff could change someone's opinion of the desert state of Arizona—it had for Charles, certainly. Yet through a nightmare, anything could take your attention away, and it was easy to ignore the tableau, despite all its horrors.

Beltran Cruz had transported the song out of our heads and into the world. Well, Charles supposed that was probably not a fair statement. The research and subsequent experimentation with the Nightmare Ballad had done that, and since Charles was head of the University's project on the recovered document—more than one person should be blamed. The song was part of the human condition; everybody's mind was married to every other's, even if they didn't realize it; and everybody shared the song between them; they heard it while they slept, but only through thought-amplification research did the contortions of the brain turn into the contortions of time and space. Just like with dreams, people accepted these perversions of reality, with the exception of those who gained the awful gift of lucidity.

Charles paid that price now. He could see the awful and strange things happening out in the playground—the place he always brought Beltran to play because the clown head reminded him of Puppet Town back in California. Everything at this playground had mental tethers with places or people Beltran had loved at some point in his life. Some of the connections Charles recognized from stories Beltran had told him: the two-dollar bill his father had given him and the Jolly Green Giant doll that he gave to Maribel Rhodes.

Which brought Charles to the rocking horse, Beltran's connection to him. While having the bluest Christmas of his life—and thoroughly sick of hearing about Maribel Rhodes—Charles had called her a *whore,* and Beltran had immediately associated the two words. Images of a horse had already been recurring in Beltran's dreams from the various experiments they'd processed thus far. Back then, Charles had no idea the Mare had chosen Beltran as its vehicle (or as the Russian translation of the song describes it, *a horse*). Back then, the Mare had been considered the fairy-tale counterpart to him and his colleagues at the school.

Others items of connection, like the red ducky and the glowing plastic toy bug, Charles had no clue about, but figured they connected to the other Rhodes family members, since Beltran missed them just as much, if not more than, his own father. The Rhodeses were obviously his ideal of a good family.

Looking closer at such things brought whispered pieces of the song into Charles' mind, and he had to shut his eyes and turn his head away. The Mare was probably judging Charles for his fear, laughing at how unsurprisingly human he was.

Charles had held on for God only knew how long (or did He *even* know?) Yes, most times Charles stared into the horror before him, hoping to learn anything to free himself from this place. He kept his ears open, kept still, kept his eyes peeled. With all his studying of the clown tunnel, it still felt new. How long ago had the clown opened its mouth and Beltran willingly crawled inside? The boy continued to sing the *Kashmaar-Pyeasnya*, the music becoming a poisonous ambience to the network of minds he had connections with, but suddenly the other sounds from the tunnel stopped, the maddening xylophone stopped as well.

A cell phone vibrated like an enormous electric razor. Unlike the previous time this had happened, with this call, this time, he could hear Beltran answer, *Dad?*—and that broke the song. Charles' brain snapped free. There wasn't any time to lose!

As he fled the bench, he saw reality slowly repossess the playground. Beltran would begin singing again soon enough, though. This time, however, the sustained interference made it possible for Charles to shake his paralysis. He flinched at the thought of leaving his stepson behind. Having been mentally connected to the boy for so long, he wondered if Beltran could hear his thoughts. The nightmares, while not as potent as in this playground, would undoubtedly follow Charles when the song reentered his mind and he would no longer have Beltran's conscious mind so nearby to call for help.

Charles would have to travel to unfamiliar places to keep the nightmare storm away from him.

He touched the curtain with a trembling hand. How long had he been sitting on that bench? Weeks? Months? What if this was the last time he had a chance to say anything to Beltran? He'd failed his

Lisa…how could he leave the only thing left of her exposed to this evil?

"Can you hear me?" he asked, not daring to turn around. "I have to go now. Whenever you can, please keep talking to your father; it's interfering with the song. Don't lose my cell phone, whatever you do. We'll call back again. *Promise*. I know it's hard, but I'll return. I'm not leaving you for good. I love you kid.

"I'm so… I shouldn't have gotten you involved in this. It'll be over soon. Just hang on. I'll bring your dad here. Maybe his nice friends, the Rhodeses, too. We will all be with you. You won't be alone. We'll make sure, Beltran. Cross my heart, son."

Charles broke out in sobs as he pushed through the black curtain.

"We'll make sure you die."

Coming Soon

Nightmare Serenade